Project Avalon

B. Alexander Howerton

Space Available Press
P.O. Box 888193
Grand Rapids, MI 49588-8193

Project Avalon

Library of Congress Catalog Card Number 98-60540

ISBN 0-9663729-0-5

First Printing 1998

The cover is an original painting by Chris Jeffries, Grand Rapid, MI.

Published by
Space Available Press

The author and the cover artist can be contacted at the address on the title page, or at **alexhow@iserv.net**

Printed in Canada

For Eliot

The world, and the stars, are yours
If only you reach for them.

*"One must still have chaos within oneself
to be able to give birth to a dancing star."*

Nietzsche, *Also Sprach Zarathustra*

Prologue: Monday, January 3, 2101

The soft rhythms pulsed gently but insistently inside Gary's head, demanding attention. He brushed distractedly at his ear, as if to bat away a mosquito, but the action had no effect on the noise. He was standing on the bridge of a massive star cruiser, observing the Eagle Nebula, one of the great cosmic nurseries of stars. Towering billows of tenuous gas rose majestically above Gary, shedding a diffuse, beautiful glow in all directions. He stared in awe at the massive star incubators, wondering if any of the stars born there would one day produce life on an orbiting planet.

The pulsations increased in intensity, and were joined by a melodic trilling that ran playfully up and down the harmonic scale. Gary yelled over his shoulder, "Can somebody take care of that blasted alarm?" There was no answer. He wheeled around, prepared to reprimand his crew for an apparent neglect of duties. The glow of the star incubators curled around him and bathed the cabin with its mystical glow. The light seemed to blur the borders of the objects on the bridge, so Gary could not distinctly perceive anything. The glow increased, until everything was awash in undefined color.

Gary's eyes popped open. Everything from the dream was gone, except for the undulating rhythm. He groggily turned his head to the right and perceived the red glow of his chronometer on the wall. 7:14. Good, he thought, I can doze for a few more minutes. He slapped the "snooze" button next to the chronometer, and rolled back over. Perhaps I can get back to the star nebula, he thought dreamily as sleep once again enfolded him in its caressing tentacles.

The next disturbance of repose was his mother's voice, coming over the intercom. "Gary? Get up, honey, or you'll be late for school. Remember, you don't want to miss today. You said so yourself."

"OK, Mom, I'm getting up now," he answered dismissively, intending to try to sleep some more. But then he in fact remembered what day it was, and sat up quickly. That's right, he thought, I don't want to miss today. Today is when we find out about my Great Grandfather Gary.

He quickly jumped out of bed and raced to the sono-shower. He closed the compartment and flipped the wall switch. Pulsations of ultra-high frequency soundwaves criss-crossed his body, shaking off loose dirt and dead skin. After two minutes, he hopped out and quickly pulled on his jumpsuit and weightboots. Although Gary was moving swiftly, an Earthbound observer would have found his movements eerily slow and dreamlike, as if Gary were moving underwater. The weightboots were not required, but Gary liked to wear them anyway, to help keep his muscled toned. His body was designed to function in Earth's gravity field, therefore it could easily atrophy under the diminished pull of the Moon. Gary never intended to go to Earth, except perhaps to visit, and then he could wear a prosthosuit, which would counteract the damaging effects of Earth's gravity. He was studying to be an asteroid miner, and was preparing for his intensive training in the heavier Martian gravity field next year. He had enrolled in the astromining program just before the holiday break, and he was due to begin formal training on Mars next cycle. He looked forward to joining the budding colony culture, floating between the shepherding orbits of Mars and Jupiter. That was the real frontier these days, and Gary longed to live and work in all its wild lawlessness and energy.

Gary sat on the edge of his bed and reached down with his long arms to fasten his boots. Although Gary was only eleven years old, he was already two meters tall, and could expect to grow to as much as two and a half meters. That was normal for him and his generation, which were born on the Moon. Freed from the restrictions of Earth's gravity, their bodies shot up to amazing heights. Gary liked to witness the awe on Earth visitors' faces when they saw the Lunans towering over them. It gave him a feeling of superiority over the "Earth-lubbers."

Gary raced out of his room and into the family common room. He grabbed the peach powerbar his mother had laid out for him, and munched on it as he scurried over to retrieve his holodisk from his workstation in the next room. "Gotta go, Mom, I don't want to be late," he mumbled through a mouthful of food, then pecked his mother on the cheek. She was several centimeters shorter than him.

"Really, Gary, you should get up in time to have a proper breakfast," she called after him as he rushed out the airlock.

He hurried out onto the promenade and dashed toward the tube entrance, where a tube car would whisk him to the schooldome. Above him, Gary noticed that the habidome was just fading into its day colors, simulating dawn. The dome's material was becoming opaque, shutting out the natural view of the stars above, and replacing it with a warm, golden glow. Soon the "sun" would rise and it would be a new day. Good thing the engineers do that, Gary reflected. Otherwise, everyone here would go supernova, with sunshine for fourteen days, then darkness for another fourteen. If I hadn't already decided on astromining, that might have been interesting work.

His long, lanky legs moved fluidly, and he seemed to float along. He pitied the Earthers, who had to endure bone-crushing jolts as they bounced up and down when they ran. Normally he did not like the two days a week students actually reported to school, preferring the days when he worked, or more often played, on his holounit at home. But today was special. Today, the first school day of the new century, they were going to begin an in-depth study of the founding of Avalon, the precursor settlement that led to the permanent habitation of the Moon.

Gary knew some of the history, but he was fuzzy on the details. Everybody knew about the Great Extermination, or Cleansing, as some sarcastically and insensitively called it, and that Avalon was, for a while, the sole standardbearer of civilization and technology. In fact, Avalon was once in grave danger of being destroyed. But they would learn about that later. Today they would examine the causes and reasons for the founding of Avalon, and what it meant to Lunan history. Gary was especially interested in the subject, because he was the great-grandson of Gary LaFey, one of the original inhabitants of Avalon, and for whom he was named. He also wanted to find out about the earlier Gary's father, Art. Gary was spoken of glowingly during clan gatherings, but Art's name was mentioned little, if ever, and Gary was curious as to why. He knew there was at one point a great conflict between Gary and his father, but no one would impart any details. Gary hoped that today's lesson would shed light on the matter.

The tube car stopped at the Luna Academy station, and Gary popped out once the translucent door slid up to let him out. "Bill! Chen! Ashmi! Floating high?"

"Light as hydrogen, Gary! You cycled?" It was the first day back from the holiday vacation, and the friends had some catching up to do. They chatted in lunaslang as they walked together through the airlock into the schooldome.

"Naw, I'm still non-linear, but that's all quadratic. I'll be vectored by lunch. Hey, can you process what's datastreaming today?"

"Yeah, we gotta download that null content social soft data about the founding of Avalon. How non-sequitor."

"No, it's gonna be supernova, you fractal! It's all about how we got here."

"You're only saying that because it's about your great grandfather."

"Valid input, but it's still gonna be max Q. We're gonna process the Great Cleansing!"

Ashmi looked around, alarmed. "Shhh! Encrypt that, droog. You want the Programmer to defrag you?"

"Well, that's what it was, no matter what they want to call it. Anyway, I'm fully booted to find out what the true story was. Oh, no! There's the sono. Come on, we're late!"

They ran down the hall and entered a holoroom. They took their places in the various gadgetry-laden seats that were arranged in a circle about a center apparatus. The Programmer was circling the apparatus, giving his introductory remarks to the students already present. He glared at the late students, but did not pause in his speech as they slipped the holohelmets over their heads, positioning the sensofeeds properly to receive the input from the central display unit.

"You have all no doubt heard bits and pieces of the history of Luna," The Programmer continued, "but probably do not have a comprehensive grasp of the events which brought us to where we are today. It is appropriate that, on this first school day of the new century, that we truly begin to understand our place in the flow of change. Today we begin to look at the founding of our colony here on the Moon, beginning with the social and political circumstances that drove people to settle the Moon in the first place. The information you are about to receive may be a little disturbing, and that is why we have waited until you have achieved a certain maturity before we presented it to you. We will spend the rest of the week discussing the implications of this history and the lessons we can learn from it. If you are all ready, I'll begin the datafeed." The students, ensconced in their holohelmets, all nodded, and the Programmer pressed a button on his belt. The story began.

One Hundred and One Years Earlier: Monday, January 3, 2000

Art LaFey was excited. He had gotten up early to view the launch of the space shuttle Endeavor on CNN before he went to work. He especially wanted to see this first launch of the new millenium, because, after many delays in the International Space Station development program, this flight would carry the United States Laboratory Module to the station, and get the whole program back on track. Art's five-year-old son Gary shared his enthusiasm for space development with him, and wanted to see the launch too. Art woke Gary up at 6:00 a.m., and without bothering to change out of their pajamas, they both rushed to fill up their cereal bowls and camp out in front of the television.

Art flicked the button on the remote control that turned on the set, and he punched in the channel that brought in CNN. An image of the shuttle appeared, mated to its massive orange external tank and two solid rocket boosters, resting expectantly on the launch pad and aiming vertically toward the heavens. Art always loved that image, which evoked power and determination. It said to him that humankind was not going to remain content scrabbling away on the surface of the Earth, was not going to be defeated by gravity, but would reach up, and out, as far as the collective will of the people of the Earth would take it. The reporter cut into his reverie.

"...just minutes away from launch here at pad 39-B at the Kennedy Space Center. This is an especially important launch of the shuttle. Not only is this the first launch of the new millenium, but also it has been delayed twice, due to unseasonably cold weather this winter here in Florida. Two other factors have delayed this launch. This is the maiden flight of the augmented main engines on the shuttle. They were supposed to have been used on a launch last summer, but last-minute problems dictated further work on the engines.

"Also, the United States Laboratory Module that is in the payload bay was due to be launched last spring, but delays in the Russian portion of the station project caused the assembly schedule to slip by several months. NASA officials hope that this flight can begin to get the program back on track. An ambitious launch schedule is planned after this, with one shuttle going up every month, on average, for the next six months. That is a very compressed timetable, because the average turnaround time between shuttle launches is about six weeks."

The reporter went on to impart details about the laboratory module and the procedure of mating it to the skeleton of the International Space Station, waiting patiently in orbit high above the Earth. He also discussed the secondary payloads, and fascinating details about the crew, their lives, and their training for this mission. Art and Gary absorbed every detail.

The reporter continued. "A word about the new millennium. Although it is generally agreed that the official beginning of the new millennium is January 1, 2001, most people around the globe are celebrating the turnover this year. We'll let one of the many civilian launch observers that have made a pilgrimage here explain it."

The camera view cut to a man, about thirty five years old, wearing a NASA baseball cap, with the erect shuttle over his left shoulder. "Yeah, sure, the new millennium is officially next year, but so what? I hit a hundred thousand miles in my Toyota truck on the way down here, but I celebrated when the numbers turned over. That's the exciting part, not the official number count, you know? Anyway, this is the first launch in the 2000s, and that's what's got me jazzed." He lifted his fist and gave a rebel war whoop, and his buddies in the background cheered.

The view cut back to the reporter. "As you can see, the observers here are excited, and blissfully uninterested in mathematical accuracy. We are now at T minus 100 seconds from launch. We'll let you listen in on the communications from the Firing Room, as it's called here at the Launch Control Center. This is where all the commands are given that lead to a shuttle launch."

The reporter stopped talking, and official-sounding voices took over. One voice announced, in ten-second increments, "T minus ninety seconds, T minus eighty seconds…"

Other voices reported conditions of the shuttle. At sixty seconds to launch, a voice said, "Hydrogen reads nominal pressure." At thirty seconds, Art and Gary heard "Terminal launch sequence engaged." Then "SRB hydraulic power units activated." At sixteen seconds, "Gimbal tests successful." At ten seconds, "Go for main engine start." The camera view had switched at thirty seconds to the bottom of the shuttle and the engines.

At the ten-second mark Art and Gary saw flames shoot in from the sides, under the three main bell nozzles of the space shuttle. Then bright blue barely-visible flames shot straight out from the engines on the shuttle. A moment later, the two solid rocket boosters on either side of the orange external tank came to life, roaring and burning brightly. The whole shuttle assembly shook slightly, then began to rise slowly, majestically, from the launch pad.

The camera image shifted to a more remote location, so the whole shuttle could be seen rising off the launch pad. The reporter said, "another spectacular launch..." Just then, a blazing white light filled the screen, and Art and Gary could not make out any details. Then the light dimmed, and the shuttle was no longer there. Instead, pieces of burning wreckage were flying in every direction. The support gantry for the shuttle was mangled, and was in the process of toppling over. The entire launch complex area appeared as if it had been bombed.

The chatter from the firing room was frenzied and indecipherable. The feed from the firing room was cut, and the reporter cleared his throat, made several mumbling attempts to speak, and finally managed to say, "It appears as if there has been a terrible accident. There has been an explosion, and the space shuttle no longer seems to be in one piece. There is wreckage and fire everywhere on the launch pad, and the officials here are scrambling to determine what precisely has happened. We'll bring you details as soon as they become available."

Art and Gary were stunned. Art had raised a bite of cereal halfway to his mouth. The spoon hovered there, dripping milk onto the carpet, as Art's jaw hung open. Gary looked at the screen, then at Art. "What happened, Daddy?"

Art put his spoon back in the bowl and turned to look at Gary. "I think the shuttle blew up again."

"Is that bad?"

"Yes it is. Very, very bad."

Chapter 1

"Those idiots! They're really going to do it!" Art screamed as he flung the newspaper across the living room.

"What is it this time?" sighed Gwen, his wife, keeping her eyes firmly on her People magazine.

"NASA has halted all space shuttle and space station operations while they investigate the shuttle explosion. They're not sure yet, but they think it had something to do with the new main engines. But on top of that, there are hearings scheduled in Congress to consider canceling crewed spaceflight altogether." Art could barely contain his frustration as he paced the room like a trapped panther. "Why did they have to put all their eggs in one basket like that? There's even talk of selling our stake in the International Space Station to the Russians!"

"Well, dear, if it upsets you so, why don't you do something about it?" The faint hint of sarcasm in Gwen's voice infuriated Art.

"Maybe I will," Art said as he stormed across the living room to grab his jacket from the doorknob of the closet. "Somehow, I will. But right now I'm going to take a walk."

"Don't be out too late. It's a work night, you know." Gwen called after him, flipping a page in her magazine.

The cool winter air caressed Art's cheeks and rustled his bright red hair as he swung the front door shut behind him and trotted down the steps of his apartment in Ballard. Art loved Seattle's non-threatening winters. There was always a hint of salty sea in the air, and a gentle mist falling constantly. Art calmed down almost instantly as he established a brisk pace down the sidewalk. I *will* do something about developing space, he thought. It's high time somebody did something. It's not happening on its own, especially now that another shuttle has blown up.

Art's mind drifted back across the years as he strolled beneath the swaying naked branches of the maples that lined the street. Art had always loved the idea of space, ever since he was a boy. He absorbed as much science fiction as he could — movies, books, television, whatever. In eighth grade science class, when the two-week session on space science arrived, Art got straight A's. He returned to his usual C minus average as soon as it ended. Mr. Haverkamp, his teacher, had asked him, "What's the deal? Why can't you get grades like that all the time?" "I guess I'm just into space," Art had replied.

As Art grew older, however, 'practical matters' took precedence, and dreams of space retreated into the crevasses of his mind. He cast about in college for a direction, dabbled in many fields, and finally gravitated toward a degree in English. He had stayed on at the University of Washington after his bachelor's degree, and enrolled in the Master of Arts in Journalism program, partly because he thought he could write well, but mostly because of a fetching music major named Gwen Evers. He was eventually degreed, and landed a job at the Arts Review, one of Seattle's alternative newspapers, as a copy editor. His ultimate goal was to acquire a job at the Seattle Press, or some other mainstream newspaper, where, as a nationally syndicated columnist on the Op-Ed page, he would set the world afire with his stunning prose and insights.

As Art reminisced, he found his feet wandering in the direction of his favorite tavern, the Valhalla, along Market Street. I love Ballard, Art mused, listening to the one long horn blast, then one short blast of a sailboat in the ship canal, requesting the drawbridge of Fifteenth Avenue to be raised so the boat could pass. Ballard, in the northwest corner of Seattle, had been settled primarily by Swedes, and retained a small-town atmosphere, even in the midst of the sprawling metropolis that Seattle had become in the early Nineties.

I've got to find a way to help make space happen, Art thought. Once he had finished his studies and was firmly ensconced in his position at the paper, his old love, space, had crept back into his mind. Art knew he needed an angle, a unique perspective, if he were to ever distinguish himself amidst the sea of columnists, pundits, and other assorted curmudgeons inhabiting the interiors of the nation's newspapers. Space had reemerged into his consciousness as a possible escape from the endless cycle of the entrenched status quo, as he saw it, battling the reactionary liberals, with both factions effectively canceling each other out, while the world decayed a little more each day.

It was difficult to develop such ideas, however, with new loves and responsibilities demanding his attention and requiring his time. He had married that demure and attractive music major, mostly for old-fashioned love, but in large part due to the no-longer concealable swelling of her belly as they both approached graduation. They were fortunate enough to find a clean but small apartment on the first floor of a house in Ballard, still one of the most inexpensive parts of the city. The rigors of motherhood, however, kept Gwen from pursuing her music career at the pace she would have preferred. She had an indefinite assignment as a replacement oboe for the

Seattle Symphony and taught several piano and oboe students, but for the most part she stayed home as Art pursued his career and supported the family. They had been married a little over five years, and the first strains of resentment were beginning to appear around the corners of Gwen's mouth whenever she spoke of her life with Art.

Art's thoughts became vague and unfocused as he turned onto Market Street and saw The Valhalla a couple blocks away. All his thoughts and emotions jumbled together, creating a confused bramble in which his mind became enmeshed. "I need a beer," was the only thought that surfaced.

He entered the tavern, crossed the smoke-filled room, and sat down on a stool at the bar. The joint was not very crowded, which was understandable for a Monday night. Art ordered a Red Hook from the ruddy bartender and studied the wrinkles of his knuckles while he waited for his pint. Half of it disappeared as soon as it arrived, and Art instantly felt his tension being washed away on the foam of a good brew.

He looked up and around to observe his surroundings. The few people in the place were playing pool or darts, or just talking and laughing. The television above the bar was running a newscast. One other fellow was seated at the bar, a couple stools down from Art. He wore a long pony tail, and the light from the television bounced off his round John Lennon glasses. The fellow noticed Art looking at him and gave him a casual half-smile of a greeting. He nodded toward the TV. "What do you think of this Patterson guy?"

Art shook off his half-daze, looked at the TV, and saw Jerry Patterson, the evangelist Christian presidential candidate, giving one of his impassioned stump speeches. "Well, I'm sure he can sucker a lot of people, but I doubt he'll get the Republican nomination. American politics is unkind to extremists."

"Don't be so sure, man. Times are weird. People will latch onto anything, if they're scared enough."

Art took a closer look at his companion. He had intense eyes that didn't waver from the location they had anchored upon.

"Sure, times are weird," Art replied, looking back at the TV. "But people are smart. They won't vote against their own self interest. We sometimes get some idiots, but for the most part, things work."

"Naw, you don't get it, man. Sure, some people are smart, but while they're arguing about the best thing to do, the idiots and the scared people listen to guys like him, and they goose-step to power. Look at Nazi Germany, man."

"Well, this isn't Nazi Germany," Art scoffed.

"Don't be so sure, man."

Art surveyed his companion, and had a high-intensity, second-long debate in his head as to whether he cared for company tonight. He reached a decision, thrust out his hand and said, "Art LaFey. Pleased to meet you."

"Likewise, dude," the stranger replied, taking Art's hand in the old hippie handshake, with the fingers on top. "I'm Perry. Perry C. Vale."

"So," Art continued after finishing his first pint and signaling the bartender, "you've got some pretty definite opinions about politics."

"I got opinions on everything. I'm a grad student."

"Oh, really? At the University? What in?"

"Comparative Literature."

"Oh yeah? What are you studying?"

"Mythology, mainly. Arthurian legends, hero's quests, that type of thing."

"And what are you going to do with this wisdom?"

"Teach, probably. And write books. I'm hoping I can help people figure out what the new mythology is."

"What do you mean?"

"Well, look around you, man. People are clueless these days. I mean, we used to be able to *believe* religion, sink right into it, you know? But science has shattered that. The stories we told ourselves, like Adam and Eve, Moses, Buddha, King Arthur, they just don't cut it anymore. They don't *mean* anything to us. I mean, I love this stuff, but it's dusty, you know? It's been replaced by Einstein, Freud, Darwin. We humans aren't special anymore. We're now just random, accidental dust mites in a vast and overpowering Cosmos. And yet we *are* special. I'm trying to figure out how."

Art felt himself getting wound up. "What do you think about space?"

"Space? As in outer? It's pretty big, cold, and lonely."

"No, I mean, about exploring it, colonizing it."

A look of disgust crossed Perry's face. "That's just some fly-boy, right stuff, military-industrial complex crap designed to milk more money from taxpayers."

Now Art was on fire. "No, no, not at all. Look, that's the way it started, no doubt about it, but now it's much more. Now it holds the hope for humanity. If we can get into space and develop the resources that are out there, we have a fighting chance of surviving and eventually reversing the damage we're doing to this planet. And we can keep the economy growing and provide more jobs for people down here, and improve conditions around the globe."

"That's exactly the kind of utopian post-industrial garbage I can't stand. How can the very polluters and rapers of the land and the people turn around and provide a cornucopia of high-tech happiness? We're probably going to blow ourselves up first, or poison the Earth."

"No, that's the wrong way to look at it, and I'd like to explain why. Can I buy you another beer?" Art called to the bartender. "Hey, buddy, two more over here." He turned back to Perry. "Let's go grab that table over there and talk about this."

When the bartender had brought the pints and Art had taken a long drink for inspiration, he launched into his defense of space development. "Let me tell you how I came to the ideas I have now. I've always been into space and science fiction and that kind of thing. But it wasn't *practical*, if you know what I mean. Sure, I could have gone into engineering or science or that type of thing, but that really wasn't me. Besides, back in the Eighties, I was your basic liberal anti-Reaganite, and I wasn't about to go to work supporting the military-industrial complex. So I got into other things, you know, writing and politics and stuff like that. But I was still *into* space.

"Then in college, around 1990, I participated in this seminar called '2020: The World Thirty Years From Now.' It was all about imagining what kind of world we wanted to live in. It was two days long; on the first day we had to envision the world in thirty years, then on the second day, we had to figure out how to get there. At the beginning, I went into this room with a buddy of mine, where we were supposed to close our eyes and describe what we saw, when we projected thirty years into the future. When I closed my eyes, it was amazing! I had a vision; I was there! I didn't have to think at all; it just leapt into my head.

"I was flying over the Earth. It was beautiful! Green everywhere, not a city in sight. Everything was farms or forests. There were no roads, at least not the concrete monstrosities we call roads, and no cars or trucks. It was an ecological paradise! Heavy industry was gone; I intuitively knew it had been moved out to space. The Earth was allowed to regreen. It had become the agricultural paradise Thomas Jefferson had dreamed of, with plenty of parks and preserves that would never be touched by development.

"There were cities, but only six, one for each continent. They were great collection and distribution centers. They were built downward, into the Earth, rather than with eye- and landscape-jarring above-ground structures. Magnetic strips fanned out like veins from each city, and goods flowed in and out along them, like a circulation system. The great trains that rode on those strips were powered by electromagnetism, rather than internal combustion, and moved at incredible speeds. Other than that, people traveled by bicycle, horse and cart, or some other tried and true method, because if you weren't going to or from a city, there was no need for extensive traveling. The world was comprised of villages of a few thousand each, or less.

"Besides being distribution centers, the great cities were spaceports. Ships were shot into low-Earth-Orbit on a laser beam, or on mag-lev rails, carrying goods and people to and from Earth. Once in space, a network of tethers slung them to the Moon, or to Mars, essentially all over the solar system. My mind's eye floated over to the Moon. It was completely developed, one huge industrial park. Every conceivable industry was there, where there was no eco-system to destroy. The far side of the Moon was reserved for science and astronomical observation.

"The whole system, both Earth and Moon, was powered by solar power satellites, which caught the light of the Sun, where all our energy ultimately comes from anyway, and beamed it to where it was needed. Fusion powered by helium three, which is an element that's just lying around on the Moon's surface, also provided a lot of local power. The neat thing about fusion, if you do it right, is that it leaves no radioactive residue, so the power systems we were using were non-polluting! Internal combustion and fossil fuels had faded away.

"Asteroid mining was going on in a big way. Bands of pioneers had turned some asteroids into their new homes, while others had constructed classic O'Neill colonies out of lunar and asteroidal material. Gerard O'Neill was an early advocate of free-floating space colonies way back in the Seventies. Ion-powered ships were exploring the outer planets, sending back valuable cargo on solar sails. They were even thinking of creating a Bernal Sphere, a type of multi-generational interstellar spacecraft, and embarking on the first interstellar expedition.

"The whole society was managed by a modular, federal system, where decisions were made at the lowest organizational level possible. It had to be done that way, because distances between the colonies and outposts were so great that the logistics of communication prevented a strong central authority. The "Earthers," as they were called, ran their affairs the same way, because there was no longer an impression of limited resources, and they didn't feel like wasting time, lives, and energy in senseless conflict. They realized there was much more to gain from cooperative interaction than conquest, which was essentially impossible, anyway. A well-directed asteroid or laser beam from the attacked party's allies in space would quickly change the aggressor's mind."

Art sat back and tossed down the rest of his pint. Perry had been mesmerized; he felt as if he had actually seen a developed Moon, a regreened Earth, and colonies floating in space. He slowly came back to himself, and slugged down his own pint. "Sounds great," he said, wiping the foam from his mouth, "But don't you think that's more of a utopian fantasy than a real possibility? Especially now that another shuttle has blown up?"

"Well, sure." Art replied, waving for another pint. "One for you, too?" Perry nodded.

"Sure it's a dream," Art continued, "and there are going to be failures and setbacks, like with the shuttle. The shuttle came out of that military-industrial complex mentality that I can't stand either. It's extremely unfortunate that those astronauts were killed, but it was inevitable, the way the whole space station program was being pushed. Still, you have to believe in something. I know that most of the stuff I was talking about can't happen in thirty years, but it's worth working toward. Look, I'll tell you another thing that pulled me into this whole idea of space development. Like I said, in my younger years I was your basic pot-smoking, free-love hippie, protesting nukes and wars and stuff.

"Then in '88, when I was a sophomore in college, Bush was running for office, and the Young Republicans on campus wanted to hold a rally. I thought this was a great opportunity to get our message out. I suggested to the anti-nuke group I was a part of at the time that we plan a debate with them, so we could show everybody what hypocritical bastards they were. The rest of the group told me I was stupid, that they weren't worth debating because it was so obvious why they were wrong. That it would just give them a platform to spout their poison. They said it would just be better to go to their rally and shout them down, even sabotage the PA system, if necessary. I said that that was wrong, that people should hear both sides and be allowed to choose, and that if our position was right, they'd choose us. I remember one guy in particular, Kurt Samuelson, said very contemptuously, 'That would be just the way you would think, Art.'

"It hit me then like a ton of bricks. These people weren't interested in making things better; they were just *against* whatever those other guys were *for*. They were anti-nukes, anti-war, anti-guns, anti-government, anti-this, anti-that. Liberals aren't *for* anything. Sure, they're for a peaceful, ecologically protected Earth, but they want to get there by destroying all the technology we've developed up until now. They just react to whatever the conservatives favor. They have no *vision*.

"The conservatives aren't much better. They have a vision, but only for an elite few. If you aren't white, rich, and male, you're pretty much out of luck. Conservatives want to preserve the status quo, get what they can while the getting's good, and not worry about the rest of the world. They preach 'no limits to growth,' but that's just a euphemism for raping the planet and letting the future generations fend for themselves, because you can't have infinite growth on Earth, which is finite in resources." Perry tapped the tip of his nose a few times. "Right on the nose," he affirmed emphatically.

"I got to thinking," Art continued, "There has to be an alternative to these approaches. One side wants to scale back technology, thereby limiting our options. The other wants to charge ahead, and damn the future. I searched my soul for a long time, trying to find an answer. Then I took that seminar I told you about, and that vision leapt into my head. *That* is the answer. We can't go backward; we've let the technological genie out of the bottle, and we can't stuff him back in. Nor can we continue to use the planet and its resources the way we have, because we'll probably deplete them before we're dead; it will be *our* problem, not some future generation's. No, we have to work *through* the problems our technology has created, and come out the other side. Space can do that. It expands our resource base to infinity. And we can start using the power of the sun directly, instead of through polluting intermediaries like fossil fuel and fission. If we can do it, the liberals and conservatives can argue their silly little issues for generations."

"Now that sounds more like it." Perry exclaimed. "There's a lot of stuff you said that I don't necessarily agree with, but it sounds to me like you're on the right track. Listen, I'm part of an ecological activist group at the University. I've been kind of having the same thoughts, about their effectiveness and all. Would you like to come to a meeting and talk to some of these guys? Maybe you'll find a receptive ear, or maybe you'll just find the same knee-jerk crowd as before."

"Sure, I'll give it a try. The worst I can do is piss them off, and they'll never invite me back, right? I'm already used to that."

"Right," Perry chuckled. "OK, our next meeting is Wednesday in the Student Union at 7:30."

"7:30. Got it." Art instinctively looked at his watch. "Oh, shit! I've got to go! I have to work in the morning. I'll see you on Wednesday, then, Perry, and we can continue this conversation. Nice meeting you." Art downed his beer while giving Perry a quick handshake, then bolted out the door.

Chapter 2

"It's incredible. You actually believe this crap," Doug said to Art, as he slapped his forehead and looked around with a sarcastic smirk at the others in the room. Doug was the most outspoken of the activists Perry had introduced Art to at the meeting of the Seattle Environmental Council that Wednesday evening. Art had explained his vision of space, and watched the faces of the group, sitting haphazardly around a student lounge, become increasingly hostile or incredulous.

Art defended himself. "No, I'm serious. If we push out into space, we have a fighting chance to save the Earth. Otherwise we're doomed. Look. We've already screwed up the environment to a severe degree, and there are no signs of industrial pressures lightening up anytime soon. On the contrary. Industry is pushing ahead, ripping more raw materials out of the ground and polluting at a greater rate. We can't turn the clock back. When has there ever been a voluntary cessation of 'progress'? Never.

"No, what we need to do is push forward, work through it. Modern technology has brought us some wonderful benefits, like improved health care and advanced agriculture. But those same things are messing us up now. Our technology has allowed the world population to explode. If we don't curb population growth, we have no hope. All those third world countries want what we have, namely, a rising standard of living. But there is no way we can sustain an ever-growing economy on a finite resource base. We've got to go to space and develop more resources to provide for all the hungry new mouths being born every day."

Someone in the back of the room shouted, "Sounds like a bunch of bourgeois bullshit to me." Chuckles rippled through the crowd of about twenty-five attendees of varying ethnicity and sex. Perry sat in a corner, his chair leaning back against the wall, and silently observed the proceedings.

"Yeah," Doug went on, "How would you stop the corporations from continuing their rape of the people, just on a grander scale?"

Art replied, "Look, moving into space is going to take a lot of energy, planning, and cooperation. Initially, it's going to be very cramped quarters. You can't engage in activity like that and not develop a deep respect and regard for other people. People will learn quickly to respect other people, and will learn what it means to be human."

A dark young man over in the corner wearing a colorful African smock and Rasta hat piped up. "Von Braun was that deep into space, and he was a Nazi!"

"Those were exceptional times," Art answered, "And these are, too. I believe we've learned the lesson the events from that era taught us. The ends never justify the means. Von Braun didn't think he had a choice. But we do. We always do. I listened to what you guys were saying, before you let me get up on my soapbox. I think you guys have thought deeply about the problems of the world, and are taking some good stabs at solving them. I'd like to join you. You could teach me a lot, and maybe I could teach you a little in return."

There were mixed mumbles of approval and dissent in the room, but Doug, who was Presiding Secretary, turned to the group and said, "Sure, why not? At the least, he'll be a sounding board of what not to do and to think. Hell, we might even win him over to our cause, and then he'd be useful. Remember he works for that one paper? He'd make a good propaganda conduit."

"That's right," Art replied. "I just got approval the other day from our Head Editor to write an opinion piece. I'm of course going to focus on what I talked about tonight, but I'll make sure to cover your concerns, and get some of your ideas in there as well."

A few heads around the room hesitantly nodded their approval, with soft comments of "OK", "Sounds Good", "Can't hurt."

"So it's settled then," Doug proclaimed, slamming his fist down as a mock gavel on the table he was sitting at. "Art's our new minister of propaganda, until he proves himself unwilling or unworthy of the role. Any other business? No? OK, do I have a motion to adjourn?"

The meeting was wrapped up in a parody of Robert's Rules of Order, and many of the members came up to Art afterwards, to argue or ask questions.

About half an hour later, Perry and Art walked out of the student union together. They turned their collars up and hunched down against the light drizzle. "Man, you sure took a beating in there," Perry said, "But you pretty much held your own."

"Thanks. Hey, you were pretty quiet in there."

"Yeah, well, I was just absorbing everything. I've been thinking about what you've said. It makes a certain weird sense."

"Hah! A convert!"

"Man, don't jump on me too fast. I just said I was thinking about it. I didn't say I was ready to move to space yet."

"Well, it always starts small."

"I could say the same about you, with the environmental thing."

"You could be right about that. My car's down this way. You need a ride?"

"No, I live just a couple blocks from here. Besides, I like the rain."

"OK. See you at the next meeting?"

"Yeah, sure thing. It's a month from tonight."

"OK. See you then. And look in the Arts Review. My opinion piece ought to come out between now and then."

"Cool. I'll be looking for it. Later."

Art's head was full of interesting and conflicting thoughts as he drove home through the soft winter rain. Seattle had received its week-long dose of annual snowfall a couple of weeks earlier. It had already melted away, and the sky had returned to its accustomed light drizzle. He was still mentally out in space, surveying the re-greened Earth, as he walked into his apartment. Consequently, Gwen's attack caught him off guard.

"Where the hell have you been? Do you know what time it is?"

Art, stunned, softly replied, "I told you I was going to a meeting tonight."

"Yes, but you didn't bother to tell me how late you were going to be. I assumed it wasn't going to be more than an hour or two. It's after eleven o'clock! I had to deal with Gary alone tonight. Although I don't know why I should mind. It seems I deal with him anyway, whether you're home or not."

"Now that's not true!" Arthur shouted.

"Be quiet!" Gwen wagged a finger in front of her lips. "Gary just went down. If you wake him..." She scowled at Art.

"Why did he go down so late?"

"He was restless. So was I. He fell asleep on the couch, watching TV with me."

Art took off his jacket and hung it up. "Sorry I'm late."

"Well, you know, Art, you are spending an awful lot of time with this space thing. You're always working on that damn computer, writing those useless space articles, or God knows what. I don't feel I know you anymore."

Art grabbed a beer from the refrigerator. "You *know* I think this is important. And it could mean a lot. I got my first opinion piece assignment."

"That's great. I'm happy for you. Really. But I just don't *see* you anymore."

After a long drink, Art set the bottle down and hugged Gwen. "I know, honey, but this will pay off. Everybody needs an angle to make it in the press these days, and this is mine. Just hang on; I'm on my way."

Gwen returned a perfunctory hug, then pulled away. "I just don't know how long we can wait. We're renting, we've got bills, we've got to take care of Gary. I just expected to be doing better by now."

"We will, you'll see, I promise."

Gwen's eyes flashed with a glint of anger. "You should stop making promises. You may not be able to keep them."

"I'm sorry, honey. I just know this is the right thing to do. It's going to work. I can *feel* it."

"I hope you're right. I'm tired. I'm going to bed." She pecked him on the cheek and headed toward the bedroom.

Art grabbed his beer bottle and went into the living room. He flopped down in the big comfy chair they had inherited from Gwen's dad and stared out the window. The rain was still gently falling, creating a multi-colored halo around the orange-pink halogen streetlamp.

I can't believe it, he thought. Just as I'm starting to achieve some successes, my personal life is falling apart. He had thrown himself into his work with the gusto of a man with a newfound mission. His plan was to cut his teeth on a few opinion pieces, and articles in magazines if he could swing it, then assemble them with some new material into a book. If possible he would like to hit the lecture circuit and promote space, like his idol Arthur C. Clarke. The Head Editor at the Arts Review, Jana Pandovar, kept tantalizing him with promises of giving him a shot, then kept delaying it for one reason or another. Subsequently, Art had thrown himself into his writing with abandon, preparing several pieces for "the big break."

This activity, however, didn't increase the paycheck, and kept him away from his wife. It seemed every month he came up just short of having enough money to pay bills. He borrowed heavily against credit cards to make ends meet. There were, as a result, few luxuries, and Gwen was starting to feel the strain. She had wanted a house very badly, a place they could settle down and raise a family. They had tried to buy a house a couple of years back, but had come up just shy of the necessary debt-to-earnings ratio to qualify for an FHA mortgage. Gwen was devastated, and that began the long, slow parting of the ways between them.

Art realized there was no way they were going to be able to afford a house on a workingman's salary. The only way was to break out of the mold somehow, and he intended to do it by writing books and articles about space, maybe a novel or two. Such projects, however, occupied an increasing amount of time, which contributed to the estrangement. Nevertheless, Art always tried to make time for Gary. Art loved Gary more than he could possibly express. The little tyke had just turned six, and was a smart as could be. He had started kindergarten this school year, and was doing wonderfully. Art was driven in his project even more by a desire to help create a world in which Gary could not only survive, but prosper and have a chance to explore the heavens. The little genius shared Art's passion for space. He already knew all of the planets and some of the moons in the solar system, and he and Art had made several simple models of spacecraft together. Gary often said, "When I grow up, I want to be an astronaut!" Nothing could have made Art prouder. When Art and Gary got together, they had the best times, playing in the park, riding bikes, reading books, and just rolling around on the floor, giggling. Gary made the whole struggle worthwhile.

Enough navel-contemplation, thought Art, throwing back the last of his beer. Feeling at the same time depressed about Gwen and elated about Gary, Art wandered off to bed.

Chapter 3

The Seattle Arts Review
February 22, 2000
"The Space Imperative"
Arthur Roy LaFey

The recent space shuttle explosion has raised doubts in many minds around the country about the viability of our space program. Many are calling for a complete cessation of space activities, claiming they are far too risky, while others assert that only the military and other specialized government personnel should be allowed in space. Such thinking is myopic, and can only ultimately lead to the decline of America and of the world in general. On the contrary, developing space can lead to incredible benefits here on Earth, and it can be conducted safely. The accident was caused by pushing forward too fast and hard in an underfunded program. If developed properly and undertaken for the right reasons, space activities can be a tremendous boon to humanity.

Space beckons to be explored and colonized. Not because it's there. Mountains are "there," and you can get plenty of excitement and adventure climbing them. And not because of some fly-boy, right-stuff desire to be the first one out there and kick some (name the enemy-du-jour) behind. No, we must go because space is, quite simply, part of our environment, part of us, and the logical next step in human development. There are several concrete reasons to develop space which I will outline in this and following articles, beginning with the economic rationale.

The greatest good a government attempts to achieve for its people is to create a climate which can enable them to work hard to create a better life for themselves. The best method that sovereign nations use to produce such a climate is an ever-growing economy. We are currently witnessing the damaging effects of stagnant or recessed economies around the globe. People who feel they have lost their opportunities for advancement, or perceive others are taking those opportunities from them, are much easier to persuade to hate, to kill, to go to war. Therefore, many governments consider it imperative that they keep the economy growing, at almost any cost.

The opening up of the eastern bloc and the ongoing development of the "third world" lend the appearance that there is much more room for growth in the global economy, but ultimately the Earth-bound economy is a closed system. If we try to keep our economy growing forever based on the finite resources of Earth, we will one day run out. The ensuing dark ages will make the last go-round seem like a holiday picnic.

Moreover, the population of the planet is experiencing an exponential increase. All attempts to curb the population growth have been unsuccessful, yet it has been discovered that the best method of population control is a rising standard of living. That is best achieved through an ever-expanding economy.

The only way to keep the economy expanding infinitely is to expand our resource base infinitely. The universe is a big place. Human ingenuity is such that we will find innumerable ways to economically prosper in space. The list of known methods is already long: solar power satellites, lunar helium-3 production, asteroid mining, hydroponic agriculture, tourism, to name a few.

We only need a few visionaries to realize the magnitude of the rewards of space development and the horrors of global depression to jump-start the space economy. The explosion of new industries and jobs created in their wake will dwarf any economic expansion that has heretofore occurred in human history. Poverty would diminish worldwide as the growing labor requirements of the new space industries put an ever-increasing number of people to work. Additionally, as we progress into space, we will discover or develop new opportunities, further compounding the positive economic effects. We will have once and for all escaped the trap of a closed, cyclical economy, and the riches of the solar system will lie before us, like fields ripe with wheat, waiting to be harvested for the benefit of all.

Another compelling reason for developing space lies in the necessity of protecting our home planet. Humans are beginning to exert great pressure on the ecosystems of Mother Earth. Even conservative population estimates predict 10 billion people by 2050, almost twice as large as our current population, with no indication of the growth rate slowing. Over half of the people living now are under 15 years old, and all of them are hungry. Food distribution is currently an economic problem, but if we cannot curb population growth, it will soon be a biological problem.

Our industry has developed to a point that we can wield amazing power and accomplish great feats. It all occurs, however, within the Earth's biosphere, so any waste products stay right here, creeping into our food chain and atmosphere.

Conservation is a noble cause, but it is ultimately a losing proposition; the best we can hope for is to slow the rate of pollution and depletion of natural resources. We merely delay the inevitable day of our own destruction. It is impossible to turn the clock back; to get out of our present dilemma, we must march forward.

Science has marched forward, and has devised possible solutions to our problems. Less-polluting energy sources, electric cars, alternative urban designs, to name a few, hold the promise of improving our lives and our chances of survival, Yet we have invested so much in our current way of doing things, both financially and psychically, that our present systems stringently resist change. The status quo rules, and will not give up without a fight.

The Earth is essentially a closed system. We have explored it all, even to the depths of the oceans. The impetus to change from which our ancestors benefited as they discovered new lands and new people is a decreasing factor in our lives. The best we can manage in the current state of affairs is an endless redistribution of resources. Our condition is like a candle; it may burn brightly now, but eventually it will run out of fuel, and snuff out.

If one approaches the human condition logically, the path we must follow is blindingly obvious. Question: How do we provide for the needs of an ever-growing population? Answer: Develop an ever-growing resource base. Question: Since the Earth is completely explored, where do we find these new resources? Answer: Where we have not yet looked: space. Question: Space is hard to reach. How will we ever develop such a resource base? Answer: As in all previous phases of human development, the pressure of an expanding population and the perception of dwindling resources, coupled with the possibility of new riches and adventure, will drive a few hardy souls to risk the unknown for the promise of a better life. The rest of civilization, perceiving new methods of obtaining profit, a rising standard of living, and other rewards, will follow in due course.

As we develop a space-based economy, we will be presented with the unrivaled opportunity to start from scratch, to develop systems as efficiently as possible, rather than incrementally imposing solutions on existing infrastructure, thus creating a palimpsest of technologies that is almost impossible to modify. Moreover, these new discoveries and inventions will filter down to Earth, improving everyone's standard of living. The benefits of an industrialized society will finally be within everyone's grasp.

There is the counter-argument that humans will take their polluting ways with them wherever they go. This may be true, but if we do *not* develop an off-world economy, we are definitely doomed to drowning in our own filth. On the contrary, as we advance into the heavens, we will learn, as we have in our past explorations, to treat our environment and our fellow humans with an increasing degree of respect and care. Human development is not a linear process. There have been tragedies and travesties, such as the extermination of most of the indigenous peoples as Europeans advanced into the "new world." No evil was perceived at the time, but we have now learned that grave lesson, and we are much less likely to inflict similar damage in the future.

One cannot advance into space without considering how to eat, how to excrete, how to breathe; in short, what it means to be *alive*. And one cannot examine those aspects of living without gaining a new appreciation for life. The advance into space will make us more ecologically aware, just as the photograph from Apollo 8 of the fragile Earth floating in a sea of black became an icon for the environmental movement. Space *is* our environment. Our molecules originated in the stars, and now our bodies, minds, and spirits must return to space, to the source of our existence. Only then will we truly be able to understand and care for our beautiful, precious Earth.

Chapter 4

"Great article, man!" Perry exclaimed, thwacking the paper with one hand. He and Art had met for coffee at Café Roma, a small neo-beatnik espresso bar on the 'Ave', the business district near the University, while they were waiting for that evening's meeting of the Seattle Environmental Council to begin.

"Yeah, I'm pretty proud of it," Art said, sipping his double latté grandé. "And there will be five more, if my editor doesn't change her mind."

"Groovy!" Art couldn't decide if Perry's constant use of archaic sixties slang was an indication that he was hopelessly out of date, or if it was a subtle, sarcastic commentary on the silliness and impermanence of all such fads. "Man, I hope you get some reaction with this." Perry said, perusing the paper.

"So do I. We'll find out when the letters start flowing in."

"Hey, look at this," Perry said, sitting up straighter, staring at the paper. "Patterson won the New Hampshire primary."

"No way!" Art leaned over to glance at the paper. "How could people be so stupid as to give that reactionary buffoon legitimacy?"

"I'm telling you, man, times are weird, and people are scared."

"Yeah, and when the going gets weird..."

They finished in unison, "The weird turn pro!" They laughed, and knocked their paper cups together in a mock toast.

Art leaned back, and Perry turned the page. "Wow. It gets weirder. That guy Moustapha Ali has taken over the Iranian parliament."

"You mean that rabid fundamentalist who wants to unify the whole Arab world against the West?"

"That's him. And they love him over there. He wants to institute a strict Islamic theocracy that would make Khomeini look like a regular playboy."

"Wow. Hey, wouldn't it be wild if Patterson got elected, and this Ali guy gained control of all the Arab countries, and they faced each other off across the world stage, or something like that?"

Perry pretended mock anxiety. "Shhh! Don't jinx us, man! We're in bad enough trouble on this planet already."

"Well, it'll never happen, anyway. Like I've said, politics is unkind to extremists."

"Man, I hope you're right. But I don't know.... Hey, we better get going, or we'll be late."

They wandered across the campus, entered the student union, and found the meeting room. As they walked in, Doug was already orating on the night's topic.

" ...and to be effective, we must target one especially grievous offender. Random press releases or protests won't have any effect, because they are too vague. We must bring to light in a focused fashion the transgressions of one company with a poor environmental record. I'm open to suggestions on that score, but my vote is to target Lindstrom Industries, right here in Seattle. As an aerospace giant, they have already participated in the military-industrial complex for decades. They use dangerous and toxic fuel mixtures and solvents, and are careless in their disposal. Three of their sites that they no longer use have been declared extremely hazardous by the Environmental Protection Agency, but the company is unresponsive to demands that they match the Superfund cleanup costs. Hell, they messed it up! They should be held fully accountable! I open the floor for discussion."

A few other members brought up other companies on which to vent the organization's spleen, but eventually, most agreed that Lindstrom was a good target. A motion was made to focus the group's efforts on a protest campaign against Lindstrom Industries, it was seconded, and most members raised their hands in assent. None dissented, but there were a few abstainers, including Art and Perry, who were leaning against the back wall and observing the proceedings.

"It passes, then." Doug resumed. "Now, we must be very unified and focused in this effort, to have the greatest impact. We should establish picket lines everyday in front of the manufacturing plant entrances, as shifts are beginning, and pass out materials to educate the workers on the damage they are contributing to. We should develop a letter-writing campaign to area papers and our local congresscritters, clearly and succinctly stating our views and demands. Art!" Doug finally noticed Art in the back of the room. Art perked up at the sound of his name. "You work for a paper, right? Can you get us some presence there?"

A little hesitantly, Art replied, "I'll see what I can do."

"Good. Thanks. We'd appreciate it. Now, we have to clearly define our position. I'll tell you my ideas, to get things started, and we can hammer out a position for the group."

The next hour and a half was spent in back-and-forth discussion, which often got heated, over the official stand of the Seattle Environmental Council on the environmental violations of Lindstrom Industries. Volunteers stepped forward to take on the various tasks necessary to coordinate the efforts, and a timetable was pieced together.

"Great," Doug finally sighed. "It seems we have a bare-bones plan we can now flesh out. At our next meeting in two weeks, we'll hear reports from our volunteers on the specific steps we should take and how to implement them, and we can look forward to starting our campaign immediately thereafter. Any other new business? No? OK, do I have a motion to adjourn?"

The motion was made, seconded, and passed, and the meeting broke up. Doug approached Art and Perry, who had remained observers in the back. "I didn't see you guys volunteering for too much back here."

"Well," Art replied, "I'm not quite sure this is the direction to take."

"You seemed pretty adamant in your opinion piece about taking action."

"You read that?"

"Yeah, it was pretty good, although maybe a little too sympathetic to big government and corporations."

"Not really. I indulged in some NASA-bashing and government-chastising."

"Well, yeah, but it doesn't really mean anything if you don't follow it up with action, does it?"

"I'm not sure what you mean."

"You've got a platform in your paper now. Why don't you use it to help us? Do some research on Lindstrom, and take them to task in an article."

Art looked down at Doug. Doug was a little shorter than most people, but the energy he exuded more than made up for his lack of stature. His stocky yet lean build and thinning black hair, coupled with his inability to stand completely still, gave him an air of a tightly-wound spring, ready to release copious amounts of energy. His gray eyes had a transparent look to them, that made them seem as if they were focusing a laser on his intended target. Art fidgeted under the penetrating gaze of those eyes.

"That would be violating a public trust. I can't just use my position as a platform for your group's ideas."

"That's just a cop-out. You're using it as a platform for your own ideas."

"Well, yeah, but I never represented it as anything different to my editor. Besides, I'm not sure if yours is the most effective course of action. I've done the protesting thing, and it didn't seem to get anywhere."

"I think it can work. Give me a chance to convince you. Let me buy you a beer at The College Inn." His unswerving eyes burned into Art's soul.

Art questioningly glanced at Perry, who subtlely shrugged, as if saying,

"What could it hurt?"

"OK, but you'll have to present a mighty strong argument."

"Oh, don't worry. Look, I'll meet you there. I've got a few things to wrap up with some people here. Order me a Red Hook."

Art and Perry had put away half a pint each in the warm, wood-trimmed surroundings of the College Inn when Doug finally showed up.

"Sorry that took so long," he said, flinging his long brown coat, covered with Salish Indian geometric designs, over the back of a chair.

"No problem," responded Perry, "We were just discussing the meeting. Are you sure...?"

"Hold that thought." Doug interjected, "I need the little boys' room."

"Are you sure," Perry continued when Doug had returned, and was taking his first sip of beer, "that your protest plan is the most effective course of action?"

"Of course," Doug answered, wiping a foam mustache away. "Look, we've got to let these guys know they're raping the planet. They've been polluting and building bombs and weapons in our name for decades now, and we've got to tell them they can't do that anymore."

"Yes," Art jumped in, "but do you think pissing them off is the best way to do that? I mean, wouldn't it be better to engage them in a dialog, and show them there are better and more profitable ways to make a buck?"

Doug sneered in disgust. "That argument is so full of holes, I barely know where to start. First, it assumes that they care enough to want to change. Second, it assumes that they *can* change, after being spoon-fed by the government for half a century. Third, you're assuming that there *is* a better way to take money away from people."

"But there is! I mean, not to rip people off, but to develop a win-win situation, in which we can all get ahead. You read my article."

"That stuff is pure fantasy. Look, your least-realistic assumption in there was that corporations are working in enlightened self-interest, and for society as a whole. But those fat cats only want to suck what they can out of the people, take the money and run, and damn the future generations. Even if we could get into space, which I doubt, it would just become one more avenue of exploitation. Look at the history of space so far. It's just been a playground for the rich countries, while the rest of the world continues to be held down and exploited."

Art felt the familiar welling of blood in his veins as he rose to the bait. "Sure, that's the way it started, because that is what the times required. But it doesn't have to continue to be that way. Look at the founding of America."

Doug rolled his eyes. "No, hear me out. Sure, when Columbus, Cortez, and the rest of the conquistadors initially explored this continent, they left a wake of dead bodies and shattered civilizations. But they also jump-started, by opening up a New World, the greatest advance of civilization the world has ever seen. We still haven't seen the end of the scientific revolution that those explorations kicked off. And when we go into space, there aren't any indigenous populations to destroy."

"Don't be so quick. What if there's life on Mars? Remember that fossil they found a few years back? Do we have the right to just go in there and tear the place up?"

"Well, the jury is still out on life on Mars. The data from the new probes we've sent to Mars haven't sent back any conclusive evidence yet, but if there is, then we must be very careful. A whole host of ethical issues raise their ugly heads if that happens."

Doug snorted. "Meaning the lifeform is toast, and it's only a matter of how guilty to feel about it."

"No, not at all. I am far from an advocate of Manifest Destiny. No, if there are lifeforms on Mars, I would strongly encourage making Mars a planetary park. You can sell the idea to eco-nuts like you guys as a conservation project, you can sell it to the scientists as a natural laboratory, and you can sell it to the industrialists by explaining that there are a lot more accessible resources on comets and asteroids, without the gravity penalty. Think of this as well. Imagine many years down the road, once space access has become commonplace, we can move heavy industry to the Moon, and into open space, and let the Earth regreen, into an ecological and agricultural paradise. Then, the indigenous peoples we've been trouncing on for centuries can reclaim their ancestral homelands, and live in harmony with nature."

Doug's face lit up a bit. "That's the first thing you've said that's made any real sense. If you really believe all this, why are you so resistant to helping us confront the mega-corporations and making them change their ways?"

"I'm not against that. I Just believe the way I want to change them and the way you want to change them are diametrically opposed. You would rather they didn't engage in developing space, don't you? You would like to see them just go out of business, am I right?"

"Well, yeah. I mean, the big corporations haven't improved our lives; they've made them worse. There is much more stress, much more pollution, and people have been divorced from their environment. If we could tear down the capitalist system and replace it with an interdependent network of agriculture-based villages, we'd all be much better off, and maybe have a real shot at surviving."

Art scoffed. "Now who's talking fantasy! We can't roll back the clock. We can't forget the things we've created. Even if we could curb technology, as you suggest, if all the cultures of the world didn't do it at the same multilateral pace (and it's highly unlikely that they would), there would be a grave temptation for one political entity to take advantage of the vulnerable position of another. Wars would break out all over the place!"

"And we don't have wars now? Look, you're assuming that the great idol 'Progress' can save us. You're assuming that there is even such a thing as 'Progress.' But look at this century. The grand dreams of 'Progress' in the Nineteenth Century led to the worst atrocities and abuses we've ever seen in the Twentieth. Remember Orwell? He said, when he looked into the future, that 'All I see is a boot stamping on a human face for eternity.' I have to say I agree. 'Progress' is just an excuse to rape the Earth and oppress people who can't defend themselves. I mean, think about it. We are destroying the planet! The stuff we're ripping out of the ground, the resources we're squandering, the pollution we're creating, no species has even come close to the devastating effects we're having on our environment. It took four billion years to create Earth, and we're using it up in a generation! We drink out of a Styrofoam cup for ten minutes, and the thing will exist in a landfill for another billion years. It's hideous! Don't you see? We're not only killing ourselves, but the whole Earth, and all the creatures on it, for all future generations. It's the greatest possible evil. If we don't curb our runaway technology, we're doomed."

"No, I couldn't disagree more. I mean, your assessment of the problem is dead on, but your proposed solution is like sticking your head in the sand, and hoping the problem will go away." Doug visibly bristled. "No, we have to walk through the hell of our own making, and come out the other side. We have to use our technology to develop non-polluting forms of energy, such as solar power satellites, helium three fusion on the Moon..."

"But only the mega corporations will profit," Doug interrupted, noticeably irate, "and the rest of the world will still be no better off. Worse, in fact, because the gulf between rich and poor will widen."

Art was getting very heated himself. He leaned forward with intensity. "Yes, but..."

"Guys, guys!" Perry, who had been listening to the whole interchange with an air of bemused detachment, leaned forward and interjected. "I think we had better agree to disagree on these interesting but divergent points. How about another round, and a game of pool?"

"Yes..." "But..." "You see..." Art and Doug stammered and yammered, trying to re-marshal their interrupted faculties to resume the fray. At about the same time, they both relaxed and leaned back into their chairs.

"I guess you're right," sighed Art with a tone of relief. "This battle will rage on and on. I do respect your position, Doug, and I'll think about the things you said."

"Then you'll still consider helping us in one of your opinion pieces?"

"Maybe. I can't promise anything."

"Good enough. I think you'll come around."

"We'll see."

Perry jumped in. "Come on, guys, the pool table's open."

They spent the rest of the evening playing and drinking and laughing and not talking about anything too important.

Art arrived home around one a.m., and caught an earful from Gwen, whom he inadvertently woke up. It was extremely difficult, and somewhat painful, to get up the next day and prepare for work.

Chapter 5

Jana Pandovar, the managing editor of the Seattle Arts Review, shook her head. "I'm sorry, Art. Your piece just didn't generate the interest we expected."

"Haven't you gotten any letters, Jana?" Art asked. He was seated in the editor's office, in front of her large old mahogany desk that was dramatically showing its age. The bustle of a Seattle street out the window behind her framed Jana's head.

"A few, and they were rather enthusiastic, but nowhere near the volume we get on other topics. In fact, more than half the letters agreed with you. We didn't generate the controversy we expected. Here, you can look at all these." She threw a bundle of letters in Art's lap. "Face it, Art, you don't have the 'sex appeal' of abortion or corporate scandal."

"Come on, you said I could run five articles."

"I just can't do it. We have a bunch of other pieces waiting to run. If the interest was there, maybe, but it just isn't."

Art felt as if the floor were falling out from under him. On the brink of success, his dream was getting snatched away from him.

"Give me one more shot. You want interest, I'll give you interest."

Jana turned her big worn leather chair toward the large picture window and surveyed the activity of the city she covered every week for her readers. Art waited on the edge of his chair in nervous anticipation. The tableau held for several interminable moments.

Jana spun back around. "OK, Art, just one more shot, in a couple of weeks. If you generate a decent amount of response, maybe we can talk about some more pieces later. Much later."

Art jumped up and reached for Jana's hand. "Thank you very much, Jana. I promise you won't regret it."

Jana took Art's hand briefly. "Yeah, yeah. Get out of here and get back to work." A half-smirk crossed her lips. "You're wasting company time."

Art snapped to mock attention and saluted. "Yes, ma'am!" He pivoted on his heel and marched out, shutting the door behind him. Jana shook her head and returned her attention to the pile of papers on her desk.

Art returned to his desk, sat down, and put his head in his hands, pushing his red hair back. So I didn't generate any interest? he pondered. What wasn't interesting about what I wrote? I only discussed the future of the planet and of the human race. Maybe it was too big, too vague. Maybe I didn't make it immediate enough. It's easy not to be interested in something that seems remote and irrelevant to daily life. I've got to make it personal and current. But what? Art racked his brain. It seemed the harder he thought, the more his mind emptied of any concrete ideas. Screw it, he concluded, I'm going to lunch.

On his way up Pine Street toward Westlake Center, the idea jumped him like a mugger. He halted in the middle of the busy sidewalk, his face brightening with revelation. Jana had said corporate scandal attracts interest. Doug wanted him to specifically attack Lindstrom. The two concepts crashed together like a wave against a pier, and Art knew what he was going to write about. Doug wasn't as far off base as I imagined, he thought, but I don't think I'll write exactly the article he wants. He resumed his pace toward lunch, feeling much better, now that he had a new mission.

The Seattle Arts Review
March 15, 2000
"A Grave Disservice"
Arthur Roy LaFey

There is an abominable travesty occurring right before our eyes. Actually, a double travesty, because the first one could be corrected and ameliorated by the second. I am speaking of the squandering of the Earth's resources and the pollution caused by big business, especially when those resources could be used to develop an infrastructure that would sustain the human population indefinitely, and lead to a cleaner Earth and a sustainable economy.

Science has now developed technologies and systems that can maintain our Western standard of living without destroying the ecosystem or causing more pollution. For example, a network of solar power satellites can be deployed, which would absorb the constant stream of energy from the Sun, convert it to microwaves, and beam it to Earth, where it would be collected and fed into the existing power grid. We could launch nuclear waste into a parking orbit around the Sun, where it would no longer harm our ecosphere. One may doubt the safety of the launch vehicles which would lift such payloads, but they can be made extremely safe and reliable; it is an engineering problem, and most of those can be solved if one throws enough money and enthusiasm at the problem.

What cannot be readily solved or created, however, is the *will* to engage in these activities. Advancing into space can solve many of the problems that face us in these early days of the Twenty-First Century, but we choose — for the most part — to pursue a quarterly return on investment instead. Such short-sightedness can only be disastrous in the long run.

A prime example of the corporate myopia plaguing our times is Lindstrom Industries, here in Seattle. This company is one of the amazing success stories of the Twentieth Century. Lindstrom was involved in developing and manufacturing airplanes early on, and has continued to lead the pack ever since. The company built much of the hardware that took men to the Moon in the sixties, and has had a hand in just about every major space project since the Space Age began. But this is by no means Lindstrom's main focus.

The company experienced a big boom during World War II, when the defense requirements of our nation skyrocketed. It never retreated from that stance, however, and has garnered the majority of its revenues from defense procurement for five decades. This seems a tragic waste for products which will hopefully never be used, and have little to no economic multiplier effect. (The economic multiplier is the number of additional jobs a certain product creates. For example, a jet airliner is sold to an airline, who then carries passengers on it. The airline needs pilots, flight crews, ground crews, and airports, with all their employees, to run the business. Moreover, the jet allows other companies to conduct business around the globe. Thus the jet exhibits a huge economic multiplier, much higher than a missile or a bomber that just sits there and waits for World War III to happen.)

In recent years, Lindstrom has lethargically, painfully, begun to swing its industrial behemoth around to deriving more of its revenues from non-defense sources. This is, however, not by choice; it is an act of desperation, a last-minute ploy necessitated by the downsizing of the Pentagon and the drying up of defense contracts. Once again, the bottom line is ruling the decisions made around the boardroom table.

The fact seems to escape Lindstrom that, as a defense contractor, it is at the mercy of one customer: the government. The executives of Lindstrom don't seem to realize that if they build a business on the expansive principle of opening the new frontier of space, rather than the very limiting one of blowing up one's enemies, while most likely getting blown up oneself, that the bottom line will increase exponentially, compared to today's current paltry returns. Of course, it takes a vast amount of capital to begin to develop space systems, but those visionary companies who do make the investment will be in a far superior position over their competitors in generating the astronomical profits that will derive from such ventures.

There are already an amazing array of profitable space businesses, such as remote sensing, global mobile telephone systems, direct-to-home television broadcasting, and global positioning systems. Many more are being developed or planned, like space tourism, lunar and asteroid mining, and the aforementioned solar power satellites. The progress is agonizingly slow, however, because companies like Lindstrom are reluctant to commit funds to these endeavors. The managers seem to reason that as long as they can keep milking the cash cow that is the United States government, there is no need to invest their own capital in building future systems.

The ultimate goal of our world economy is to produce an ever-growing supply of goods and services, so that all citizens of the planet may benefit from the industrial and post-industrial movements. However, except for a few civil servants supported at exorbitant costs on the International Space Station (and recent events have led to a call to curtail even this modest activity), the entire human economy takes place on this planet. How can we sustain an ever-growing economy with a finite resource base? We can't; it is fundamentally impossible. If we stay on the planet, we *will* one day reach the limits of growth.

When faced with such a budget shortfall, an organization can implement one of two alternatives: 1) decrease spending, or 2) increase revenues. Decreasing spending is out of the question. The population of the world is growing at an astronomical rate, with no signs of abatement. Moreover, each and every one of those new mouths is hungry. Curbing global spending necessarily dictates implementing draconian population control measures. Putting the obvious moral and ethical questions of such tactics aside, they would produce innumerable revolutions, increasing anarchy, and a deteriorating world economy. In short, curbing spending would result in the precise scenario we would be trying to avoid.

The only viable alternative is to increase revenues. How can we do that, when we have essentially explored the Earth, and can quantify its resource base? The answer is obvious: look up. The Earth is one mere speck of dirt amongst the planets and stars. There is a reservoir of untapped resources, vast beyond our imaginations, just above the cloud tops. We only need to get there. The resulting boom in the economy would be able to sustain populations thousands of times larger than at present. More importantly, however, it will give us the opportunity, the breathing space, to truly solve the questions of population and growth. We would have the unparalleled opportunity to raise the general standard of living on the planet while we develop rational methods of curbing the population. As it stands now, we are desperately rushing around, trying to snatch up as many resources as we can, or trying to prevent someone else from taking what we already have. That is no way for a truly intelligent species to live.

Lindstrom Industries and the other aerospace giants should be focusing their long-range planning on such activities, instead of supporting the war machine, as they currently do, that will ultimately destroy us all. If we fail this grand experiment called Humanity, the blame will rest firmly on their shoulders, for they will have doomed us, when they had it within their grasp to save us, and profit handsomely in the process.

*****

"Not bad, for an evil capitalist." Doug nodded approvingly as he folded and set down the paper. "Now, are you willing to put your money where your mouth is?"

"Huh? What do you mean?"

Doug, Perry, Art, and a few other members of the Seattle Environmental Council were sharing their second pitcher at the College Inn, after a meeting of the SEC. Art looked around the table, and noticed a decidedly conspiratorial air about his companions.

"Well," Doug replied, "We've come up with a plan, and we want you to be a part of it."

"Plan?"

"Yeah." Doug leaned forward, his eyes intensely staring at Art. "We're going to make an example of Lindstrom."

"What do you mean?" Art asked warily.

"Lindstrom is the target of an act of civil disobedience we have planned. We want to grab some headlines, and make a name for ourselves."

Art looked hesitantly around the table. Even Perry seemed to be in on the conspiracy. "What...what are you going to do?"

"We want to get buckets of red paint, symbolizing the blood of the people that Lindstrom's weapons have killed, and throw it all over the front doors of their corporate headquarters. Then we want to strew the place with Monopoly money, to represent all the wasted money that could have been spent on feeding those same people. Naturally, we would let the media know we were doing this, so that they could document it. After we've left, of course."

Art's eyes widened with shock. "I can't do that! I'll get arrested. Look, most of you are single. I'd lose my job, and wouldn't be able to support my family."

Doug slumped back in his seat in disgust. He threw up one arm in exasperation. "I knew it. You talk tough, but you won't back up your convictions with actions. You're just like one of them!"

Perry piped up. "Look, Art, you wouldn't have to actually *do* anything. We just need someone to drive the car. All of us are students; you're the only one with a car. You'll just sit there, we'll do our thing, and you get us out of there. Simple stuff."

Art grabbed his beer glass and finished it with one gulp. He looked around at his cohorts. They were all gazing expectantly at him.

They're right, he thought. If I don't act on my convictions, I'm just a whiner. But Gwen. What would she think? Do I care? And Gary. I have to support him. There's no way we can pull this off without getting busted. But would Gary have less respect for me if I did — or if I didn't — do this?

As he stared at Doug, a vision coalesced in Art's mind. He saw himself many years later, doing the same editorial work at the same paper. He had to stay there; the conditions of the world economy were getting increasingly worse. Gary was grown, and was having trouble finding a job. Space development had fallen off, and there were little to no opportunities for even bright, educated young people. "If only I had taken a stand, and fought for what I believed in, maybe things would be different," the older Art of the vision lamented.

Art snapped back to reality. "Well…?" Doug asked.

"OK, I'll do it! I only have to drive, right?"

"All right!" There were sporadic high-fives around the table.

"Just don't get us busted, OK?" Art said nervously to Doug as he took a long drink from the glass Perry had refilled.

Chapter 6

A couple weeks later, Art was sitting at a table outside an espresso bar in the open plaza at the Westlake Center in downtown Seattle, sipping a caffé latté and reading the Seattle Press, one of the city's major papers, on a cool late March afternoon. It was an uncharacteristically warm day for March, and the espresso bar employees had optimistically set up the outside tables, in hopes of attracting more customers. The sky was cloudy and threatened rain, but every now and then the sun peeked through the heavy clouds.

Art was proud of the picture and headline on the front page of the paper: ECOLOGICAL ACTIVISTS VANDALIZE LINDSTROM. The paper had splurged; the picture was in color, and depicted the great double glass front doors of Lindstrom corporate headquarters, awash in red and strewn with play money. There was a note taped to the doors, but it was not discernible. The caption transcribed it: "This represents all the blood your weapons have spilled and all the money your fat-cat contracting has wasted." The accompanying article explained that no one had claimed responsibility, but Lindstrom would not rest until they had apprehended the perpetrators.

Art quietly chuckled as he read the article. It had been a perfect caper, pulled off without a hitch. Art had stopped at a gas station just before the incident, to let Doug call various newspaper and television reporters (Art had informed him of the best ones to contact) and tell them to get down to Lindstrom as quickly as possible for "a big surprise." Once they had begun implementing their prank, the security guards had come running immediately, but it was so well-planned that Doug, Perry, and the other SEC member involved finished their work and were back in Art's car in less than a minute. Art made Doug spend the rest of the night scrubbing the small splotches of red paint off his car's upholstery with paint thinner.

Art's nerves had been on edge the whole time. "I will never, ever, do anything like that again!" he had vowed as Doug scrubbed.

"Yeah, but it was a rush, wasn't it?"

"Sure, but I can easily pass on rushes like that."

As Art read the article for the third time, two men in dark gray suits and Ray-Ban sunglasses quietly slipped into the chairs on either side of him. Art hadn't really noticed them before he was startled when one asked, "You Art LaFey?"

"Who wants to know?" asked Art, suddenly very nervous.

The other one answered, "We want to have a talk with you, down at Mr. Lindstrom's office."

Art knew he was busted. "Sorry, guys, I'm busy." Before he had finished speaking, he pushed the table over, sending his coffee cup, napkins, and newspaper sections flying, and jumped up to scramble over it.

"Hey!" shouted the man on the right. The one on the left grabbed at Art's pant leg, but didn't get a firm grip. Art hit the ground on the other side of the table, started running, and pulled free of the grasp.

The two men followed immediately. Art ran as fast as he could out of the table area, knocking over chairs as he rushed past. He made it to the sidewalk and quickly glanced about. To his right, he saw the huge neon 'Public Market Center' sign, two blocks away. I can lose them there, he thought frantically, and ran as quickly as he could in that direction. He didn't dare look behind him, to see if he were being pursued, but he didn't need to; he could hear running feet behind him.

He dodged in and out of the crowd on the sidewalk, occasionally and accidentally knocking shopping bags out of pedestrians' hands. All the better of a delay, he concluded. What am I going to do?

Fortunately, the light was with him at the first intersection. He charged across the street and kept running at top speed. He was not used to running; he was getting tired, and was not sure how much longer he could go on. The sound of slapping feet behind him, however, lent him the necessary motivation.

He was not so fortunate at the next corner. The light was red, but he sailed out into the street anyway. Horns blared and tires screeched, but Art didn't care. The front of one car stopped right in his path. He put his hand on the hood, did a semi-vault over it, and kept going. He was now in the market, and was forced to slow down by the pressing crowd. He became extremely anxious, fearing that his pursuers would certainly catch him now. He ducked and dodged through the crowd as best he could, but it was slow going.

He was not precisely sure where he was heading, or what his plan was, but he dared not stop. He reached the central fish market, where the fish handlers would yell out customers' orders and toss large fish across impossible distances to each other. As he was pushing his way past, he felt a hand fall heavily on his shoulder. "Gotcha!" exclaimed his assailant. Just then a voice yelled "Coho!", and the hand lost its grip on Art. As he kept pushing forward, he risked a backward glance. The man in the gray suit had fallen down, a huge salmon covering his face. One of the fish market employees apparently had thrown a fish and struck the pursuer. He quickly glanced over at the worker behind the counter, who returned a wink. That must have been on purpose, Art thought.

Art was quickly approaching a panic. What the hell do I do now? he worried. He saw the stairs that ultimately led down the steep hill to the wharves and the waterfront. Without a plan, he raced down the steps. He didn't hear any feet running behind him, but he dared not slow down. He jumped three stairs at a time in his haste. He came around the corner of a building and could see the pier area below him. He saw the trolley that carried tourists back and forth along the shops and restaurants on the piers. Maybe if I can catch the trolley, I can get away, Art thought, racing down the stairs with renewed purpose.

He reached the bottom of the stairs and ran toward the green trolley, whose decor was reminiscent of the 1890s. It was just pulling away from a stop where several passengers had descended. The trolley was free in this area, to encourage tourist traffic. Art used his last burst of energy to chase the receding trolley. He caught the back rail just before it sped out of reach, and swung himself onto the back step. He turned around and leaned on the back railing, panting heavily to catch his breath. After a few deep breaths, he looked up and back along the trolley's tracks. The two gray-suited pursuers were chasing the trolley, but had no hope of catching it. They were yelling and pointing at Art. Art smiled and waved good-bye to them.

Well, that's that, Art noted mentally. But what now? They know who I am, and they'll keep looking for me. God, I've really blown it. I knew we were going to get caught! Why did I agree to help in that idiot plan! Were those guys cops? They couldn't have been; they said Mr. Lindstrom wanted to talk to me. Oh shit! I've pissed off the big man! How did they know I was in on it? What are they going to do now? What am *I* going to do now?

He turned around to see where the trolley was headed, and caught a glimpse of the Space Needle over the tops of the downtown buildings. I'll go up there and hide in plain sight, he concluded. There's only one elevator up that thing. They'd never suspect I'd go somewhere I couldn't easily get away from. I'll stay up there a few hours, until they stop looking for me, and ponder my next move.

The trolley stopped at the north end of its run, and Art hopped off and rapidly walked (he was too tired to run anymore) the few uphill blocks to the Space Needle. It's incredible, he thought, I've lived here seven years, and have only been up this thing one other time, when I first got here. It's funny how the natives rarely do the things that are the first priorities of the tourists.

He bought his ticket and rode the glass elevator to the observation deck.

As the car ascended, Art glanced all around, searching the streets for his pursuers. He saw no sign of them. A feeling of relief washed over him. He visibly relaxed, and leaned his forehead against the glass for the rest of the ride to the top.

He exited the elevator and walked out to the observation deck. He strolled slowly around the periphery, still trying to gain a glimpse of the dark-suited men on the ground far below. He did not find them, but the cage around the rim of the deck prevented him from seeing the blocks immediately surrounding the Space Needle. Well, I'll just wait up here for about two hours. By then they will have given up looking for me. He glanced at his watch. 12:58. Oh shit! I guess I'm not making it back to work this afternoon. I'd better call Jana.

He went back into the central area and phoned his editor.

"Something important has come up, Jana. I'll be in in the morning."

"Hell, Art, OK, if you can still get that MacMillan piece done by tomorrow afternoon."

"Consider it done. I'll work on it at home tonight if I have to. I've been wanting to try out my modem connection to the server anyway. Thanks, Jana."

He hung up the phone and went back out to the deck. He was finally calming down, and his mind wandered through all the possibilities and consequences that this episode implied. He happened to be facing southward, looking over downtown Seattle, its skyscrapers rising majestically beside Elliott Bay. Out on the water, the outbound ferry to Bainbridge Island was just passing the inbound one. The ferries reminded Art of Gwen's sister Sarah, who lived on Bainbridge Island, and he wondered if Gwen and Gary were on that ferry to go visit her, which they often did. No, it's a weekday. Gary is in school. He thought of Gwen sitting home with not much to do, now that Gary had started school. She was called for replacement in the Seattle Symphony just often enough to not want to look for another job. She had a few oboe and piano students, but her days were still pretty empty, and she resented Art's constantly working and all the schemes he came up with to improve their situation. If only I can make some real money with one of those plans, Art pondered, maybe everything will change.

Beyond downtown, Art could see the Port of Seattle, with its mammoth orange cranes, standing ready to load and unload box cars from cargo ships and attach them to trains, bound for countless inland destinations. Beyond the cranes he could see the top of a building that he identified as the control tower at Lindstrom Field. The whole complex, where Lindstrom Industries built and tested many of its military and commercial aircraft, sprawled out to the south of Seattle, out of sight to Art.

A wave of disgust passed over Art. Look at this city, he reflected. It's beautiful from up here, but get down into those streets, and the ugliness of humanity starts poking through. Homelessness. Drugs. Gangs. Crime. Poverty. The city is getting more crowded all the time. And this is supposed to be one of the most livable cites. And look at these buildings. These businesses try to build up and out of the grime, or disperse out to the periphery, like Lindstrom out there. Don't they realize they can't escape it? It will always grow to catch them. And as we expand the markets of the world, pretty soon there will be no more markets to develop. The game will be up, and we'll sink into a worldwide depression. Don't they get it?

The only way out is to develop more resources. Doing that will provide jobs to those 'great unwashed' who would otherwise be indigent. We have to increase the general standard of living for the whole world, so we can educate as many people as possible and stop fornicating ourselves out of room on this planet. We've got to develop space! Is it really that hard to comprehend? But greedy opportunists like Lindstrom down there are only chasing their bucks, and screw the rest of us! I guess the main problem is that we've got to find the one thing that will motivate us to go. We need that one initial money-maker that will open the floodgates. What could it be?...

Just then, a heavy hand fell on Art's shoulder. Art whipped around. The two gray-suited men stood immobile before him, their eyes hidden behind the impenetrable shades. There was no escape this time.

"How....how did you..."

One of the men pointed down at Art's left leg. Art looked down at it.

"What...?"

"Look around behind."

Art pivoted his leg. On the back of the pants, near the cuff, a small electronic device was attached.

"He tagged you back at the coffee shop, when you first ran," the one on the left said.

"Just call me Marlin Perkins," the other joked.

"OK," Art sighed, "You got me. What's next?"

"Come," they both said, and grabbed Art's upper arms, one on either side.

They rode down the elevator in silence. They reached ground level and walked out of the Space Needle. A black stretch limousine was waiting at the curb. The two men tugged Art unceremoniously into the back seat, and surrounded him on either side. The limousine pulled away.

They rode in silence. As the limousine wended its way through the city, one of the mysterious men removed the tag from Art's pant leg. Art could tell they were traveling south, and guessed they were heading toward Lindstrom Industries. A thousand different thoughts raced through his mind, and his tension mounted. He could feel his cheeks beginning to burn with anxiety.

Chapter 7

The limousine pulled up to the main double glass doors of the corporate headquarters at Lindstrom Industries. As Art was tugged from the Limousine, he noticed there was no trace of paint anywhere, even though the incident had only occurred the night before. The Ray-Banned men hauled him through several doors and labyrinthine corridors. He was finally shoved through two massive oaken doors. In a richly appointed office, Art found himself standing in front of a mammoth mahogany desk. A giant burgundy leather chair on the other side of the desk slowly turned, to reveal an old, very large man, with a tube wrapped around his head and under his nose, which led to an oxygen tank by the side of the desk. There was, however, a vibrant glint in his eye.

"You must be that young fool Arthur LaFey who dowsed my building with fake blood," the old man wheezed.

Art decided it would be better not to correct him on the finer points of the matter. "You must be Merle Lindstrom," Art replied, more than a little awestruck. "How did you know it was me?"

"Oh, come now," answered Lindstrom, "It's pretty obvious. You derided my company pretty severely in your paper a couple of weeks ago. Besides, you didn't take the obvious precaution of changing your license plates."

Art mentally kicked himself for such a simple oversight. "Now I suppose you're going to turn me over to the cops and have me locked up for life, aren't you?"

"I really should, you ballsy little bastard! But I see something in you, something I haven't seen in young people for a long time. Now's your chance, sonny; you're face to face with me. Tell me all that tripe you've been writing about me, plus the crap they won't let you print, if you've got the guts."

Art stared at the old man for what seemed an eternity. What kind of game is he playing? he questioned. He decided he was trapped anyway, so why not let the old geezer have it. Still, there was a lump in his throat that made his voice crack as he started speaking.

"Well, sir (he couldn't help saying 'sir'), you've wasted a perfect potential. You could have spent a mere fraction of the money you've received from highly overvalued government contracts to develop a private space infrastructure. Instead, you kept bidding on weapons systems, and producing massive cost overruns on cost-plus contracts, which you proceeded to keep. You gave lip service to defense conversion, but your earnings statements show that your company has shifted maybe ten percent of real assets away from defense, still leaving you as one of the largest defense contractors. To top it all off, your company manufactured some of the key components on the shuttle that are suspected of contributing to the recent explosion."

Art could tell the old man was getting more and more furious as he talked, but Art felt his blood well up, and he was on a roll. Finally the old man slammed the great mahogany desk with a violence that seemed impossible to have emanated from that flabby frame. "God damn it, you little shit! What do you know about anything?! My grandfather started this company two years after the Wright brothers flew at Kitty Hawk. He dreamt of flying as high as possible. He tried to help his good buddy Bob Goddard get even higher, into space. My granpappy dreamed of flying to the Moon before you were even a spit in the cup!

"Then the Big War came. My granpappy was old, and my father took over. We had to build machines to beat that bastard Hitler. We had to save this country, so you could be born, to grow up and say that crap to me!" Lindstrom's eyes shot through Art's soul like fire. Art felt like he was standing behind himself, watching someone else get berated. "By the time I took over this company, after my tour of duty in 'Nam, defense contracting was so deeply ingrained into this company that nothing could change it. It was profitable, and at the time, *it was the right thing to do*! Those damn Russkies were breathing down our necks, and it was *my* duty to save *your* ass! I am proud of everything I did in those years. We did damn fine work."

Lindstrom softened a bit, and his eyes lost their focus on Art and seemed to look far away. "Trouble is, I remember when I was a kid, taking walks at night with my granpappy. 'See that star? That one, right there,' he'd say. 'That's your star, and someday I'm going to take you there.' My granpappy died in 1960, one God damn year before we sent a man into space, using some of *his* best work. My father didn't share a love of space like we did; he just saw NASA as another cash cow. But I'll *never* forget." The old man's voice trailed off.

Art fidgeted as the old man stared off into a corner for a few moments. Then, with an abrupt jerk, his full attention was back on Art. "But now I have a chance. You can see I'm not a young man anymore, nor am I in good health. I was a good boy. I ran the company like my father wanted me to. But I am retiring next year, and I won't have to do another God damn thing that those bastards on the board want me to do!" All of a sudden, Lindstrom got as excited as a ten-year-old who had found a frog in a swamp. He leaned forward, very animated. "I'm going to do it. I'm going to fulfill granpappy's dream!"

He looked Art up and down, as if assessing him. "You have a dream, too, don't you, son?" Art could only slowly, almost imperceptibly, nod once or twice. Lindstrom fumbled in a drawer, eager to find something. He pulled out six wooden matches and threw them on the desk toward Art. "That's your test, me lad, your 'sword in the stone,' if you will. Pass the test, and we'll dream together. Fail, and I'm going to lock you up so long, you'll be older than I am now before they let you out! Take those six matches and make four equilateral triangles, without breaking them or altering them in any way." The old man sat back deliberately and icily stared at Art.

Art returned Lindstrom's gaze, a thousand different thoughts racing through his head. All of a sudden he lost all ability to think or remember anything, and he stared blankly at the matches. He looked up at the old man, who was now a cold, marble statue. He glanced over his shoulder at the great oaken doors, contemplating bolting, but he knew the two goons who brought him here were probably right outside the doors. He looked back at the matches, and realized his only way out was *through* the problem, not by retreating or trickery.

The universe collapsed into just those six matches, and Art's mind searched for a solution. He created a thousand different patterns in his head, but none of them worked. He even tentatively reached toward the matches, intending to experiment, but he glanced up at the immobile creature behind the desk, and pulled his hand just as slowly back. Sweat began to run down his temples and into his eyebrows. Art hated when that happened, but he was too petrified to wipe the sweat away.

This is a puzzle, Art thought, and I love puzzles. Just treat this with a sense of adventure. Yeah, right, I'm on the edge, and the Old Man has me by the balls. I wonder what he means by a 'dream?' He says I have a dream, too. Does that mean it's the same dream? His granpappy obviously loved space, and instilled a love of space into him. He knows I love space. Does he mean we'll go to space together? If he does, he's a crazy old fart. 'I'm going to do it,' he said. Do what? Go to space? If anybody has the cash and the means, he does. How does he intend to do it?

As it always does when he thinks about space, Art's mind began to wander the void, gracefully sweeping around planets and moons, floating in the interplanetary sea. His eyes were staring at the matches, but his mind was out at the orbit of Saturn, contemplating the majestic rings. In his inner vision he saw immense ships carrying precious cargo in toward the inner planets, and outward again. He saw ferries leave the great ships and descend to the surface of a moon, or to a free-floating colony, and return with the goods fabricated by the colonists.

Suddenly, his mind clicked. "Of course!" he shouted, leaping at the matches. "We're never getting off this planet if we think two-dimensionally." He quickly arranged three matches so that they formed a triangle on the desk. He then tried to stand the other three, one at a time with one hand. He used his other hand to hold the matches in place, up from the three corners of the triangle on the desk, so that the opposite ends rising from the desk met at a point. In his nervousness, he fumbled and dropped the matches several times, but the stone figure did not budge.

Finally, Art achieved his goal: The three matches on the desk formed one triangle, and three more were formed in the space above the desk by the three matches that were standing up, in a three-dimensional symmetrical figure of four equally sized, equilateral triangles. Art stood back, sighed heavily, and finally dared to wipe the sweat from his forehead.

The stone melted, and Lindstrom came back to life. "Congratulations, me boy! I knew you could do it! Otherwise, I would not have invited you here. You had to think unconventionally to pull that trick off. You're exactly what I need in the Project. Come with me." Lindstrom struggled to his feet and ambled over to an obscure corner of the office, dragging the cart with his oxygen tank behind him. There, where Art had not seen it before, was a large table, covered with a plain-looking gray box. A silver chain was attached to the top of the box, and it ran up to the ceiling, over to the wall, then down it, to end in a velvet handle.

The old man struggled over and grabbed the handle. Holding it, he turned to Art. "Judging from your writings, lad, you've put a lot of thought into the world's problems, and how to solve them. Tell me, what is the biggest problem we face?" There was a change in the old man's demeanor, as if he had found someone in which he could finally confide.

Art looked at the man with incredulity, but the answer leapt into his head. "We've run out of frontiers," he replied. "We've entered the Age of Claustrophobia. All other problems stem from that."

"Very incisive, young lad. I've thought the same thing myself... not exactly in those terms, however. What would you say if I could provide, shall we say, an escape valve?"

"What do you mean?" Art whispered, afraid of the answer.

In response, the old man tugged on the chain, and the box rose from the table top. Lindstrom wrapped the chain around a knob on the wall, so as to hold the box aloft, and flipped a light switch. All of a sudden, a vision appeared to Art. He saw, nestled among the rocks of a lunar landscape, a large, curving dome, encasing a complex arrangement of tubes and domes, planes and angles, lights and shadows. It was a fully developed lunar settlement! The detail was so intricate that it took Art a full minute to realize he was looking at a model.

"What..." Art could barely breathe, "is that?"

"Lindstrom Base," Lindstrom responded, defiant and proud.

"But...is it real?"

"As real as you want it to be, lad."

The two men stood motionless for a minute, each thinking quite different thoughts.

"I mean, does it really exist..."Art finally whispered, "...up there?"

"No, you dolt!" Lindstrom exploded violently. "It exists up here!" he shouted, slapping the side of his head. "I mean to make it exist, up there." His finger shot straight up. "Just like I yanked the Sneaker attack jet out of my head, just like I brought the SeaPup mini-sub to life. I'm going to *build* it!" Lindstrom's eyes shone with a maniacal glint.

Art couldn't figure out whether he'd encountered a madman or a saint. Is it possible, he asked himself, that this war-monger actually wants to create what he, Art, had dreamt of and had longed for? There must be an angle.

"There must be an angle," Art said.

"Of course there is, my boy! TANSTAAFL!"

The strange word echoed in Art's head, and for the first time, a tingling arose in his belly, that first twinge of excitement that always let Art know he was doing the right thing, chasing the right dream. The old coot has read Heinlein, he realized. TANSTAAFL: There Ain't No Such Thing As A Free Lunch.

"So..." was all Art could say.

"You're going to help me do it, me boy!" The old man boomed. "You and me, we're going to save this shit-encrusted planet!"

"Me...?"

"Well, no, not you, specifically, boy! I got engineers coming out my ass. But none of them have *soul*!" As if punctuating the sentence, the old man's eyes burned into Art's soul. "Not one God damn one of them ever knows what they're really doing. I *have* to keep them all in the dark, to preserve confidentiality. They need to be guided, like sheep. You!" The finger thrust straight at Art's chest. "You know what to do with something like this." The finger flashed toward the model. "I've read your stuff, and I've *heard* what you have to say!"

Art was stunned. For years, he had been pushing. He had pictured himself as the lone voice in the wilderness, had even somewhat enjoyed the martyr complex that accompanied that perception. Now, when he had expected to get tossed in jail, suddenly his dream was revealed to him, in greater detail than even his imagination could conjure. Art felt like the obstacle he had been pushing against was instantly removed, and he had to catch himself from falling over.

"What...what am I supposed to do?"

"You have to breathe life into this husk. You know as well as I do that this world is going to hell in a handbasket. We've got to save it. We've got to export our civilization, so that it survives. That was one of the first lessons my granpappy taught me: you've got to export to survive. Hell, even if we're wrong, even if the world keeps on spinning, and we don't blow ourselves up, this would be an ideal base for off-world operations, eh?" Art was vaguely disturbed at the conspiratorial tone the old man had adopted, as if Art was miraculously and instantly accepted into Lindstrom's Old Boy network.

"How the hell are you going to build that thing?"

Lindstrom puffed up like an indignant peacock. "Hell, boy, you don't operate in the aerospace industry for fifty years without acquiring a few strings to pull. I've got connections all throughout the military, in Congress, in every administration that comes along, all throughout industry. Lord, some of those people would unquestioningly give me their lives! I practically built NORAD. A few turns of the head from the radar screen, a few fudged launch reports, and we'd have all the materials on the Moon that we'd need to survive a century!"

"But...why?"

"Oh, you idiot! What the hell have we been talking about for the past half-hour?" Lindstrom sidled very close to Art. His breath stank of old cigars, and Art could examine the quality of the old man's cavity fillings. "Immortality, you boob. I could slap my name on the side of just about everything on this planet, but if the whole shithouse goes up in flames, what good is it?" I want to own the *future*!" Lindstrom backed up, looked Art up and down, and turned to slowly amble back toward his huge leather chair.

"It's more than that, though, and that's why I had you brought here. I know I've lived at the pinnacle of civilization. You've obviously observed the state of the world around you. It's downhill from here, unless *we* change it. I have ... a vested interest in seeing the world continue." The old man was about to sit down, but suddenly became agitated. "Damn it, don't you see!? Alexander, Caesar, Ming, Charlemagne, Napoleon! When their times were up, they were through! Except for a few daring exploits, they left nothing behind. Nothing! I want the world to remember me! And not as some grotesque monster, like Hitler! I want to be known as the savior of the world!" Lindstrom's two arms rose upward, as if lifting the planet. " I want to lead my children to the promised land! I want there to be a future!" Lindstrom's arms dropped to his side, and he looked at Art, defiant, yet with an air of defeat. "I only want to do what my granpappy taught me. I only want to live a good life, and leave something for my children." He slumped into the folds of the leather chair. A beam of light glancing off the dome of the lunar base model shone through his silvery hair.

Art didn't know what to think. During the whole encounter, he had stood relatively motionless in the center of the great office. He was less inclined to move now. They remained where they were for uncountable moments, Art standing, Lindstrom sitting.

Art finally dared whisper, "But... what can I do to help?"

Suddenly Lindstrom animated and became the efficient businessman. He sat up, laid his hands, arms outstretched, on the wide mahogany desk, and rattled out instructions. "Your job is to make sure the activity at Lindstrom Base is not just about dollars and technology, but about people. Your primary duty will be to ensure that Lindstrom Base will be a place where people will *want* to live. I'm imagining recreation, cultural events, art, music, dance, sports, all the things that make life worth living. As an initial project, I want you to begin a catalog of the great works of art and literature, anything essential to a great library or museum. This includes," he recited, ticking them off on his fingers, "literature, music, paintings, sculpture, film, theater, philosophy, religion, anything that portrays Man's struggle to know himself. Of course, the original works will be very difficult to transport, so you will transcribe everything possible to some sort of electronic storage medium. You may export, say, ten percent of your choices in each category in their original format, but each item must be approved by me."

Lindstrom carried on for the next half hour, outlining in ambitious, ambiguous brush strokes his vision for Lindstrom Base, as he called it, and Art's role in the whole project. After a while, Art gathered that his job was to infuse the whole project with meaning and spirit, and to develop a general cultural and education program for the inhabitants. But why me? he thought. What special contribution can I make? He nevertheless listened intently as the old man talked, or more often wheezed. Before the end of Lindstrom's monologue, Art had been granted a $50,000-a-year stipend, an unlimited expense account (subject to broad oversight by Lindstrom, of course), and had been instructed to quit his job and free up his schedule.

"Now, get out of here, you little turd. Report back in a week with an outline of your plan to humanize this project. You'll meet the other members of the team then. My secretary will furnish you with the time and place on your way out. She'll be your main point of contact with the Project. She'll get you anything you require. I trust you can keep all this confidential?" He stared at Art through his thick white eyebrows.

"Oh… yes sir, I can. May I consult with anybody?" Art had not talked for so long, he had almost forgotten how.

"Well, hell, boy, of course you'll have to consult with people. You will be nominally working for the Lindstrom Philanthropic Foundation. You will be acquiring your items for charitable donations to museums and schools. You just can't tell anyone where those institutions will be." Lindstrom winked slyly. "Well, that's it for now. Now get out of here, and get to work."

As Art opened the thick oak door to leave Lindstrom's office, he saw the two gray-suited men, sitting in the reception office outside Lindstrom's. Both gave Art a brief smile and a casual salute.

Lindstrom's secretary handed him a thick envelope. "You must be a very lucky man, Mr. LaFey. Most people come out of that office looking like they've been hit by a tornado. You must have said just the right thing." There was a glint in her eye as she said, "You must be some sort of philosopher."

"Thank you… I think." Art said, a little hesitantly. He was a bit taken aback at the general change of attitude toward him since he had been brought forcefully in. He looked closer at the secretary. Art was struck by her casual beauty. "Thank you…."

"Mara." She flashed him a smile. "I look forward to working with you." She extended her hand for a handshake.

"Yes, me too." Art shook her hand and turned to go.

One of the Ray-Banned gentlemen got up to lead Art back out of the building. "I'm your shadow now." He did not turn as he spoke. "I will always be there to protect you, if you need it." They walked on a few paces. The man wheeled around suddenly, and Art almost barreled into him. "Or protect Lindstrom from you. Remember that." He turned again, and kept walking. Art was shaken, but kept following.

They walked out the infamous front doors, and Art got back into the waiting limousine. The sun was setting; Art had been with Lindstrom all afternoon, and into the evening. It had not seemed that long to Art. As the limousine drove him home, Art opened the packet from the secretary. Included was a memo informing Art that the initial meeting of the board of the Lindstrom Philanthropic Society was Thursday, April 6, 2000, at 7:00 p.m., in Lindstrom's boardroom. Art also found several pamphlets of Lindstrom corporate propaganda (no doubt to ameliorate my opinion of the company, thought Art), and a check for $10,000.00. Art slapped his forehead in disbelief. Maybe I ought to engage in civil disobedience more often, he mused.

Chapter 8

"Hi, honey, I'm home."

"About time, too. Where have you been all afternoon? Your office called, wondering where you were."

"I called Jana and told her what I was doing. She must not have told everyone else."

"Still, it's after eight. Where have you been?"

"Well, I had some stuff to take care of. I'll tell you about it later. Is Gary still up?"

"I just put him down. You should go tuck him in. Really, Art, you've been out a lot lately. I get so tired."

"Look, some special things are happening right now. I'll tell you all about it soon."

"Don't bother. You obviously care more about your 'projects' than you do about this family, so just go on about your business. *I'll* take care of the family."

"Now that's unfair! I'm working hard, and I've got something big brewing. I just don't want to tell you about it until I'm sure of the way things will turn out. You know how you hate it when I say something, then it doesn't happen. Well, this is *big*."

"You always say that, and it never works out. You are such a dreamer, Art. Good night. I'm going to bed. Go see your son."

Art went into Gary's bedroom and lay down beside him.

"Hi, pooky. You still up?"

"Hi, Daddy. How are you today?"

"Just fine. Did you have fun at kindergarten today?"

"Yeah."

"What did you do?"

"Don't know."

"Don't know? Of course you do. Did you play games?"

"Hmm... Yeah."

"What games did you play?"

"Don't know."

"Sure you do. Did you play 'Duck, duck, goose?"

"Yeah, and I was the goose!"

"You were? I bet you were a good goose."

"Hmm... Yeah."

"What else did you do?"

"Don't know."

"Aw, come on now. Did you sing songs?"

"Yeah. We sang my favorite! 'Oh, I'm a workin' on a railroad, all a live long daaaaaay. I'm a workin' on a railroad, just to pass the time awaaaaaaay. Dinah won't you blow....' "

"No, like this: 'Can't you hear the whistle blowing...' "

"Noooooo! I get to sing it!"

"OK, you sing it."

" 'Dinah won't you blow, Dinah won't you blow, Dinah won't you blow your hor...or...orn.' The end."

Art chuckled. "Hey, do you want me to read you a night-night story?"

"Yeah! Yeah! Read 'Wizard of Oz!' "

"OK. Now where were we?"

"Don't know."

"Well, let's look at the pictures, and we'll figure out where we were in the story."

"OK. Let me look at the front. There's Dorothy, and there's Toto, and there's the Tin Woodman...Hey, Where's the....Where is... he doesn't.... where's his... he's got a funnel for a hat...where is it?"

"Don't know, pooky. It must have fallen off in the grass, and he's looking for it."

"Oh. And there's the Scarecrow. He has his hat on the ground, because he doesn't need to wear it when he's sitting down."

"That's right. OK, here we are. 'Dorothy sat up and noticed that the house was not moving; nor was it dark, for the bright sunshine came in at the window, flooding the little room...' "

"Daddy, I love you."

"Aw. I love you too, Gary."

Art gave Gary a big hug.

"OK, now, you try to get sleepy. I'll read to you for just a little while."

"OK, you read for a couple of more whiles."

Art chuckled again, and rubbed Gary's head. "You little pooky bear. OK. 'She sprang up from her bed and with Toto at her heels ran and opened the door. The little girl gave a cry of amazement and looked about her, her eyes growing bigger and bigger at the wonderful sights she saw....' "

After Gary was fast asleep, Art tucked the blanket around him, adjusted his pillow, kissed his forehead, and shut the door most of the way, open just enough to let in a little of the hall light. He went to the living room, flopped down on the couch, grabbed the remote control, and turned the television on to CNN.

"...the Republican primary here in California. In an amazing upset, although many would claim it was no surprise, it appears that Jerry Patterson of the Christian Union is winning the primary and could very well become the front runner for the nomination of the party. The race is still very tight, however. We turn to Mitchell Heiligmann for analysis."

"Well, George, all the precincts have not reported yet, but the contest is too close to call. As you know, Patterson's organization has campaigned heavily here, as they have in all the other key states. It seems that, on the local level, conservative Christians are very well organized, passing out information through churches and school boards, and motivating people with similar values to get out and vote. They characterize it as a fight for the moral fiber of America, almost a crusade, if you will. Although Patterson has been the second runner-up in many primaries and caucuses, he has won enough states to give the front runner Nelson Blindich a real run for his money.

"As you can see behind me, here at a rally for Patterson in downtown San Diego, Patterson generates almost a fanatical degree of support. The moderate faction of the Republican party, which backs Blindich, is calling the tactics of the Christian Union, Patterson's main support group, machiavellian and borderline unethical, and is characterizing this whole movement as nothing less than usurpation of the leadership of the Republican party. Meanwhile the Christian conservatives claim they represent the true opinion of the country, and it's time to break the moderates' 'old money' stranglehold on the party. This promises to be the most exciting primary season in decades. This is Mitchell Heiligmann reporting from San Diego. Back to you, George."

"Thank you, Mitchell. In international news, Moustapha Ali has been named Imam, or supreme leader, for life in Egypt. After many unsure months following the mysterious death of Egypt's past Premiere, Wali Al Faddah, the power struggle seems to have resolved itself. During the ceremony today in which Ali was installed, he vowed a return to the traditional ways of Islam, and complete intolerance of corrupting Western culture. Ali has already been named Ayatollah in Iran, and is popular in many other Arab states. He seems to have the ability to unify Arabs across national boundaries. There is as yet no official reaction from Israel, but it is reported that security has been tightened and the military has been put on alert, especially along southern bases.

"We turn now to Bernie Laninga for sports news…."

Disgusted with the news, Art flipped off the TV and went to bed.

Chapter 9

"Man, you are *not* going to believe this!" Art said as he sat down on the couch in Perry's apartment. "Nice couch," he remarked, patting the faded off-green and threadbare upholstery.

"Thanks. Goodwill special. Beer?"

"Sure." Art took a long drink from the Red Hook Perry offered him. "You know, for a broke college student, you sure have expensive taste in beer."

"Hey. Some things just aren't worth compromising on. So what's up?"

"OK, check this out. You remember our little escapade the other night?"

"Do I?! It was all over the papers and the local news the next day! We really pulled it off. Good thing we didn't get busted."

"Well...."

"What?" Perry looked worried. "Are you in trouble?"

"Not exactly. Look, I have to swear you to secrecy. I'm exploding, and I have to tell someone. You could, however, be in danger of your life if you let on to anyone that you know about this. Can you keep a secret?"

"Hell, I can keep the Pope's underwear color a secret if it's going to get me killed. I can tell by the way you look that something big is up. Come on, man, spill the beans!"

Art surveyed Perry, wondering whether he should divulge his knowledge, teetering on the brink between the magnitude of his information and consequent gravity of revealing it, and a burning need to share it with a trusted co-conspirator. At last he made a snap decision, and launched into the events of three days previous. Perry's eyes grew wider through the whole story, and he emitted an intermittent "Woah!" and "No way!" when Art reached the most incredible parts.

At the conclusion of Art's tale, Perry sat back for a moment, drank a long slow sip of Red Hook, and whispered "Avalon...."

"Sorry?..."

"You guys want to build Avalon." Perry said with a tone of realization.

"What are you talking about?"

"Do you know what Avalon is?"

"Yeah. A ballroom in Jersey. An album by Roxy Music. A movie with Burt Lancaster. A car. So what?"

"No, no, I mean the *real* Avalon. King Arthur's final resting place."

"You *are* making a leap! What does King Arthur have to do with a lunar colony?"

"Everything. Look, if there's one thing I've learned in my Comparative Literature studies, it's that the eternal themes recur, and men undertake the same quests, generation after generation. Do you know the story of King Arthur?"

"Well, I know what everyone knows. The sword in the stone, Lancelot and Gwynevere, Camelot, so on and so forth. There was a pretty cool movie about the knights of the round table when I was a kid. 'Excalibur,' I think it was called."

"Let me tell you the real story of King Arthur. It happens to be my specialty; I'm writing my dissertation on the subject. This could take several beers, mind you."

"That's fine. Gwen took Gary off to her sister Sarah's on Bainbridge Island for the weekend. I've got nothing but time. Good thing it's Friday night."

"OK. Just kick back and bear with me. I think you'll see how this relates to your situation before too long."

Perry shifted into a professorial tone. "Arthur was King of England in its golden days. He gathered about him valiant knights, whose duty it was to uphold chivalry and honor." Perry paced as he talked, waving his arms with a flourish to accentuate his points. "He was the son of Uther Pendragon, who was king before him, but Uther was killed prematurely, and Arthur was raised by peasants, knowing nothing of his lineage.

"After Uther's death, the dukes and earls fought bitterly, and England was splintered. It was prophesied that whosoever could pull the sword from the magnificent stone that had mysteriously appeared in the yard of a church in London would be king. There was a great tournament, and all the dukes and princes fought for the right to attempt to remove the sword, but of course none could. Arthur, who was at that time the squire of his (unknown to him) adoptive brother, was looking for a sword for his brother to use in the tournament, for he had misplaced the one they brought. He casually pulled the sword from the stone, thinking nothing of it, but all the people dropped to their knees and honored Arthur as king." Art was amazed at the transformation in Perry; he was in his element, speaking very eloquently, carried away by his subject.

"Arthur accepted the honor, along with the challenge of uniting England. He spent many years fighting wars to unify England, and succeeded in establishing Camelot, in which he had a great round table brought in where all his knights would sit, so all were equal, and none was held to be superior to another, except by deeds of valor-at-arms." Perry turned toward Art with a gleeful grin. "I love telling the tale this way. I like to imagine I'm a bard entertaining his king on a cold winter's evening."

He resumed his pacing and gesticulations. "For many years, life at Camelot was good, and the knights went out on many quests and encountered many adventures, which they then recounted at Camelot through the cold winter months. The greatest of these quests was for the Holy Grail, that holiest of chalices which was purported to be the cup from which Jesus drank at The Last Supper. The Grail had been brought to England, so it was generally believed, by Joseph of Arimathea. He had, according to popular accounts, entombed Jesus, and had taken magical and powerful relics of His, among them the Holy Grail, to prove to others that the mystery and message of Jesus Christ was true. Whosoever looked on the Grail would know peace, wisdom, and God. Only one knight, Sir Galahad, was worthy of the quest, and he never returned to Camelot. The beauty of his vision when he beheld the grail lifted him directly to heaven.

"However, the seed of Camelot's dissolution had long since been planted. The very moment that the greatest of the knights, Lancelot, gazed upon Gwynevere, Arthur's queen, his heart never again knew rest. He rarely came to Camelot, for fear that his heart would betray him. Of course, it did. After a particularly stringent tournament in which Lancelot was wounded, Arthur insisted that he stay at Camelot to recover. As fate would have it, Gwynevere reciprocated Lancelot's affections, and they secretly spent as many hours as possible together.

"This did not go unnoticed by the more observant of Arthur's knights, in particular to Mordred, the King's nephew. Mordred, who had designs of his own, hatched a plot to trap Lancelot and Gwynevere in their tryst. Lancelot fought his way free, and fled Camelot. Gwynevere, however, was captured, put on trial for treason, and sentenced to burn at the stake. Lancelot, hearing of this, desperately rode into the courtyard, killed several knights, and rode off with Gwynevere back to his native lands in France. Arthur, driven to fury, raised an army, pursued Lancelot, and pillaged the French countryside for months. He besieged Lancelot in his castle, but could not win a decisive victory.

"Meanwhile, Mordred cultivated his own dark plans. Arthur had named him regent of England in his absence, and Mordred took this opportunity to usurp the throne. Arthur caught wind of this, abandoned his siege of Lancelot, and rushed back to England to recapture his throne. There was a tremendous battle between the forces of Arthur and Mordred, and even Lancelot, due to his chivalrous nature and love of his former king, returned to fight for Arthur. In the end, almost everyone was killed. Finally, as the sun was setting, Arthur and Mordred met face to face. They fought viciously. Arthur finally skewered Mordred on a lance, but with his last ounce of energy, Mordred slid down the lance and split Arthur's head open with his sword.

"The king was dying, and the land with him. One of the last knights alive, Sir Gawain, stayed with Arthur in the twilight, by the side of the sea. In the fading light, he saw a boat approach, with three fair women aboard. They told Gawain they would take Arthur to the isle of Avalon, where Arthur's wounds would be healed, and he would return to lead England to greatness again. One of the women was Morgan Le Fay, who, in the shining noontime of Camelot, had been a bit of a trickster, weaving spells and misleading knights, and generally causing a nuisance.

"Le Fay. That's my name!"

"Le Fay is old French for 'the fairy'. Who knows? Maybe you're descended from her. Maybe you have the blood of the Good People, the fairies of Ireland, running through you," Perry joked, saluting Art with his beer. "Anyway, that was how the people of medieval England knew her. In older myths she was known as Morgana, the high priestess of the feminine mystery cult, and in even older tales as the Morrigan, the three-headed goddess of war and conflict. But now, in the waning of the day, she was the healer, the mother, the goddess, who would restore health and life to Arthur. Wait..."

Perry quickly turned to his bookshelf and began rummaging through his books. "Here," he announced, triumphantly holding up a worn book. "This will tell it better than I can." He flipped through a few pages, found the right one, and read:

"Arthur was wounded wondrously sore,
And these words spoke he with sorrowful heart,
'And I shall fare to Avalon to the fairest of all maidens,
To Argante the queen, a fay most fair,
And she will make sound all my wounds,
And make me all whole with healing potions;
And afterward I shall come again to my kingdom,
And dwell with the Britons in very great joy.' "

Perry appeared wistful as he stared out the window. Art, who had been mesmerized by Perry's tale, was also a bit moved.

"That's from a guy named Layamon, who wrote this about 1200 A.D., easily six hundred years after Arthur lived. Argante is a variation of Morgana, and 'fay' means fairy in old English. That was just the beginning. Arthur's story grew until it became the national legend of England."

Art was confused. "But what has all this got to do with lunar bases?"

"Patience. I'll get to that. Of course, a factual Arthur didn't live the life we read about in, say, Malory's Le Morte D'Arthur. Arthur, the Knights of the Round Table, Camelot, and all the rest are symbols of something much deeper, something that resonates deep within the soul. Oh, there probably was some great warrior at the fall of the Roman Empire who gained a respite against invading barbarians. Some scholars have even unearthed a few likely candidates. But dwelling on the factual reality of Arthur is missing the much deeper point. We have to go even farther back to the beginnings of The Great Struggle to really understand what the Arthurian cycle is all about.

"Back at the dawn of time, when the proto-men and women were experiencing the first glimmerings of consciousness, they started to ponder what it meant to be alive, and what it meant to die. They would witness a comrade, who yesterday was walking and laughing and hunting, but today lies so still and does not move. The next day he begins to stink a little. What has happened? It was next to impossible for these primitive beings to imagine that their comrade's life energy just went away, so they began to make up stories about where their friend went. These stories, of course, are colored by their world and their experiences in it.

"Initially, these early humans were primarily hunters, for they were just coming out of an ice age, and the world was cooler, and large game, such as the Woolly Mammoth, was abundant. So the early stories, the proto-religions, if you will, modeled life, death, and life after death on The Great Hunt, or the Quest. Since this world was fickle and did not provide a constant food supply, their friend obviously had departed for a realm where game was always plentiful and the climate was always temperate. Thus we get the first glimmerings of a Heaven. Another beer?"

"Sure."

"Of course, men excelled at the hunt, so early tribes became male-dominated. The hunt was very goal-oriented, so early men tended to develop a linear view of time in which individuals played a significant role. Thus the model of life became the Quest, in which an individual is born, struggles heroically through life, and is ultimately rewarded with the Great Boon, or fruition of his hunt. This is the ultimate source for the myths of Zeus and Hercules, Odin and Thor, and Arthur and Lancelot. A hunt, of course, had to take place during daylight hours, so the Sun became a symbol of this growing body of myth. The hunter's conception of life is very male, linear, animalistic, and in the daylight world.

"The Hunt ruled men's conscious and sub-conscious minds for millennia. But then another culture began to emerge. As the men would wander off in quest of game, the women would stay back at camp and gather what fruits, vegetables, and nuts they could find. Of course they would drop some on the way back to camp, and they would take root. It probably took countless centuries of noticing and forgetting until some of the women figured out that the plant that grew in the path was a direct result of dropping a bean or a nut. But once they acquired that knowledge, the women began to grow in power, until they superseded the men.

"For you see, the women could grow a more stable food supply than the men could bring back from the hunt. It was feast or famine with the men, but the women provided for the clan, year in and year out. Since plants grew in a cyclical manner with the seasons, that is the way the female-led cultures began to view the cosmos. They also needed a way to predict the cycle of the crops, so they turned to the steady rhythms of the stars and planets to inform them when to plant and when to reap. Thus, the night becomes the source of power, the realm of women. And the Moon dominates the night. The Moon became a symbol for women and their power, because it waxed and waned every twenty-nine days, pretty much matching a woman's menstrual cycle. In fact, menstrual means moon. Both words stem from the Latin mensis, meaning moon or month.

"Once the women gained ascendancy, they of course did not want to hand back power to the men, so they developed a hierarchical culture ruled by priests and kings. Of course the King was ruled by a Queen; this phenomenon survives in chess, where the king is the center of power, but he is weak and must be protected by the Queen. The priests developed a cyclical, mysterious, agricultural, many-layered religion that only Initiates who had passed the various levels could comprehend. In addition, agriculture is necessarily a collective exercise, so this is when slavery began, and the world was first divided into the haves and have-nots.

"The central mystery of the feminine religions was that of the continuity of life. The plants died every autumn, but would mysteriously spring back to life in the spring, once again providing sustenance to the tribe. How could this be? Moreover, they pondered the central mystery that to live, one must kill and eat other living things, both plant and animal. They noticed that new human life grew in the bellies of already existing life, and that women had to eat much more food to get nourishment to those growing beings in their bellies. They concluded that the life force must pass from being to being, and continually cycles through Earth, plant, animal, human, and then when we die, back to the Earth, to begin the cycle again. This is the first inkling of the sublime Hindu notion of reincarnation."

Art shook his head. "Hunts, priests, reincarnation... I don't get it. What's that got to do with King Arthur? And how does any of this relate to Lindstrom?"

"Patience, my good man. You should feel lucky that I'm trying to encapsulate the entire cultural history of humanity in one night. It took me several years of research and heavy student loans to fill my head up with this stuff. Where was I? Oh, yeah. Although the feminine agricultural societies could provide more steadily for their people than could the masculine hunting cultures, nonetheless there were famines, droughts, and bad harvests. The priestesses hit upon the notion that perhaps they could coax along the growing cycle if they infused more life energy into the process, so they started sacrificing higher orders of life to the lower, in hopes the Earth would pick up the energy and become more abundant. Of course, the highest level of life energy was concentrated in a human being and the highest order of human was a king in the prime of his life. Thus began the ritual sacrifice of a king, the pinnacle of the pyramid of life, so that his energy, in the form of his draining blood, could return to the Earth and re-energize it to grow more abundantly for the whole community. It was a small price to pay, especially for the vitality of the community. There was no perception of an injustice being done to an individual, because life was viewed as cyclical, and just like the plants and the children growing in women's bellies, the energy that was the king would return someday and manifest itself in a new king. Besides, the concept of an individual, if you will recall, belonged to the masculine, hunt-oriented societies.

"Well, the macho hunters weren't going to take this state of affairs lying down. As the world warmed, the feminine cyclical cultures tended to concentrate toward the equator, where the most fertile land was located, and the masculine cultures were increasingly marginalized toward the poles, where the large beasts of the hunt still thrived. The male-led nomadic hunting bands wandered endlessly in the more extreme climes. But then the development of animal domestication took place, and the male cultures could begin to provide as well as the agricultural societies. The Great Struggle commenced, as each type of culture vied for dominance in various parts of the world. It was a vicious, bloody conflict that raged for centuries, even millennia.

"This is the origin of the myth of Cain and Abel. The story doesn't make any sense until you evaluate it in this context. Abel was a shepherd, and Cain was a farmer. Each offered to the Lord, but the Lord preferred Abel's offering. Why? The bible doesn't say. But buried in one line, almost a throwaway, lies centuries of struggle, which the nomads-turned-herders obviously won, at least in ancient Palestine. So Cain slew Abel and was banished by the Lord. In other words, the hunters kicked the farmers' butts and sent them running, but not before they experienced their own heavy losses. The Lord put a mark on Cain. This symbol represents the mysterious subtle powers of the feminine cultures, with their rituals and magic and astronomy. Even though the hunters generally won the struggle, they did not understand the power of the feminine culture, were still terrified by it, and wished to avoid it."

Art looked pensive. "I think I'm beginning to get it..." he said slowly.

"Good. Now we have the groundwork to understand what went on in the Arthurian cycle. Through the civilizing influences of the Indian, Persian, Greek, and Roman cultures, these two mythic complexes spread over the known world. As I said earlier, the feminine cultures gravitated toward the tropical regions, while the nomads and pastoralists moved generally toward the north.

"As part of these migrations, the Celts ended up in the British Isles. The Celts were a nomadic hunting people, so they were marginalized toward the north, and at that time, Britain was pretty north. But they moved in over a previously established population, which was definitely of feminine, agricultural origins. As had occurred in Palestine, there was a centuries-long conflict for dominance, which the Celts eventually won. Once again, however, they could not eradicate the mysterious Goddess, and they feared her. The feminine culture became the substratum, the underpinnings, of the masculine culture. The myths and legends of The Great Struggle were told and retold, and, as such stories do, they became more fantastic and magical with each retelling. The Irish tale of The Cattle Raid of Cooley is an excellent example of the Great Struggle, but there's no way we have time for that tonight.

"Finally, with the Roman invasion, we reach a semi-literate age, in which history (for the Britains) began. As the Romans retreated, around 400 A.D., many barbarian tribes seized their opportunity and invaded Britain. Some surviving documents tell of a great general who fought off these invaders for a time, and instituted a brief period of peace. He undertook a campaign in

Brittany, in western France, to help an ally, and he never returned. Remember Arthur's campaign against Lancelot in France? There was infighting among his lieutenants that he left behind, the fragile peace cracked, and Britain sank into the Dark Ages. This general was the historical figure on whom Arthur was based. Since he disappeared without a trace on his French campaign, his people held out hope that he might one day return to save them. You can see how the legend began to grow. Hey, your beer is empty. Here."

"Thanks."

"This shadowy historical figure came along at just the right time to become a magnet for the fading legends of the Celts. They had been pushed back to the far reaches of the British Isles by the Romans, and their way of life was losing vitality. The proto-Arthur gave them one last hope of glory, and they seized upon him, more subconsciously than consciously, and made him their returning king, who would lead his people once again to greatness. But this promising general disappeared mysteriously, without recreating a golden age.

"The disappointed Celts could not give up hope. They constructed legends of yet another return (the cyclical wheel keeps turning), and appended their ancient tales to him in the form of the Knights of the Round Table. They waxed nostalgic for Camelot, a golden age that never was, perhaps dimly reflecting Roman glory, and that would come again in some distant time. Arthur became the divine king, whose character and nobility supported the land and the people.

"Remember, however, that in the feminine cyclical myths which circulated just beneath the surface of the Celtic culture, the king must be killed so that his vitality can reenter the land and sustain the people. Arthur and his knights were hunters, forever questing, and living in the daylight world. In this male-dominated realm, a figure such as the sorceress Morgana was mysterious, mischievous, even wicked. She was forever plotting and fouling up the grand designs of Camelot, for that was her role and her duty. And Gwynevere was ultimately the agent of Camelot's fall. Leave it to men to always find a way to blame women for their own misfortunes!

"Arthur was sacrificed in a great noble battle, and his blood ran back into the land. Morgana guided the boat that took Arthur to Avalon to be healed. Now that the stable, male-dominated sunlight world had drawn to a close, Morgana transformed from a counterproductive mischief-maker to the one true healer, the sister-mother-healer-goddess, the only hope of salvation. The feminine culture concurrently supports and undermines the male world, but in the end, when the men have spent their energy on futile war and material strife, the women take over, and support, nurture, and heal. The Isle of Avalon, forever shrouded in night and bathed by moonlight, where Morgana took Arthur, is analogous to the womb. This is the sacred healing place where Arthur will recycle and be born again, once again to establish his brief reign of the male, sunlit golden age, only to sink back once again and rest in the bosom of woman. The wheel turns, the cycle is ever thus."

With a very smug, confident look on his face, Perry, who had been agitatedly punctuating his soliloquy with all manner of gestures and body language, flopped down in the big old burgundy overstuffed chair, with such force that it lost more of its stuffing from its various rips and tears, and looked at Art with an air of self-satisfaction.

Art stared at Perry with a blank look on his face. He finally said, "But... what has any of that got to do with Lindstrom's project?"

Perry jumped up again, agitated as ever. "Don't you get it, man? That moonbase *is* Avalon! That Old Man Lindstrom has looked around, and seen that the male-dominated, sunlit world he's helped create is falling apart, and it's time to mellow out and heal a while. He wants to build a retreat where people can rest and regenerate, meditate, get their shit together, and try to get it right once they've calmed down a bit. But this is the wild part: he doesn't just want to retreat to some moonlight-bathed island; he actually wants to retreat *to the Moon itself*!"

Perry started shaking his hands in excitement. "Man, this is great! Without even knowing it, he's living out the ancient myths that have seeped into his unconscious." Perry stopped pacing, and suddenly looked somewhat concerned. "But if he's going to pull it off right, he better make sure he gets plenty of women up there, as many as the men. Because if the place is run only by men, the whole male dominance trip will start up again too early, and there won't be any healing, and we'll all *really* be doomed!"

Art was stunned. The whole picture had suddenly congealed in his mind, like a great tapestry depicting the course of western civilization. "So... you mean, this isn't new?"

"Hell, no! Well, the technology is, no doubt, but this dream is as ancient as Odysseus spending several years on Circe's island. Men (and it's usually men) have to retreat from the world for awhile, to gather their strength and get in touch with the feminine aspects of their psyche. They then come back stronger, more mature, less warlike, and ready to try to build something permanent.

"You say you've been tapped to develop a cultural library for this place? I would love to help you with that. We would want to make sure we acquired a balanced set of materials that reflected both sides of The Great Struggle, all the way back to the beginning of culture, so that we could truly foster the healing process."

Art pushed his hair back. "Whew. This is going to be a massive project, much bigger than I had imagined. I thought I was just going to have to collect a few books and paintings. I will definitely need your help." Art was struck with an inspiration. "Hey! Maybe I can get you together with the Old Man. I'm sure he would love to have your expertise on the Project."

Perry started bouncing around like a little kid. "Would you? That would be great! Man, this is going to be a blast!"

They both opened new beers, chinked their bottles in a toast, and took big gulps. They then sat down and began plotting their collection of cultural artifacts. The houses were turning purple in the first light of day before they ran out of steam, and Art crashed on Perry's couch.

Chapter 10

The next Thursday, Art took Perry with him to the first official meeting of the Lindstrom Foundation.

"Nice to see you again, Mr. LaFey," Mara said with a wry smile as Art entered the reception area outside Lindstrom's office. "I was beginning to worry we might have scared you off earlier."

"Hello, Mara. I must admit I was shaken, but excited, too. I don't know what to think of it all just yet."

"I'm sure you'll figure it out in due time. And who might this be?" Mara asked, glancing at Perry, who had followed Art into the office.

"This is my friend Perry. He has some excellent ideas for the, ah, Foundation, that we would like to present to Mr. Lindstrom."

Perry jumped forward, hand extended, with the enthusiasm of a schoolboy. "Perry C. Vale, ma'am. Pleased to make your acquaintance."

Mara took his hand with a warm chuckle. "I'm happy to meet you, Perry, but I'm not the one you have to impress. You might want to save your energy for Mr. Lindstrom."

"Is he in?" asked Art. "I'd like to talk with him, if I could, before the main meeting gets started."

"Yes, he's in, and deeply wrapped in thought over the Project. He usually doesn't like unannounced visitors, but he told me to extend you every possible courtesy. You've really impressed him, Mr. LaFey. I'm going to have to find out sometime what's so special about you."

"I would be more than happy to oblige." Art replied, and returned Mara's gaze. Is she just being friendly, he asked himself, or is something beginning to happen here? He snapped back from his brief reverie and asked, "Uh, can we just go on in?"

"Of course," Mara answered, with the soft smile of someone who knew she had put someone else off guard, and was enjoying it. "the door is open."

Art, still looking at Mara, reached for the doorhandle and missed, causing him to stumble slightly. He directed a little embarrassed grin to Mara, groped for the handle again, and finally got hold of it. Mara watched the whole incident with a Mona Lisa smile.

"Uh, see you later."

"I'm sure you will. Bye."

Art and Perry entered Lindstrom's office, which was just as impressive on second viewing. Perry looked around at the mahogany paneling and the rows of books with his jaw slightly hanging. Art looked toward the massive desk, and saw that the great leather chair was turned away from him, allowing Lindstrom to look out the window. The oxygen apparatus next to the desk was humming, and a hose led from it to the chair, disappearing behind it. A male nurse was attending to the oxygen apparatus, apparently making sure it was in good working order.

"Uh, hello again, Mr. Lindstrom, sir," Art said, somewhat nervously.

The chair whipped around. "Art, me boy, how are you doing?" Lindstrom's look of welcome changed to consternation, then irritation, as he noticed a second person in the room. "Who the hell is this?"

"This is my friend Perry, sir. I brought him to meet you, because he's helped me a lot in refining my ideas for the Foundation."

Perry leapt forward, just like with Mara earlier, hand extended. "Perry C. Vale, sir, pleased to make your acquaintance."

"That's it, sir," the nurse interjected. "You're set for a couple of weeks.

"Thank you, John," Lindstrom answered as the nurse left the room, then turned the full weight of his gaze on Perry.

Perry held out his hand for a few more seconds, then hesitantly withdrew it. "Well, sir," he began again, his voice nervously cracking a little on the first word, "Like Art said, I've got a lot of ideas for your Foundation. First let me say that I think it is highly noble of you to offer to provide schoolchildren around the country a better way of accessing and interacting with art and culture, and I think your idea to do it electronically on the Internet is excellent." Art had forewarned Perry to talk in code, because he didn't know how Lindstrom would react to Perry and his ideas, and he didn't want the Old Man to know that he had told Perry the whole plan. "Of course, that implies a lot of up front legwork. First we'll have to catalog the world's art, literature, and cultural artifacts, then we'll have to do a triage to decide what is really important for the kids to become familiar with, then we'll have to acquire the electronic rights, which won't necessarily be easy, because Bill Gates and the other nouveau riche have already snapped a bunch of them up. But I'm sure with your prodigious influence and the weight of a noble cause behind you, it wouldn't be too hard to acquire certain licenses from them..."

"Get out!" Lindstrom bellowed. He had become increasingly livid as Perry's exposition continued, and he had finally exploded. Perry blinked a couple of times, and just stared back. Art looked back and forth between the two several times. "Sir...?" he questioned tentatively.

"Out! Now! Get out of my office! Go!" Lindstrom's face was cherry red.

"Here, take my car," Art almost whispered, handing Perry his car keys. "I'll talk to you later."

"Yeah, later. Good idea." Perry was backing slowly away from Lindstrom's desk, totally at a loss as to how to react to his outburst. Lindstrom's gaze was nearly burning a hole in him. "Nice meeting you, sir," he said sheepishly as he backed out the door. As the door clicked shut, Lindstrom turned his burning stare onto Art.

"How dare you bring someone here without asking me first?"

"I…I just…"

"Did you tell him the real story?" He leaned forward intensely.

Art's mind raced through his options at lightning speed. He decided to lie, not quite sure if it was the best idea, but too scared to do anything else. "No, sir! He doesn't know anything except the children's education story." He felt as if his cheeks were on fire, and he prayed that it didn't actually show on his face. He stood motionless, feeling like a trapped animal, as Lindstrom examined him.

Finally he leaned back and said, "I hope you're not lying to me, boy! If he knows, we'll have to kill him." Art could tell that he was not joking. "Don't you ever do that again without my permission! Of course you're going to need help, but I need to approve the people first, so our real cause is not compromised. We have to maintain the Foundation front as strictly as possible, or none of this will happen." He reached for the intercom on his desk and slapped a button. "Mara!"

"Yes, sir."

"Put a tail on that hippie that was just in here. Have him followed for two weeks. Report on any unauthorized activity."

"Yes sir."

Lindstrom stared at Art for a minute in silence. Art nervously twitched, looked around the room, and shifted his weight several times on his feet. He thought of a thousand things to say, almost started speaking several times, but in the end just gazed nervously back at Lindstrom.

Lindstrom finally spoke. "You've got to realize, boy, this whole thing *is* me. If this fails, my whole life is a waste. Sure, I've been a successful businessman, but so what? So have thousands of others. This is unique, this is history! I will not have it compromised because some overzealous kid got overconfident. I know you meant well. I know you want this to work as much as I do. But you're in the big leagues now. We can't afford mistakes. I'll allow you this one oversight, but I want you to *think* about what you're doing in the future. Come: it's time you found out exactly what you are involved in. Give me your arm."

It was almost painful for Art to unfreeze, but he managed to, and walked over to Lindstrom. He held out his arm, bent at the elbow, and Lindstrom grabbed hold of it. It took several attempts, but Lindstrom finally boosted himself out of the great leather chair. With his other hand, he grabbed the handle of the oxygen apparatus and dragged it behind him as they walked slowly toward one end of the office.

"You see, lad, it's not just you and me we're doing this for. It's for the world. Oh, sure, we're going to have the fun and profit, but everyone in the end will benefit. But to really make it happen, we need all kinds of people from all different industries and professions cooperating, and they all want their slice of the pie, and they would be extremely upset if the Project were derailed because of a careless error in judgment. It's time you met the Foundation."

They had reached the mahogany-paneled wall. Art was wondering just what they were doing, when Lindstrom reached up and slapped the nose of a bust of Einstein on a bookshelf. The mahogany panel slowly slid aside to reveal a boardroom as richly appointed as Lindstrom's office. Several gentlemen and a few women in expensive-looking suits were seated or standing around the large round oak table in the center of the room, and they all turned to greet Lindstrom as he entered with Art.

"Hello, Mr. Lindstrom."

"Good to see you, sir."

"Hope you're feeling well, Merle."

"Ladies, gentlemen, thank you all for coming. Shall we begin the first official meeting of the Lindstrom Foundation?"

Chapter 11

Lindstrom ambled over and sat heavily down in the largest of the burgundy leather chairs surrounding the mammoth table, and all the others took that as their cue to take their seats as well. Art, dressed only in casual street clothes, felt very uncomfortable and out of place amongst the power suits, and lingered close to a wall. Lindstrom glanced around the room to see that everyone was ready to begin, his gaze finally resting on Art. "Sit down, lad. You're part of this."

Several of the attendees now took notice of Art as he sheepishly slid into a chair, and he wished attention had not been called to himself. One gentleman in a charcoal gray suit, two seats down from Lindstrom and across the table from Art, gazed longer at him than all the rest. Art was sure he noticed a cold expression in his black eyes. His thinning black hair was combed straight back and moussed in place, and the angle of his dark eyebrows gave him a decidedly malevolent appearance, in Art's opinion. Art was very glad when Lindstrom started talking, and everyone's attention was turned away from him toward the old man.

"Well, since this is the first time we've all officially met together, I believe it is appropriate that we all introduce ourselves." Lindstrom nodded to his left. "Let's start with you, Larry."

"Larry Dulak, Executive Vice-President of Business Development, Energy Development Corporation. For those of you unfamiliar with our firm, EnerCo is a diversified energy production company. We specialize in oil, natural gas, and nuclear energy, but we are always interested in developing alternative energy sources. We're here to provide our company's energy expertise to the Project, and to learn what we can about space-based energy production."

The malevolent-looking man was next. "Morris Dredson, Senior Vice-President, Marketing, EnerCo. I'm pleased to offer whatever I am able to the Project."

Next was a fellow dressed in full military uniform. Four silver stars gleamed on his collar. "General William Devere, Commanding Officer, United States Space Command. I'm here to see we get these birds aloft."

As the introductions traveled around the table, Art felt increasingly ill at ease and out of place. These were high-powered executives. What could he possibly offer to this project? He almost jumped when he felt a hand on his forearm. He turned to see Mara sliding into the empty chair beside him. She flashed him a warm smile as she sat down. Art instantly felt a little more comfortable. Mara began arranging the papers, pens, and tape recorder she had brought with her. She was obviously going to record the proceedings.

"Art?" Lindstrom's voice questioned from the end of the long table.

Art instantly realized that he had been staring at Mara, and had completely missed his cue to introduce himself. Again he felt everyone's attention on him, and again he felt very sheepish and small.

"Uh, Art LaFey, Editor, Seattle Arts Review. I'm here to, ah... to, ah...."

Lindstrom burst in. "Art's here to provide the human touch, to keep us big money boys from going off the deep end. His specific job is to develop a cultural library for the inhabitants and eventual visitors of Lindstrom Base. All work and no play will drive our people nuts."

Art was thankful for Lindstrom's intercession, but he wondered if he really had anything to contribute to this group.

The introductions continued around the table until they reached back to the old man. "Good," he said. "Now that we have broken the ice, we can get down to business. I've spoken with all of you individually, so we are all aware of why we're here, but I want to reiterate it so there can be no doubt. We are going to build a lunar base. We will spend a lot of money doing it, mostly mine, and the payoff is much farther out than what we are accustomed to, but the eventual profit will one day dwarf any other activity we could possibly undertake.

"I dare say I shall not live to see the fruits of our labors. You may ask why a crazy old coot like me would want to throw his money away on an impossible dream. Well, you know: 'You can't take it with you.' I want to build something of lasting value, the biggest monument in history, and, yes, I want my name plastered all over it. I want to be the most famous man in history, and I don't care if it's a posthumous distinction. If we pull this off, gentlemen, our names will be uttered in the same breath with the pyramid builders, Caesar, Columbus, and the like. I propose nothing less than to change the course of history."

Lindstrom coughed weakly, and paused to wheeze a few breaths from his oxygen mask. "A grandiose dream, to be sure, but what mundane steps shall we take to bring it to pass? Well, as some of you know, the paperwork has been filed to create the Lindstrom Foundation. The ostensible purpose of this organization is to foster excellence in education and research. We will offer scholarships and stipends to gifted students at all levels of academia, in all subjects, but especially mathematics and the sciences. And when we find the best and brightest, we will recruit them to our cause, and we will assemble the finest pool of talent and knowledge ever assembled.

"But more importantly, the Foundation will be a front for the rather large expenditures we will need to make to build our base and the supporting infrastructure. As you are all aware, this project will need to be kept in extreme confidence; the Foundation will give us the cover we need to avoid undue scrutiny. As for the details of the construction of the Base, I'll turn it over to our Chief of Operations, Larry Dulak."

Lindstrom nodded toward Dulak, who stood to address the gathering. "Thank you, Merle. As I'm sure you're all aware, this is a momentous occasion, and if you are privileged enough to be sitting in this room, you are blessed with the opportunity to change the course of history, and become immensely wealthy in the process. Let me present to you our plan for Lindstrom Base."

Dulak fiddled with a remote control in front of him, and the lights dimmed while the oaken panel on the wall behind him lifted to reveal a screen. On the screen appeared a painting of an installation which could only be on the Moon, and Art recognized it instantly as another rendering of the model Lindstrom had shown him during their first encounter.

"Lindstrom Base will be completed in three years' time, and will house up to seventy full-time occupants plus one hundred guests when fully operational. It will be completed in five phases, each one accommodating more power, capability, and staff." Dulak pressed a button, and the image changed to accompany his speech. "During Phase One, we will design and develop all the necessary systems and hardware to construct Lindstrom Base. This initial work will take about two years.

"Phase Two will consist of a habitat formed out of four inflatable modular domes launched to the Moon by rocket. They will be placed side by side, in a square pattern. Interconnecting hatchways and tubes will create four interlinked yet completely sealable compartments, capable of accommodating a crew of six plus various experimental and operational equipment. This cutaway view shows the layout of Phase Two, but the entire structure will be partially buried under a few meters of lunar regolith to anchor the installation and help shield against radiation. Even at this early stage, human presence will be necessary, but as much work as possible will be done robotically. Phase Two will be completed quickly, in about one or two months."

The slide changed. "Phase Three will be brought about by encircling the original habitat with a ring of eight more domes, launched by rocket and inflated on the surface. This ring will attach to Phase Two at the four corners of the 'square' formed by the original habitat. This phase will accommodate up to twenty full-time and four visiting staff. We will complete this phase in about two to four months." The image once again shifted. "Phase Four will concentrate on developing the supporting infrastructure of a permanent lunar settlement. We will require a spaceport, several current and redundant systems of power generation, and the implementation of lunar agriculture, as well as development of the goods and services we can sell at a profit. At this point, excavation below the domed structures will begin. These sub-lunar tunnels and caves will become the basis of our permanent habitat, and will provide raw material for extracting lunar oxygen, or lunox, and other processes we have planned."

Once again the slide changed. "Phase Five will begin to use local resources to develop the expansion of the base. Notice the extensive use of robots and automated machinery. Phase Five will culminate in the doming and pressurizing of the crater originally chosen for settlement. This final phase will accommodate the full complement of seventy inhabitants, and it will be at this time that we can consider opening the settlement up to non-essential personnel and the development of offshoot colonies. Phases Four and Five will be ongoing and will provide continuous upgrades to our systems and capacity. When we have successfully reached this point, we can announce our presence to the world, can begin selling our products, and can accept applications for habitation and visitation from individuals outside of our present organization."

The slide changed again, showing a montage of paintings representing lunar activities. Dulak continued. "What will our primary purposes and activities be? First, to begin to develop local resources as quickly as possible. Our location near the south pole of the Moon will give us a prime opportunity to search the surrounding craters for ice from cometary impacts. Some areas of these craters have never seen sunlight, and may very well contain ice. The discovery of local water supplies would go a long way to making the base self-sufficient.

"Second, to develop a local power supply as quickly as possible. The south pole location is also very advantageous for constructing a solar power system. Towers supporting photovoltaic arrays will be erected, which can be rotated to always receive maximum exposure to sunlight, thereby constantly producing energy. Any other location on the Moon, except the north pole, would be in darkness fourteen days out of a month, severely curtailing energy production capability. As we expand these 'sun farms', we will increasingly be able to reduce our dependency on the nuclear generators which we will initially be relying upon for power. Once we have a steady and growing power supply, we can commence the manufacture of Lunox, or lunar oxygen, which will have a tremendous impact on the operations of the Base in the form of breathable air, rocket fuel, and a basis for creating water with imported hydrogen. Our excess Lunox also has the potential to be a highly profitable export.

"An even more exciting energy project, our 'holy grail,' if you will, is the harvesting and refining of helium three. This is a substance which has been demonstrated to be the optimal fuel for generation of power from nuclear fusion. The benefits of the process are that it produces much less radioactivity than fission, making it a more benign energy source, and it once again reduces our dependency on energy imported from Earth. The big drawback is that we have not yet produced a net energy gain from the fusion process. Concurrent with the Lindstrom Base development project will be several research projects conducted here on Earth, the primary one being the development of helium three fusion techniques. It is theoretically possible, but a great deal of research remains to be done. The abundance of helium three on the Moon will make our research infinitely easier. If we can achieve a net power gain from fusion, however, our excess energy may well be one of our first and most valuable exports back to Earth.

"Other projects include the development of a mass driver to get bulk material into space. A mass driver is a long railway, powered by magnetic levitation, which can propel a vehicle at great speeds and 'sling' it off the surface. The G forces that are generated prevent humans from using the system, but once in place, it would be a much cheaper means than rockets to get raw material into orbit. Why? So we can begin to construct solar power satellites for collecting and distributing more energy, and, ultimately, for the construction of space stations. The long-term goal is to develop the infrastructure to take on projects such as asteroid mining and free-floating space factories, the profits from which will keep the revenue stream flowing quite nicely.

"Finally, once the Base has reached Phase Five, and all systems are nominally operational and the bugs have been worked out, we can seriously consider opening it up for tourism. The high-end adventure travel business is a proven and stable multi-billion dollar industry. We can sell bragging rights to people with a large amount of disposable income to experience one of the first vacations on the Moon. Activities could include lunar education and sightseeing, amateur astronomy, space sports, both adapted from terrestrial sports, and completely new inventions, and one-of-a-kind romantic getaways for honeymooners and others wanting to experience the ultimate, ah, low gravity thrill, if you follow my meaning." Quiet snickers traveled around the table. "As the frequency of visitors increases and economies of scale become effective, we will be able to lower our prices for a trip to the Moon, and begin offering it to the general public.

"This is just a brief overview of what we intend to accomplish, presented to inform you of what you are getting involved in. Your specific duties and responsibilities will be elaborated on as we progress deeper into the project. Of course, if you have been paying attention, one critically important element has heretofore been omitted from the discussion: how are we going to get to the Moon? To answer this question, I'll turn it over to General Devere."

Art's head was swimming. This whole thing was bigger than he could have conceived. Rushes of sheer excitement periodically raced through his body. How could he possibly be so lucky, he wondered, to be included on such a venture? This was his wildest fantasy, laid out before him, not as a suggestion of a possibility, but as an actual project, with real money and deadlines and managers behind it. He shook his head to bring himself back to the present, and focused on General Devere, who had already begun talking.

"...will require several flights to LEO, or low-Earth-orbit, and the Moon to get all necessary supplies, equipment and personnel in place. I, as Commander in Chief of the United States Space Command, am prepared to offer this support to the Project, because it has definite defense ramifications, and is the quickest way to begin operations on the Moon, which has long been a goal of the Air Force.

"You may wonder why I am not content to work through the proper funding channels of the congressional budget process to establish a moon base. Primarily because defense funding has been on a downward spiral for several years, and speculative space projects such as this were the first to go. Second, if we can establish any one of our energy goals, namely lunar solar power collectors, helium three-based fusion, or solar power satellites, we will have access to an unlimited supply of power, which would give us a definitive defensive advantage over any other military entity. If this were done through normal congressional means, it would inevitably get public, and we will have lost our element of surprise. Sun Tzu, in The Art of War, identified surprise as the supreme military advantage, and I for one agree.

"We have an experimental launch complex on Baker Island, 2500 kilometers southwest of Hawaii and practically on the equator. We propose using approximately every fourth launch from this facility to be dedicated to the Lindstrom Base Project. As an adjunct to our conventional expendable launchers, we are close to finishing development on a vehicle we call Dark Stallion. This craft will be able to take off from a traditional runway, like existing aircraft, and fly to sixty thousand feet. At that altitude, it will rendezvous with a refueling plane which will supply it with the oxydizer necessary to achieve LEO. Once in orbit, it will dock with a space station, refuel again, perhaps undergo modifications and take on supplies, then continue to the Moon. Dark Stallion will nominally carry two passengers and two thousand kilograms of payload to the lunar surface. We have also designed a modular unit that will fit in the cargo bay, allowing four other passengers to ride to the Moon. The craft will be able to be piloted, or flown remotely.

"As I said, the vehicle is experimental. We have agreed to devote a large percentage of the early flights to the Lindstrom Base Project, because this gives us real-world operating parameters, and because we would not be risking essential military payloads on an experimental vehicle. Moreover, it gives my old friend Merle the quickest access to space he'll ever find." The General winked at the old man.

"Our first goal will be to construct a small LEO station, named Oasis, for Orbital Assist Station In Space, primarily for refueling and maintenance. This facility will be based on the same inflatable module technology as the dome units intended for Lindstrom Base, and will house a crew of two on a two-month tour of duty. Every month one of the crew will be replaced, creating a rolling turnover of personnel to provide continuity of training and services. Initially material and fuel will be lofted on several Atlas expendable launchers and assembled robotically, but once Oasis becomes habitable, Dark Stallion will loft personnel and the more sensitive equipment.

"After station operations become nominal, the primary task of the station crew will shift to retrofitting two Dark Stallion vehicles for flight to the Moon. These vehicles will shuttle between Oasis and the surface of the Moon, and will never enter the Earth's atmosphere again. Some flights will carry cargo, while others later in the program will ferry passengers. This, ladies and gentleman, is how we propose to go to the Moon."

Enthusiastic clapping broke out around the table, and Art found himself applauding louder than just about anybody. After letting the appreciation continue for a while, Lindstrom raised his hands and indicated that he would like the clapping to cease. When it finally died down, he began speaking.

"I appreciate your enthusiasm, and I don't doubt that with the fine talent assembled here, we have every chance of success. Now I would like to take questions, if there are any."

A gentleman to Art's right asked, "This sounds like a big project. How are we going to keep it confidential?"

"That's a very good question," Lindstrom replied. "As most of you know, you have been issued stock in this venture. Of course, this stock is worthless right now, but when we eventually do go public, this stock will have attained immense value. If anyone leaks information about this project, however, we will lose the opportunity to complete it, and the stock will remain worthless. Also, I believe General Devere has a point to make in this regard."

"Yes, thank you, Merle. Gentlemen, to accomplish what I have just outlined to you, I have begun assembling an organization within an organization at the U.S. Space Command. One of the first issues I addressed was security. There is, I believe, a vital and critical defensive role in this project, and I wish to see it succeed. Anyone suspected of compromising the confidentiality of the project will be permanently silenced. I state this not as a threat, but as a fact. But I know many of you, and I trust we are all here voluntarily, and that this matter will remain a non-issue."

"There you have it," Lindstrom resumed. "The carrot and the stick. I trust everyone is comfortable with this arrangement?"

Murmurs of assent circulated around the table. Art, remembering the Old Man's outburst at Perry, became a little nervous at this talk, but he had been entranced by the plans for the Base, and he resolved not to be a problem for the Project.

Another question was asked. "What are the legal ramifications of what we are doing? Aren't most of these plans illegal?"

Lindstrom nodded to a fellow three seats to his right and said, "I'll defer that question to our General Counsel, Hector Maris."

The small bald man pushed his thick black horn-rimmed glasses up his large, hooked nose, noisily cleared his throat, and began speaking in a high, nasally voice, as he referred to several sheets of legal paper that he incessantly shuffled. "We have a team of attorneys working on that very problem. Of course, our first line of defense is to keep the project as confidential as possible. When we do go public, we intend to use the reasoning, as far as possible, that there are not yet laws governing what we are doing. Finally, once we do actually start turning a profit, we intend to pay our full tax burden, and stipulate to the international community that our activities are in the interest of the Common Heritage of Mankind, as stipulated in the United Nations' Outer Space Treaty of 1967. We intend to prove this, for example, by selling our surplus power to developing nations at a fraction of current costs. These and other such activities will, we hope, win the good will of the citizens of the world. We are still refining our strategy, however, so if you have concrete suggestions, please see me privately afterwards."

Several other questions were asked and answered by various members of the organization. Art didn't hear most of them. He had focused on the image of the finished, domed base that had been left on the screen, daydreaming about what life at the Base would actually be like when it was finished and inhabited. His reverie was broken by the sense of some attention directed toward him, and he glanced down to see Morris Dredson, the energy company vice-president, staring at him with what Art interpreted as a decidedly cold gaze. The last question had just been answered, and Lindstrom asked, "Any other questions?"

Without breaking his stare at Art, Dredson asked, in a cold, measured tone. "Yes, Merle. I still don't understand why we are including non-essential personnel in the Project. It seems to me that it compromises the whole character and security of our mission."

Lindstrom fumed, noticing the direction of Dredson's stare. "God damn it, Morris, we've gone over this before! Lindstrom Base isn't just about new technologies and profit. True, in the beginning, we have to concentrate on those things, but eventually we want to open it up to the world. This is ultimately about the future of humanity, about the next great step into the cosmos. If we're myopically focused on the bottom line, if we value money and technology over people, we won't win the hearts and minds of the people we want to serve, and we'll have a useless shell that no one will want to use. That is one thing I've learned in my fifty years in this industry.

"Consider Art LaFey here." He waved his hand in Art's general direction, and Art felt uncomfortable under the sudden amassed attention of the room. "Art is like an ambassador of the people, if you will. His task is to keep the project on a human scale, to make sure the Base is a place where people will want to work and live. If we don't have that, we might as well just send robots to do the work. And I want no part of a project like that." Lindstrom's gaze fell full force onto Dredson, who finally broke his stare at Art to confront the old man's powerful personality. "Hell, my money's funding this project, and I'll invite anybody onto the board I damn well please. If you don't like it, if any of you don't like it, you can leave now!"

Dredson glowered back at Lindstrom. The moments dragged agonizingly on in the tomb-silent boardroom. Art felt extremely uncomfortable, knowing this showdown concerned him. Finally, Dredson seemed to soften, and said quietly, "Well, thank you for explaining matters so clearly, Merle. You've answered my question. You know EnerCo is behind you one hundred percent, and we will support you all the way, because we see mutual benefit. The project is, of course, in need of EnerCo's expertise to most efficiently develop the Base's energy systems, and we hope that will be kept in mind as planning progresses."

Dulak, sitting beside Dredson, put his hand on the other's arm and said, "OK, Morris, you've made your point." The two commenced talking in whispers, and Lindstrom slowly turned his attention back to the group at large.

"Any other questions or concerns?" After a moment's silence, "Good. Don't forget, we are serving cocktails and hors d'ouevres afterwards, so we can all have a chance to get to know each other better. Also, in two weeks, on the 22nd, which is a Saturday, I am hosting an open house at my estate, which will officially kick off the activities of the Foundation. I have invited various members of the media and the community at large in order to generate goodwill for our 'work.' Of course, this is all in aid of developing a credible cover for our real project. I would be delighted to welcome any of you who wish to lend support to our public image. The tighter we can construct our facade, the more efficiently we'll be able to conduct our real operations. Contact my secretary Mara Gann for directions or other information you may need." The old man waved his hand carelessly in the direction of Mara, sitting next to Art.

"Well, that's about it. Oh, one last thing. We don't have an official name for our Project yet. We'll need to be able to refer to it amongst ourselves. Any ideas?"

"Sir?" Art couldn't believe he was actually speaking up, after the tension of the past few moments that he felt sure he had caused. "How about Project Avalon?" He rushed into an explanation, wanting to get as much as he could out before being cut off, as he was sure would happen. "Avalon is the mythical island that King Arthur retreated to after his final battle, to heal himself and regenerate his powers, before he returned to the land of reality to once again save his people. It seems that in a way, we are proposing the same kind of thing. We're planning to build a moonbase for developing the technologies that could make the world a better place to live." Art was amazed he was allowed to finish.

Lindstrom rubbed his chin in concentration. "Project Avalon. I like it. Any objections?" No one objected, although Dredson's scowl became darker.

"Good. Project Avalon it is. See, Dredson, he's been good for something already. This meeting is adjourned."

Chapter 12

"Well, that's the first official meeting." Mara said to Art with an air of completion. "I have to wrap things up with Mr. Lindstrom. Go and get yourself a drink."

The attendees of the meeting were getting up from the board table and gathering in groups of two or three. They generally drifted toward one end of the room, where a bar had appeared, and a bartender was taking drink orders. Art had not noticed the bar and the hors d'oeuvres tray being wheeled in, and was once again impressed by Lindstrom's efficiency. He ambled over to the bar and ordered a vodka and tonic. He sipped it appreciatively as he moved off to one side to allow others to come up to get a drink.

The low murmur of conversation could be heard throughout the room, and some small groups looked very intent in their discussions. Art looked around and politely smiled at some of his fellow boardmembers, and exchanged small comments like "good meeting" and "pretty exciting stuff, eh?", but never really got engaged in a real conversation. He soon found himself standing against one wall, sipping his drink and looking around pointlessly. It seemed everyone had forgotten about him, or did not have anything of significance to say to him. He remembered he had loaned his car to Perry, and began to wonder about how he was going to get home.

"So, what do you think of it all?"

Art turned, and there was Mara, smiling warmly at him. Art relaxed instantly, discovering that he had not realized that he was getting slowly more tense.

"I think it's fantastic! I mean, I hope it can really happen. But I'm not quite sure what I can do in all this."

Mara laughed softly and put her hand on Art's forearm. "Don't worry about that. Mr. Lindstrom has faith in you, and knows you have something to contribute, or else he would not have invited you here."

"Yeah, maybe, but it seems like I've blown it ever since I showed up. First that thing with Perry, then that Dredson guy sure took a disliking to me."

"He'll come around. You just stick to your cultural catalog project, and things will work out fine."

There was something very reassuring in Mara's tone. Art felt instantly put at ease.

"Well, I ought to be getting home," he remarked, glancing at his watch.

"Is there a phone I can use to call a taxi?"

"Why don't you let me drive you home? I'm ready to go anyway. I don't much care for these cocktail hours. Mr. Lindstrom always hosts one after his meetings, and everyone tends to get so stuffy about their businesses."

"Oh, no, I couldn't trouble you. It's probably out of your way."

"Where do you live?"

"Ballard. I'll just take a cab."

"It's no bother, really, I live up in Edmonds. Ballard is pretty much on the way. We could stop and get a cup of coffee on the way, if you'd like. If we're going to work together, we should get to know one another."

"Well, thank you, that would be very nice. Yes, let's go get coffee. I'm buying. I insist."

They stopped at The Java Hut in Wallingford, a small, pleasant neighborhood on the north shore of Lake Union, the central lake in Seattle, and just east of Ballard. The coffee house was warm and inviting with its rich wood paneling and soft indirect lighting. The place was full of university students, some talking, some studying, and rhythmic African-sounding music was being played on the stereo behind the bar.

After ordering double mochas, they sat at a table by the main large picture window, where they could observe passers-by and other street activity. They gingerly sipped their coffees in the vain attempt not to be scalded by the first contact with the hot liquid, in the semi-awkward silence of two people who barely knew each other, but found themselves alone together with no preprogrammed plan of interaction. They had expended their small talk on the ride to the coffee house.

"So," Art started, wiping the whipped cream from his lip, "what do you think of all this space stuff?"

"Oh, I think it's fascinating. I'm certainly keen on the idea, but I'm not as obsessed about it as the rest of you seem to be."

"Oh? What do you mean?"

"Well, it's all very interesting, but it's not as if it's the end of the world or anything. You men always seem to take everything so seriously." For the first time, Art seemed to notice something slightly peculiar about the way Mara talked. The last word had sounded more like "sarioosley."

"Well, this is serious stuff. And I beg to differ with you. We could be witnessing the beginnings of the end of the world, if things keep going like they are these days."

"You can beg all you want, but it won't change anything," she retorted with a wry smile on her (very attractive, Art mused) face. "The world will unfold as it will, no matter what toys you boys build, nor how important or serious you all think you are."

"Now wait a moment. Don't you think Lindstrom Base is a worthwhile project?"

"Certainly. But you must keep things in perspective. I mean, life will go on down here, while you boys are playing up there. Earth is the cradle of life, after all, and that will never change."

Art was rising to the bait. "Exactly. And that's why it's so important that we do this. Of course we want to see life and civilization survive here on Earth. Not just survive, but thrive. But we have to have an escape hatch, a safety valve, a lifeboat, in case things get dicey down here."

Mara's laugh was warm and good-naturedly patronizing. "Now I see why the Old Man likes you. You share his megalomania. And his paranoia." She continued chuckling as she sipped from her mocha.

There was something so disarming about Mara that Art didn't feel the slightest bit annoyed, even though she was pushing all of his buttons. He knew she was just playing with him.

"Well, nonetheless, it is very important work, perhaps the most important, and it will have wide-ranging benefits, for everyone."

"Oh, I'm sure it will." Her eyes twinkled with merry ridicule.

"You're making fun of me!" Art declared in mock indignation.

"Of course I am. You're taking yourself much too seriously."

"OK, if you're so skeptical, how come you're so deeply involved in the Project?"

"It's my job. I'm Lindstrom's executive assistant. And I've already told you: I think it's fascinating. Not just the Project itself, but the way you lads go about carrying it out as well. Someone has to watch after you, and clean up and bandage your knees when you skin them."

Art was intrigued by her use of the word 'lads'. "I can't help but notice," he said, suddenly desiring to change the subject, "You seem to express yourself differently than most people. You have a most intriguing accent. Are you from here, originally?"

"How very observant of you. As a matter of fact, no. I was born and lived the early part of my life in Ireland."

"That's it! I've been trying to place your accent for a while."

"Oh, darn. I thought I covered it well, after all these years in America."

"Oh, no, it's wonderful. Don't ever lose it. It sounds so refreshing. So you grew up in Ireland?"

"Yes, until I was eight. Then I moved to the States."

"With your parents?"

"No, actually, I was an orphan. I suppose I may as well tell you. My parents died in a car accident when I was seven, and I lived in the town orphanage for a year. They fed and clothed me, but I sold flowers in the street to earn extra money. Mr. Lindstrom and his wife, on one of their frequent trips to Ireland (his mother's family is Irish, you know), spotted me and were so taken with me that they adopted me and brought me to America. I spent the rest of my childhood growing up in Mr. Lindstrom's house as his daughter."

Art was mildly stunned. "I would have never guessed...."

"Oh yes, Mr. Lindstrom loves children. I am the only one he ever adopted, but he has helped many children throughout his life. Many people owe their college educations to him. The Lindstrom Foundation isn't a complete sham. He honestly intends that a significant portion of its activities will be directed toward genuinely helping children in need and promoting education."

"Well, I'll be damned! The old coot! And this whole time I've just thought of him as an old profiteering warmonger."

"Well, he is that, too, but that can't be helped. He's a man, after all."

"There you go again!" Art flicked a small fingernailful of whipped cream at Mara. She dodged, it flew over her shoulder, and they laughed.

"Well, you seem to have come through your misfortunes in prime form," Art said after he caught his breath. "You seem so naturally suited to be Lindstrom's assistant. It is almost as if you run the place, in a certain way. Have you been there long?"

"Since I graduated from the University."

"Here in town? U Dub?" Mara nodded, indicating she had attended the University of Washington.

"And do you intend to stay on with Lindstrom? Do you have any other plans or ambitions? Do you have a significant other, or anything like that?"

"No, not really. I've had a few relationships, but nothing serious.... Hey, tell me about your boy. Gary, right?"

"Yeah, Gary. Here, I've got to show you these pictures." He dug out his wallet. "I took them at the zoo. I just got them back." He passed them over to Mara.

"Aw, he is darling," she cooed, slowly flipping through them. "Look at that one with the otters. He looks so amazed."

"Yeah, he loves otters. He says he wants to be one."

"That's precious."

"Yeah, I'd do anything for that little guy."

They talked a while longer, then Mara drove Art home.

"Goodnight, Mara. Thanks for the ride home," Art said as he got out of her red Honda Accord.

"My pleasure. Thank you for the coffee."

"I'll see you at the Foundation party, then?"

"I look forward to it." She smiled at him.

He shut the door, and she drove off. Art stood for a moment, watching the receding car and relishing the warm afterglow of time spent with good company. He then turned to walk into his apartment, and saw Gwen at the window, watching him. Oh boy, here we go, he thought as he turned the door handle.

"Hi honey, I'm home." He pecked Gwen on the cheek.

"It's about time you got home. You're always out so late with those friends of yours. And who was that who dropped you off? Where's your car?"

"I loaned it to Perry. Lindstrom didn't like him and kicked him out. That was Lindstrom's secretary."

"Secretary, hmmm?"

"Oh, for Christ's sake, Gwen, we're just friends."

"I hope for your sake you're telling the truth." Her voice began to tremble. "I get so tired waiting for you, and now strange women are bringing you home." She turned, not wanting Art to see her tears.

"Oh, honey, I'm sorry." He walked over and put his arms around her waist. He felt her shoulders sink against his chest, while her lower body pulled away. Art sighed. "I told you this new job with the Foundation was going to take a lot of time and energy at first. It'll get better, I promise."

"It's just that I don't see much of you any more. And when you're home, you're not really home. We just don't seem to have that much in common anymore."

Art ached to tell her the whole truth about Project Avalon, but he didn't dare, especially after the incident with Perry. He had given Gwen the Lindstrom Foundation story. She had agreed it was important work, and was impressed by his new salary, but none of it seemed to bring them at all closer together.

"Say, I've got a surprise for you," he said, wheeling her around and holding her by the shoulders. "Lindstrom is throwing a gala ball in two weeks to kick off the activities of the Foundation. Let's see if Gary can stay overnight with your sister Sarah, get all dressed up and go have a really good time. How about that?"

Gwen's eyes were misty. "You mean that?" She hugged him and put her head on his shoulder. "I would love that. I really would."

They held each other for a while in the soft orange glow of the streetlamp shining through the window, then went off to bed. They made love that night for the first time in a long time. It was pleasant and tender, but Art felt vaguely dissatisfied, as if there were something lost or missing. He could tell by Gwen's behavior that she felt the same way.

Chapter 13

Art knew Lindstrom was wealthy, yet he was nevertheless amazed and impressed as he drove up the long, winding driveway through tall Douglas firs to Lindstrom's estate. It was the night of the Foundation gala. Paper chinese lanterns had been strung along the length of the drive, giving the impression of driving through a lighted tunnel. Art kept catching glimpses of the mansion through the trees, which he then lost again, until it jumped into prominence as the car rounded the last bend. It was mammoth. It had four floors, with easily twenty windows spread across each floor. It had a white neo-classical facade, with four great pillars framing the main entrance. The guests had already begun to arrive. A few were milling about outside, most were entering the mansion. Valets were parking the cars.

"Oh, Art, this is wonderful!" Gwen exclaimed, looking around at the mansion, the flaming torches ringing the grounds, and the guests and their attire. "We've never done anything like this before. I'm so thrilled!"

"Yes, very impressive," Art responded.

They stopped at the front of the mansion, and a valet courteously offered to park their car. They walked up the wide steps to the front entrance, Gwen's arm wrapped around Art's forearm, and into the mansion. Art had rented a white tuxedo, and Gwen was wearing the dress she had gone out and purchased especially for this occasion, a white, rather snug, low-cut dress that accentuated her figure and reached to her ankles. She completed her attire with her mother's string of pearls, and her hair was styled into an intricate bun, with curled strands of her brunette hair strategically escaping the coif.

They were instantly dazzled by the opulence of their surroundings. A wide, red-carpeted stairway dominated the entrance hall, and a great crystal chandelier hung over them. A valet in the costume of an eighteenth century servant, complete with powdered wig and knee-breeches, indicated that they turn and proceed to their left. They turned, trying not to gawk overly much, and strolled through a wide doorway, to see the ballroom laid out before them. They were up on a balcony, and could view the whole scene. The ballroom was long, with a high ceiling, and could easily fit an average-sized house inside it. The decor was of a pseudo-Versailles style, with a black-and-white checkered floor, gilt-edged mirrors all around the room, and ornately-carved molding around the perimeter of the ceiling. Three chandeliers, each bigger than the one in the entranceway, lit the room with a dazzling brilliance. The ceiling was covered with imitations of Michelangelo and other classical painters. Guests in fine attire were circulating around the ballroom, chatting and drinking. Some were partaking of the bar with three silver punchbowls, or of the immense buffet laid out along one wall, with every imaginable food item arranged in intricate patterns. A large swan carved out of ice rose from the center of the table. A string quartet was playing Vivaldi on the stage at one end of the ballroom. They were likewise dressed in eighteenth century regalia. Gwen audibly gasped, so taken was she with the whole image.

"Your names, please?" A valet had approached them.

"Art and Gwen LaFey," Art answered.

"Is that Arthur and Gwendolin?"

"Uh, yes."

"Follow me, please."

They were led to the top of the red-carpeted staircase that led down from the balcony. There they paused while the valet announced them. "Arthur and Gwendolin LaFey." He then led them down the stairs, stopped at the bottom, bowed, and graciously extended his arm, palm upward, toward the guests, indicating that they were to join them. Art and Gwen were both awestruck at this cordial and dignified treatment. They looked around, trying to decide what to do and where to go first.

"Art! Art! Glad you could make it!" Lindstrom was calling to him from amongst a small crowd of guests. He waved his hand frantically. "Come here, come here, and bring that lovely creature with you."

Art looked at Gwen, who was glowing from the compliment. "Come on. It's high time you meet our new benefactor."

They approached the group. Lindstrom was seated in a wheelchair in the middle of it, his oxygen tank mounted to the back. With him were Larry Dulak, General Devere, a couple other people from the board meeting whose names escaped Art, and a couple others Art had never met before.

Lindstrom began speaking as they walked up. "This must be your wife Gwen. She certainly is ravishing! It is a pleasure to meet you, my dear." He held out his hand.

"The pleasure's all mine," she returned with a slight curtsey and taking his hand. "You have a marvelous estate here. I love this ballroom!"

"Why, thank you, young lady. Art, how are you?"

"Fine, sir. Thank you for inviting us here." They shook hands.

"You must forgive the wheelchair," Lindstrom continued. "I could be on my feet for this, but I would get so tired, and have to turn in early."

"Understandable, sir."

"Let me introduce everyone here. Art, you know some of these people from our first board meeting. General Devere."

"Hello." The General shook Art's hand, then Gwen's.

"Larry Dulak, our Executive Director."

"Good evening to both of you." He shook Art's hand. "And a pleasure it is to meet you, Gwen." He took Gwen's hand into both of his. "Your husband holds much promise for our organization. You should be proud."

"Oh, I am," answered Gwen a little nervously, returning Dulak's intense gaze. A second before the scene would have become awkward, Dulak released Gwen's hand and stepped back.

Lindstrom continued the introductions. "John Brandiles."

"Hello. Nice to see you again."

"Henry Sagramor."

"Good evening."

"Bill Barnett."

"Pleased to meet you."

"And John Tuttle."

"Hello there."

Lindstrom started to speak again, but a cough overcame him. He recovered, and tried again. "Excuse me. Well, I bet you two are hungry and thirsty. Why don't you go get some refreshments? But please do come back, Art. There are some things I would like to discuss with you."

Dulak chimed in. "Why don't I take Gwen over and get us all some refreshments, and Art can stay here and get to know the others?"

Gwen looked questioningly at Art.

"Sure. That would be fine."

"My dear," Dulak said, offering his arm to Gwen. She took it, and they were off through the crowd. A couple other members of the small group broke away, leaving Lindstrom, General Devere, and Art together.

Lindstrom glanced around briefly to observe who was in earshot. "Good, I'm glad we have a chance to talk. Later, we'll be making speeches for the general public and media consumption, and there will be questions and interviews and all sorts of things. We'll have to be on our guard to present a unified front, and not let the real purpose slip. I wanted you, General Devere, to get to know Art a little better. After getting to know both of you somewhat, it seems to me you two, although from completely different backgrounds, have similar ideas for directions and purposes of Avalon." Art got a small rush of excitement from hearing Lindstrom use his proposed name for the Project. "General Devere's primary aim is, of course, defensive in nature. Art, if I've understood you and your writings correctly, you want to preserve civilization, get all the eggs out of one basket, so to speak. These seem to me to be very similar goals."

"Well, yes," Art replied. "But I don't advocate weapons in space or anything like that."

"Nor do I," General Devere responded. He was dressed in full military uniform, countless medals blazing across his chest. "You see, my deepest opinion is that, once you have started shooting, you have already lost the war."

"That is an uncommon attitude from a military man."

"Not at all. Think about it: what is the goal of defense? To defend our land, our people, our property, correct?"

"Yes."

"Well, if you start shooting at an enemy, they are bound to shoot back at you. You may win whatever given battle in which you are engaged, but the conditions of modern warfare are such that the victor comes out nearly as damaged as the vanquished."

A rather large matronly woman burst upon their group. "Merle, you have positively outdone yourself this time!"

"Thank you, Marjory. I wanted the Lindstrom Foundation to be kicked off right."

"Albert is dying to talk with you." She leaned in closer and loudly whispered, "he's getting up in years, you know, He's taken a seat against the wall."

"Well, let's go see the old codger. Gentleman, if you'll excuse me." Lindstrom wheeled off with Marjory, leaving the General and Art alone.

"Well, General," Art continued, "if you don't propose putting weapons in space, how do you intend to derive a defensive advantage from our project?"

"Defense isn't just weapons, son. Congress is fixated on that idea, and I have a devil of a time trying to convince them otherwise. They love big weapons projects, because it means pork for their districts."

"This is amazing," Art said with a wry smile. "A general arguing against pork barrel politics."

"Don't get me wrong, son. I believe we should have a robust and growing defense budget. I just believe there are more effective ways to spend it than on just another smarter bomb. Wouldn't you agree that the best defense would be to get the enemy to capitulate without a fight?"

"Of course."

"And how could you accomplish that?"

"I suppose by being so superior in every respect that the enemy would fear fighting you, or calculate that the risk was not worth it."

"Precisely. And how do you think you could accomplish that?"

"More firepower?"

"Certainly you have to have a superior degree of armaments. But think about it: when each side has enough warheads to annihilate the world twenty-five thousand times over, doesn't the policy of Mutually Assured Destruction reach a limit in its ability to deter aggression? Besides, all those bombs didn't help us in Viet Nam. A surgical scalpel is often more effective when a big stick is useless."

"So, what do you want, if not bigger bombs?"

"You tell me. What advantage could we derive from space-based operations?"

"Well, increased communications and observation ability, for one."

"Exactly. Any others?"

"A base beyond the reach of the enemy?"

"Very good. But that is useless in and of itself. What could you do with that base to gain a defensive advantage?"

"Gosh, I'm not a military strategist. I don't know."

Devere rolled his eyes. "Now do you see how hard my task is? Your imagination fails you. This is the precise problem I have with all those wonks in Washington. They just want what we've got now, only bigger and better. They pooh-pooh any new idea, until it is proven to be effective, then they say 'You see? I told you it would work all along.' The situation has gotten even worse after the shuttle incident. All new space project starts have been postponed pending the completion of the investigation and recommendations of the Griffin Commission. That is why I have hooked up with Lindstrom. He knows the value of going out on the cutting edge, and making investments that aren't going to pay off for a decade or more. I'll tell you what I expect to gain from Lindstrom Base."

A valet approached them with a tray of full champagne glasses. Art and the General each took one and sipped from them.

The General resumed his explanation. "First, the research and development going into constructing the base will produce new technologies, mostly in communications, materials, and systems. These will be directly and indirectly applicable to military operations. Second, we will have a base of operations beyond the reach of the enemy, because we will see any threat coming with at least three days' warning. That's how long it takes to get to the Moon with current technology. This gives us plenty of breathing room to develop and perfect new systems and operations. Chief among them are energy production. As you heard in our first board meeting, there are three forms of energy which can be derived from lunar operations. One, lunar solar power collectors. Two, helium three fusion. Three, solar power satellites. If even one of these can be made viable, we will have a surplus of energy over any potential enemy. If all three come online, we will have practically no limit to available energy.

"The third reason Lindstrom Base is valuable to defense is the spur to the economy and education lunar operations will provide. Project Avalon will lay the groundwork for a space-based economy. A robust economy is always better prepared to take defensive measures than a sagging one, and is less likely to go looking for a war. I've read your articles. Lindstrom calls them 'required reading.' " Art was amazed to hear this. He had believed that Lindstrom hated those pieces. "You are correct that the root cause of any war is ultimately economic. Korea, Viet Nam, the Persian Gulf, even the Pacific Theater of World War II were all primarily waged to open up new markets to the U.S. economy. If we keep sinking a greater percentage of our budget into weapons, we will have less and less for developing new products and services for those markets, and our economy will sink into a chronic recession. Weapons systems are notoriously bad economic multipliers. If we can expand our economy and thereby produce a greater tax revenue base, we will naturally gain in defense spending, relative to other countries. You look surprised, probably because a General of the United States Air Force is talking this way. Yes, we all are familiar with these arguments. Most of my colleagues, however, choose to ignore such reasoning, and prefer to maintain the status quo. It's much easier that way, especially when one is approaching retirement. Officially I act that way, too. This is just a side project for me. If it goes, fantastic. If it fails, I return to status quo procedures."

Art opened his mouth to speak, but the General cut in. "Let me finish my explanation. If we can develop an off-world economy, we gain three principal benefits. One, we will be less inclined to engage another entity in war, because it will be much more advantageous to develop new markets than tussle for existing ones. Two, the benefits in research and development will keep our economy strong and enable us to more effectively withstand an assault from an enemy, either economically or militarily. Three, our increased economic activity and the example of our peaceful expansion will have a positive spin-off effect on other economies around the globe, spurring their space development, and we will one day compete economically in space, rather than militarily on Earth."

"You mean to say you'd be willing to allow other countries, perhaps hostile ones, to engage in space activities?"

"Yes, if they adhere to the strict guidelines that would be formed by an agency such as the U.N."

"But you are involved with this Project, which is secret and doesn't adhere to any such code."

"That's the beauty of it. We will have our systems and operations in place before such laws and regulations have been formulated. He who gets there first gets to develop the standards."

"So you are in essence saying the ends justify the means?"

"Not at all. The end is a peaceful, growing, space-based economy. Nothing we are doing runs counter to that goal."

"But you are violating laws."

"Don't forget to include yourself in this, son. You're part of Project Avalon, too."

"But I haven't broken any laws."

"Oh, really? I seem to recall a very interesting story Merle told me the other day about red paint."

Art blushed and looked down.

"Look, son, laws are tools. Just like any other tool, if they're right for the job, you use them. If they're not, you use different tools. And if they don't work, you discard them and get new ones."

Art regained his composure. "That seems a rather cavalier attitude, coming from a government official."

"It may be, but my position as Commander of U.S. Space Command is governed by several books of laws and regulations, each as thick as three Seattle phone directories. I have a full-time staff of thirteen just to keep up with the yearly changes congress makes in those laws. Hell, some of the new ones outright contradict the old ones. If Congress can't use the tool of law properly, how am I supposed to? The only way to accomplish anything and stay true to my mission to uphold and defend the Constitution of the United States of America, which, by the way, is an excellent example of the proper use of the tool of law, is to attach myself to a higher mission. Project Avalon suits that mission perfectly. Have you ever read Plato? Or Nietsche?"

"No, I can't say that I have."

Just then Gwen and Dulak came bursting through the crowd, laughing.

"Oh, Art, this party is wonderful! The quartet just started playing a waltz, and Larry promised he'd teach me how to waltz. Do you mind?"

Art was deeply engrossed in his conversation with General Devere, and barely noticed the two. "No, that's fine. Go have fun." They whirled away, back into the sea of partiers.

"You were saying, General?"

"First, I need another drink." He signaled to a valet, who approached with his tray of champagne glasses. Both took new full glasses and replaced them with their empty ones.

"That's the trouble these days. Everyone is so focused on the present, on the latest movie or the latest quarter's financial statement, that classical education has been abandoned. You really ought to correct that omission, and probably many others, if you are to develop a cultural library for Lindstrom Base.

"You see, Plato addressed this exact question twenty-five hundred years ago. Actually, Plato always 'reported' for Socrates. In The Republic, Socrates and his protégés discussed the nature of justice and a just society. They generally concluded that one could not find it in the world as it then existed, but that one was compelled to construct an ideal republic to represent and uphold it."

"Are you saying we are without justice today?"

"I am saying that without a goal, without a higher mission, it is nearly impossible to keep yourself focused on the necessary things, and to defend and uphold the society."

"And that gives you the right to pick and choose which laws you will follow?"

"No, I take that right myself. If there were a commission to examine the performance of my duties as an officer of the United States Air Force, it would find exemplary conduct and adherence to the highest standards. Such a commission always has; that is why I am a four-star general. This project is a crap-shoot into the future. If it works, it may just be the beginning of the next great step of the human race; if it fails, no one and no institutions will be harmed. There are no deleterious means here, therefore no need to justify them with the intended end."

"Then what is your long-term hope for the project, if I may ask, General?"

"Well, that gets back to Plato again. Have you looked at the state of affairs in the world lately, Art? Of course you have; your editorials reflect that. You see, we have reached such a state of development that to build new systems, to create new institutions, would be nearly impossible, because of the resistance of the status quo. Yes, yes, I know; in one way I *am* the status quo. But If we are to truly create a new society which will improve and augment the old one, we need a clean slate, so to speak. The Moon is a *tabula rasa* in its current condition. If we can plant the seeds of a new civilization there, and begin its governance properly, we could bypass centuries of earth-bound revolution to achieve a higher order of social organization. We need to strip ourselves of our preconceived notions and build our structure from the foundation. We must examine the great thought on these issues, from Plato through Nietsche and beyond, to determine what we should and should not try.

"Socrates undertook to arrange such a society. Early on, the discussion in The Republic centered on the nature of men and their roles in an ideal society. He recognized that all men are *not* created equal. Now that doesn't mean we should have slaves and masters. That means we should institute a proper education curriculum which will enhance children's natural skills and talents and guide them to their most well-suited occupation early on.

"Now, Socrates advocated censorship. Sometimes an examination of philosophers is worthwhile, if only to hone one's thinking and reach the conclusion that one disagrees. A certain amount of censorship is necessary in some defensive situations, such as the construction of Project Avalon (it would be hell to try to pull this off in public, eh?), but otherwise the communication and exchange of ideas in a society should be as open and free as possible, for it is in this context that the grist for change arises.

"Socrates advocated that the defenders of the republic be the highest category of citizen, for without the defenders, the city would fall. However, I take a broader view than Plato as to the nature and scope of the defenders. As I was saying earlier, not only the soldiers who can fire guns, but also the educators, the business leaders, anyone who is lending to the strength of the institutions which make up the society are the defenders.

"In fact, what we should create at the moobase are several guilds, if you will, which cover the various functions of a society: education, energy production, defense, and so on. Each guild would elect a leader, or president, or guildmaster, or whatever you wanted to call that person. This person would also participate in a council of guildmasters, who would administer the general affairs of the society. This council of guildmasters would then elect a prime minister, or some such official. This arrangement preserves a relative amount of autonomy for each guild, and doesn't concentrate too much power at the top. You would have the benefits of tribalism within your guild, but the benefits of collective action through the guild council."

"That is utterly fascinating," Art said reflectively. "I never conceived of Project Avalon as the beginnings of a completely new government. Go on, please."

"Nietzsche's thought has a bearing on our project as well. He wrote of the Last Man, the man at the end of history who would be content with the status quo, who would niggle away at the small projects of his life, and never again think a great thought. Nietzsche believed most people of his time were Last Men. In contrast, he conceived of the Superman, who would be the next great evolutionary step of man. We current humans are just a preparation for the Superman. He wrote nebulously of some great goal, some great project, that would cause the Superman to appear. I believe Project Avalon is that project.

"Now, many have argued against the idea of the Superman. They say that concept was the basis of Hitler's Third Reich. Keep in mind, however, that Hitler believed that the ends justify the means, whereas we have established that they do not. Besides, don't you think that such tirades against the idea of the Superman are merely the whinings of Last Men, who do not want to raise their heads and look higher than their own meager existences?"

Art felt a tingle rush through his body as he returned General Devere's intense gaze. The General's last speech alternately thrilled and repulsed him. He could not decide if he agreed, but he knew he was hearing the crucial motivation of the General.

Devere continued. "Nietzsche did not seek peace; he sought struggle, because he believed only in struggle can one be truly alive, can one truly create. Look around at the world. Society is becoming complacent. Bureaucracy is taking over, choking the life out of people. I should know; I work for one of the largest bureaucracies ever created. Nietzsche said a man wants danger and play, and I agree. He believed gravity was the highest evil. Wait; give me a moment.... 'The devil is the spirit of gravity,' he said. And the Will is the antithesis of gravity. Our will to struggle to the highest height, to overcome the trap of gravity, that is the ultimate good a man can achieve. That is why we are colonizing the Moon.

"These concepts are nonetheless beyond the idea of good and evil. Such concepts are yet again tools for use in specific circumstances." Art's brow furrowed in the attempt to comprehend the General's last comment. "Think about it. This century we have fought the good wars: World Wars One and Two, Korea, Viet Nam, Persian Gulf, Bosnia. We either won them or fought to a standstill on enemy territory, and we have achieved the highest level of peace and security ever. Obviously, by conventional standards, a good achievement.

"And yet what have we done with this great boon? Look at the state of our youth. They demand jobs and material goods, they think they are entitled to unearned rights, they are squandering our victories in aimless materialism. Is this what we fought for? In a strict interpretation, yes, we achieved our goal, but it turns out our highest good is now our greatest evil. We must now fight the last battle against ourselves and our inertia. With the world explored and the frontiers conquered, we can only look forward to devolving into slothful, wired video-junkies who find more meaning in virtual reality than real life.

"If we define the parameters of our existence in the traditional terms of good and evil, we are stuck in this dead-end forever. We must break out into space, where we can define new terms of good and evil, namely, that gravity and entropy are consummate evil, and the will to power the ultimate good. This kind of talk, however, is more than the average person can take. What do you think, Art?" Devere deliberately stared at Art, assessing him as he sipped from his champagne.

Art was nervously silent for a bit. He glanced around the room at the other party attendees, trying to absorb the nonchalance of his surroundings, and taking furtive sips from his drink. "Well... ahh... yes..." He started several times before he gathered his words. "There is a lot to contemplate in what you just said, General. I don't quite know what to make of it all. I guess I hadn't taken my thinking to such extremes, but I can see your points. I'll have to think about it, maybe pick up some Nietzsche and read it...."

"General! Come here, please. It's time to put on our show." Lindstrom's wheelchair burst through the crowd. "Oh, I see you two have hit it off. Splendid! I hope this is the beginning of a long and fruitful relationship amongst us all. Art, you'll excuse us, but it's time for our dog-and-pony show for the media. Stick around and enjoy the fun!"

General Devere thrust out his hand. "It was a pleasure talking with you, Art. I hope we can continue this conversation sometime."

"Yes, so do I," Art said, vigorously returning the handshake.

Devere and Lindstrom headed off together, chatting and making their way toward one end of the room, where a podium had been erected on a stage.

Art felt a sudden need to cut down on his stimuli and get some fresh air. He made his way in the opposite direction, toward the end of the ballroom where the string quartet had just finished playing. Tall french doors stood at the end of the room, leading out onto a broad, shrub-lined verandah. Art walked through the doors and leaned on the stone railing, looking out over Lindstrom's broad lawn to its edge, where it abruptly dropped away to reveal the Puget Sound beyond, the half-moon's reflection glittering on the water.

"Enjoying the view?" Art recognized Mara's voice, which then transformed into feigned concern. "Please don't jump. You have so much to live for."

Art looked down over the railing and saw that the ground was about three feet below the floor of the balcony. Chuckling, he turned. "Hello, Mara...." He had to forcefully restrain himself from dropping his jaw. She was gorgeous. She was smiling a wide, radiant smile, her eyes glittering in the reflected moonlight. She was wearing a long, flowing, dark green velvet gown, with a low cut, snug but not-too-revealing bodice. Her dark wavy shoulder-length hair framed her face beautifully. "You look... wonderful!" he finally stammered.

"Thank you. You look rather nice yourself. That's a smart tuxedo you've got on."

"This? Oh, I rented it. I have to have it back tomorrow. And my car turns into a pumpkin at midnight." Impossibly, she smiled even wider than before. Art felt the dangerous tingling in his belly that informed him of feelings greater than friendship for her.

She tossed her head toward the ballroom. "Aren't you interested in all the hoopla in there?"

"Yes... well, not really... I just had the most interesting conversation with General Devere, and I just wanted to come out here and get some fresh air and digest it. You know, get out of the crowd."

"Yes, I know. Mr. Lindstrom has been showing me off like a prize pony. He's really enjoying himself, you know."

"Yes, I can tell."

"Isn't your wife here?"

"My wife?" Art suddenly realized he hadn't seen Gwen for quite some time. He scanned the crowd of revelers, bobbing and weaving his head, trying to catch a glimpse of her. "I can't seem to see her."

"Well, I'm sure she'll turn up, and I'll meet her then." She turned, leaned on the rail, and looked out to the Sound. "Isn't it beautiful?"

Art's gaze lingered on Mara for a moment, then turned to the moonlit scene. "Yes, it is."

"Has the Old Man... I mean, Mr. Lindstrom ever shown you around?"

"No, this is the first time I've been here."

"Come on then, let me take you to the cliff. The view is absolutely breathtaking."

They walked slowly along the verandah to one end, where stone stairs led in a graceful sweep down to the lawn. They strolled through the grass, chatting about the party, the guests, the decorations. They reached the cliff, high over the Puget Sound, and Art was genuinely impressed. The wide expanse of water opened before him, and a thousand moons danced and played in the waters. Here and there sailboats were anchored for the night, and a long row of brightly lit windows shone out from a ferry, returning from the other side of the Sound. "This is fantastic." He said appreciatively, after observing the scene for a while.

"Yes, I love to come here. It is a good place to gather one's thoughts, to relax, to try to gain some peace. Mr. Lindstrom often has lawn parties in the summer. I'm sure he'll be inviting the Project Avalon team here a few times."

"That would be a lot of fun." He turned and looked at her, noticing they were standing closer than two casual friends usually stand. She gazed back at him, searching his face. The tableau froze for an instant, then, with the inevitability of two magnets attracting each other, their lips slowly came together and met. After the briefest of kisses, they separated, both with a look of surprise on their faces. A moment later, their arms were holding each other, and they shared a longer, more passionate kiss.

Art put his hands on her shoulders and pushed away. "I… I can't do this. I'm married."

Mara looked down and occupied herself with straightening the wrinkles in her gown. "Yes, this isn't right. I'm sorry."

Art took Mara's shoulders again. "No, no, it wasn't you, it was me. You're just so… beautiful."

Mara swiftly turned and started back toward the mansion. "We really should get back to the party."

"Yes, you're right. Good idea."

As they returned to the mansion, farther apart than when they walked out, Mara folded her hands in front of her, and Art thrust his hands deep into his pockets. They walked in silence, gazing down at the ground.

They climbed the stairs back to the verandah. "I need to go powder my nose," Mara said, and she was off into the crowd. Art slowly sauntered back into the midst of the revelers, hoping his face didn't appear as red as it felt. Suddenly overwhelmed with the urge for a drink, he made a beeline for the bar.

He ordered a rum and coke, and he sipped it as he turned away from the bar. The rush of alcohol instantly calmed him. He was going to make his way toward the podium to catch the end of the Lindstrom Foundation speeches, when suddenly a face appeared before his. It was Morris Dredson. He did not look at all pleased.

"You don't belong here, LaFey. You should just leave."

Art was stunned into silence. Dredson continued, with a snarl on his lips. "You have absolutely nothing to offer this Project. You are a drag and a hindrance. I want you to know I am going to do everything in my power to have you thrown off the board. I'm telling you this now, to give you a chance to go quietly, without fuss or embarrassment."

"I… I really don't…"

"Save it, LaFey. I don't care for more mindless prattle. Somehow you conned Lindstrom into thinking you were worth something, but I see right through you. How much do you make in a year? Thirty Grand? Forty Grand? I could buy your whole life, and not even dent my expense account. You are obviously looking for a free ride, and I don't like it. You're wasting valuable time and money, and I want you out!" Dredson accentuated the last three words with his finger, poking Art's chest.

Art had no idea whatsoever how to react. He stared incredulously at Dredson, who had simultaneously intimidated and angered him. Suddenly, the accumulated stimuli of the evening bore down on him, and he felt an overpowering urge to leave the party. With all the tact and grace he could muster, he muttered "Excuse me" through clenched teeth. He turned and sped off into the crowd, not looking back. He frantically searched the sea of faces for Gwen, and became increasingly disoriented. After fifteen minutes, which seemed like fifteen hours, of wandering around in seemingly endless circles, he found Gwen with Larry Dulak nestled in an antique-looking love seat in a small alcove off the ballroom. They each had an arm around the other, giggling and drinking.

"Oh, there you are, Art, darling. I wondered where you ran off to."

"Come on, Gwen, we have to go."

"So soon? But I was just starting to have fun."

"We have to go *now*!" He reached forward, grabbed her free arm, and tried to pull her up from the love seat. Larry shot Art an indignant look.

"All right, all right! Jeez, you don't have to get violent." She started gathering up her purse and straightening her dress. Art glanced frantically around, praying he wouldn't see Dredson again.

Gwen finally stood up, and took a couple of seconds to get her balance. She turned to Larry, blew him a kiss, and said, "Thank you for all the wonderful dances, sweetie. I had a *marvelous* time. I hope we can do it again sometime."

"Come on, Gwen," Art growled through gritted teeth as he took her hand and began dragging her toward the stairway that led out of the ballroom.

"OK, OK, calm down. What's your rush, anyway?" She slurred, stumbling after him.

"You're drunk!"

"Yeah, so what? You don't take me out much. I'm going to have fun when I get the chance."

They walked swiftly in silence the rest of the way through the crowd, up the stairs, and out the front door. Art impatiently paced as he waited for the valet to return with his car. Gwen leaned against a pillar for support, but still couldn't prevent herself from bobbing and weaving a couple of times.

Raindrops began to hit the windshield as Art drove down the long driveway, increasing in intensity into a torrent. Gwen nodded off, while Art hunched over the wheel, trying to make out his way through the swishing wipers and beating rain. One thought kept dominating his mind: "What have I gotten myself into?"

Chapter 14

"Hello, Mara." Art gingerly opened and closed the door to Lindstrom's reception office, as if he was afraid of breaking the glass in the door. Mara looked up, then quickly looked back down. "Hello. Nice to see you."

Art stood there, his hands folded in front of him, not sure of what to say. Mara shuffled papers on her desk. "Listen," he finally offered, "I've got a meeting with the Old Man right now, but I'd like to talk to you afterwards, if that would be all right."

"Yes, that would be fine." Mara looked up with an expressionless face, but the soft intensity of her eyes melted Art's heart.

Art sidled toward Lindstrom's office door. "So, I'll see you in a little bit?"

"OK."

Art quickly slipped into Lindstrom's office, glad to have run that gauntlet.

"Art, me boy, come on in! Good to see you! Did you enjoy the party? I didn't see you after the speeches."

"I left early, sir. Gwen had a little too much fun, if you know what I mean."

"Oh, yes. Doesn't get out much, eh?"

"No sir. I guess not." Art stood there again, in embarrassed silence, his hands folded in front of him.

"So what is it you wanted to see me about, lad?"

"Well, sir," Art said, after a pause and swallowing hard, "I am really sorry to have to say this, but I have decided to drop out of Project Avalon."

"What?" The old man nearly exploded out of his chair. "What's this nonsense?"

"Well, you see, sir, I really don't feel I'm qualified to participate in this Project. I mean, I really have nothing of significance to offer, and...."

"Did that little creep Dredson get to you?"

Art was startled. "How... how did you know?"

"It's no secret he doesn't like you, and wants you off the Project. But I didn't think your spine would melt at first heat. Come here. Sit down." He waived to an overstuffed leather chair beside the desk. "I want to tell you a couple of things."

Art sat down as if he expected iron spikes to come shooting through the seat.

Lindstrom leaned in close. "Art, this is between you and me and this desk. If you reveal any of it to anyone, I'll deny it, and kick you off the Project myself. I hate that little twerp Dredson, but I need him. He is disgustingly well-connected in the energy business, and if we're going to make a real go of it with Lindstrom Base, we'll need all the energy muscle behind us we can get, at least initially. But I'm not building it for slime like him and his cronies, I'm building it for you."

He threw up one arm and wagged his head. "Well, not for you specifically, but for people like you, for the ordinary people of the world with dreams and hopes of seeing tomorrow. You are their representative. You especially, because you see the value of all this. You *know* what this is all about. If you quit, in my mind the Project isn't worth doing. I have a million other ways to make faster, easier money. Stick around, hang in there, lad. The fun is just beginning." He leaned back and caught his breath, as if he had just greatly exerted himself.

Art sat in stunned silence for a minute. "I... I really don't know what to say, sir. I really don't see myself as that important."

"Well, you're not, really. But I like you. I have confidence in you, that someday you'll make a contribution far beyond what anyone would expect. I've made a lot of gambles in my business dealings. Some failed, but most succeeded. That's why I'm here today. I can sense these things. I told you about my boy, who died in Desert Storm. Did I tell you you remind me a lot of him?"

"No, sir, I'm honored."

"Art, this thing is bigger than both of us. Ultimately, you, me, Dredson, we mean nothing. Do we know who the first fish were that floundered up onto shore to become airbreathers? Of course not. But I do know what I like and who I like, and it's my money, for the most part, that's building this thing. I want you around. Will you stay?"

Art felt a warm rush overtake him, and he knew what his answer was. "Yes, sir, and I'll try to do justice to the honor you do me."

Lindstrom waved his hand at Art. "Oh, cut that ass-kissing shit and go pour us a couple of brandies."

They laughed and drank for half an hour, then Lindstrom dismissed Art to tend to some business. Art was grateful for the brandy, because it gave him fortification for his encounter with Mara.

He walked back into the reception office, a rosy glow overtaking his cheeks. "Hello again, Mara."

"Hello again, Art." She turned away from her computer, folded her hands on the desk, and looked directly into his eyes. Art felt as if a powerful wind were blowing into him. He sat down in a chair next to the desk, for fear of falling over.

"Look, about the other night, I am really sorry I took advantage of you."

"You couldn't do that, even if you wanted to." Somehow he knew she meant it.

"Well, OK, but what I mean is, well, I was going to say goodbye, that it was good to know you. I came here to resign from Avalon, but the Old Man talked me into staying."

"Yes, he does have a way about him, doesn't he?"

(Those dancing, merry eyes, Art thought. She's not making this easy.)

"Well, so now I guess I'm going to stick around, and that, uh, means we're still going to have to work together."

"I look forward to it."

"Yes, well, but we must maintain a certain, ah, professional demeanor, don't you think?"

"Oh, of course."

(My God, she's beautiful.)

"Look, Mara, I have to tell you I'm attracted to you, but I'm married, and I just can't, well, get involved beyond a professional level."

Mara put her hand gently on Art's. "I would expect nothing less from a gentleman such as yourself." She patted his hand, then pulled hers back.

Art stared at his hand. "So, you're OK with all this?"

"Perfectly."

(But am I?)

Art stood up. "OK, then. Well, I'm looking forward to this, then. Shall we get together Thursday and do some planning?"

"Thursday is fine."

"OK, I'll call you."

"I'll be waiting."

"Bye."

"Bye."

Art closed the door behind him. How does she turn me into a blithering idiot like that? he thought, heading to the parking lot. His thoughts kept turning to Mara and Project Avalon as he drove to pick up Gary from school to take him to the Pacific Science Center, which was currently running a special exhibit on Mars.

Chapter 15

Events seemed to take on a life of their own after that. The media attention on The Lindstrom Foundation ran its course and died down, and Project Avalon got underway in earnest. The board met once a quarter, reviewed progress, and planned future direction. Art always sat as far away from Dredson as he could, and often looked to the old man for encouragement. Lindstrom often winked at Art, as if to say, "Don't worry. I'm on your side." Art took comfort in that. Dredson would occasionally scowl in Art's direction, but he never directly confronted him again.

Art kept Perry abreast of the progress. A couple of nights after Lindstrom had talked Art into staying on the Project, Art and Perry had discussed Avalon at length over Red Hooks at The College Inn. Perry was initially at a loss to understand why Lindstrom was so rough with him, but Art filled him in on the general details of what had transpired at the first board meeting, and Perry said, "Woah! This is way bigger than I had imagined. I guess I'm kind of glad I don't have a major role." After swearing Perry once again to ultimate secrecy, he assured him that he would keep him up to speed on developments. "I'm going to need your input, Perry. You've already helped me to understand what this is really all about. I feel your perspective will keep me focused. I'll need someone I can trust outside the Project that I can confide in, or I'll explode."

"You got it, dude." They chinked their half-full pints together, downed them, and ordered another round.

Art and Mara began to work on a catalog of the major works of art and literature for the Moonbase, and started devising an organizational structure for it. They developed a multi-tiered hierarchy, with essential classics at the top that should be present in their original form, if possible, such as fine editions of Dante's Divine Comedy and early Jules Verne ("Nothing is more wonderful than the smell of an old, dusty book," the old man remarked once. "We can't deprive our lunar cave dwellers of such simple pleasures."), followed by information that would easily and without deterioration of quality be accommodated on CD-ROM, such as basic reference material. They included plans for Internet links, but they determined that they also wanted an independent catalog of materials, in the event that their Internet access was lost.

Art and Mara worked well together. There was obviously a deep and growing friendship between them. The first few working sessions were slightly awkward as they silently defined their personal boundaries, but after they became comfortable with each other, they both looked forward to their time together. The hint of romance had disappeared, or at least been suppressed, and they laughed together like old friends as they worked. Art, without letting the Old Man know, consulted heavily with Perry on the Project. Art, Perry, and Mara would occasionally go out to dinner together and discuss the finer points of the information catalog. Mara, distrustful of any outsiders at first, grew to like and trust Perry, and did not mind that he knew of Project Avalon. "He's so… refreshingly odd," she told Art after one of their nights out. "He makes me laugh."

At the third board meeting, Lindstrom took the board to an obscure plant buried in the back of the Lindstrom grounds. "Ladies and gentlemen," he said with his hand on the door handle, "this is where Avalon is being built." They entered and were instantly amazed. Before them was a full-scale mock up of Phase Two of Lindstrom Base. Domed structures were arranged in a square pattern, connected by round tubes large enough for a person to walk through. A crew of white-jacketed technicians was scurrying around, performing all sorts of indecipherable tasks. One rather short technician turned, saw the board members, and approached. The technician took off a white hair net and goggles to reveal a young, rather attractive Japanese woman. Lindstrom introduced the woman to the board. "This is Sukati Matsukawa, the chief engineer on Project Avalon."

"Call me Scotty, if you'd like. That's what everybody around here calls me." She said with a broad smile, reaching forward to shake boardmembers' hands. Art happened to be first.

"Like in the old *Star Trek* show," he said.

"Right," she responded, laughing.

"Show us around," Lindstrom requested of Scotty after the introductions were complete. Scotty gave them a guided tour, and Art was completely overwhelmed. The technical aspects of the base had progressed rather far, obviously with help from Lindstrom's space station work. Art asked the most questions, and Scotty seemed to respond to him best. She revealed that amongst the projects the team was working on was cold fusion using helium three. "If we can perfect it, we will have eliminated our dependence on outside energy." Art risked a quick glance at Dredson, across the crowd from him. He was scowling, obviously not enjoying that piece of news.

Lindstrom always hosted a cocktail hour after the board meetings. Art casually got to know some of the other boardmembers, but he always seemed to have short, significant interchanges with General Devere. Art considered him his closest friend on the board, outside of Lindstrom. If Art ever got in the vicinity of Dredson, he would scowl at Art, and Art would find some pretense to move quickly away. Art talked to Larry Dulak a few times, but it was always cursory and on the surface. Both men conveniently ignored the events of the gala.

Art stopped going to the meetings of the Seattle Environmental Council, but he felt a strange compulsion to convince Doug of the effectiveness of his actions. Doug occasionally joined Art and Perry for a night at the College Inn, or some other U District tavern. Without revealing the true nature of what they were involved in, Art, with help from Perry, tried to persuade Doug that developing space was the only long-term solution to solving the Earth's environmental problems. "That may be, although I don't quite buy it," he would answer, "but nonetheless, I could never leave the Earth. It is the cradle of life, the source of our existence. How could you give up trees, and rivers, and all the wildlife? It's just not natural." Art nevertheless kept trying, and he and Doug formed a unique friendship, wherein both agreed to disagree.

Art found his relationship with Gwen becoming increasingly frosty. They never spoke of the night of the gala. Their communications were almost exclusively of an informational nature. Gwen began spending more and longer weekends with her sister Sarah on Bainbridge Island. Sometimes she would take Gary, sometimes she would leave him with Art for the weekend. After a while, she stopped telling Art she was going; Art would assume that she had gone to Bainbridge, and took it in stride. He cherished his weekends with Gary. They went to parks, rode bikes, worked on beginning math and word books, and just rolled around and tickled each other, giggling like crazy.

The actual supporting infrastructure of Avalon started to take shape. General Devere announced at a board meeting that the first inflatable elements of the space maintenance station Oasis were soon to be launched, and that final tests on the Dark Stallion reusable vehicle were being conducted. In a matter of months, he said, they would be prepared to launch the first crew of two to Oasis. Lindstrom looked as gleeful as a child at his birthday party upon hearing the news. Although the name of the lunar base was still officially Lindstrom Base, the boardmembers and other insiders increasingly referred to the Project in general as Avalon. Lindstrom himself would go back and forth, using one term then the other, but he too finally alighted on Avalon as the common designation.

Project Avalon dominated most of Art's thoughts, but the wider world kept making incursions from time to time. Art was amazed at the progress

Jerry Patterson made in capturing the Republican nomination. He had infused the party at all levels with operatives from his Christian Union, and they dominated the party platform negotiations. He waged a bitter and vicious campaign against his Democratic opponent Jim Stanton. Allegations of sexual harassment, draft-dodging, and a checkered past of drug use and defaulted loans surfaced at the most inopportune times. When Patterson actually captured the White House, no one was really surprised, although heads were shaking all over the country, regretting that politics had become so nasty and divisive. Due to the tight organization of the Christian Union, Republicans also captured control of the House and the Senate, although by very narrow margins. Patterson, claiming a God-given mandate, immediately began pushing a sweeping social and economic agenda, which most Americans were either fervently for or vehemently against.

One of Patterson's first official acts was to condemn the tactics of Moustapha Ali and his Party of Allah. Ali was gaining popular support in the Middle East in a Pan-Arab movement whose focus was non-negotiation with Israel. Ali claimed that the peace with the Palestinians was a false one, and that they were little more than slaves, trapped inside an Israeli protectorate. No official ties could be established between the Party of Allah and the various radical Arab terrorist groups, but no one doubted the cause of the increase of bombings, shootings, and other terrorist activities inside Israel's borders. The Israeli government cracked down on its Palestinian citizenry and raided southern Lebanon periodically, but they could not diminish the frequency or intensity of the attacks.

Ali traveled the Arab world, preaching unity against the West. He never outright claimed the mantle, but his followers declared that he was the twelfth imam, returned from days of yore to inaugurate "The Arab Century." Crowds thronged wherever he spoke. Patterson publicly pledged full support of Israel, and warned that, if necessary, he would come after Ali. Ali, for his part, warned the West in general and Patterson in particular not to meddle in local affairs. He hinted that oil might become scarce if his conditions were not met.

In the spring of 2001, President Patterson addressed the nation on live television with the results of the Griffin Commission's findings on the space shuttle explosion. He announced that the panel had concluded that the immediate cause was a design flaw in the recently upgraded main engines of the shuttle, but that serious institutional problems had been uncovered, relating to how hard and fast NASA had pushed to make up for schedule slips in the International Space Station program.

"We've spent tens of billons of dollars over two decades on the program, and what do we have to show for it?" Patterson asked in his most sincere and authoritative tone. "An incomplete skeleton, a useless framework of a space station that we can no longer reach because our shuttle system is inadequate and unsafe. This is the second explosion that has claimed an entire crew. It is time we abandon this space folly and turn our attention and resources back to Earth. I am proposing legislation to Congress tomorrow that we sell what there is of the space station to Russia, disband NASA, and reallocate the funds to prison construction and veterans programs. Rest assured, our military space programs under the Department of Defense budget will remain intact. We will be safe and secure on Earth, but we will no longer invade God's domain of space. God never intended us to fly in space. The two shuttle explosions prove that, and we should heed the warning." Art was infuriated and disgusted, and thanked his own God that he had been privileged enough to be included in Project Avalon.

The slew of environmental disasters that struck within three weeks of each other shortly thereafter convinced Doug that he was right about the evils of technology, and he told Art and Perry as much. First, the biggest oil spill in history occurred in the Gulf of Mexico, just outside of the Panama Canal, killing wildlife and contaminating coastline from Costa Rica to Columbia. Two days after that, a chemical processing plant in Southern China exploded, wiping out a city of 300,000 unsuspecting people. As if that was not enough, a week later the National Geographic Society reported that the giant Tortoises of Galapagos had been poached to near-extinction, and seventy-eight other species had disappeared within the last ten years, or were in a very precarious situation, on Darwin's favorite islands.

In light of these events and Patterson's speech, Art became even more committed to Project Avalon. He had regular meetings with Lindstrom to discuss progress on his aspect of the Project, and the conversation would inevitably turn to the hopes and dreams each had for Avalon. "You know, Art," the old man said one time, "I'm looking at the way the world is going, and I can't help thinking that we're just possibly building a new Noah's Ark, if you will. Perhaps what we're doing will turn out to be the last great hope of mankind."

"I've had similar thoughts, sir," Art responded.

"Well, then, that gives your project added urgency. You have to ensure, just in case, that the collected wisdom of the Earth survives." Art felt the weight of great responsibility sink onto his shoulders.

Lindstrom threw several parties and cookouts at his estate for a select group of his favorite Avalon people. Art and Mara were always invited, as were Scotty and some of her engineers. Every now and then board members would be there, but not often. "I prefer all these young enthusiastic kids to those stuffed shirts I usually have to deal with," Lindstrom leaned over and said to Art and Mara at one party. When the weather was nice, the parties were held on the great lawn overlooking Puget Sound. Art and Mara enjoyed each others' company at these events, surrounded by close friends. Their feelings for each other deepened. Eventually they began taking long walks along the cliff and into the surrounding woods, holding hands and talking. They felt comfortable with each other and were content with their friendship, not pushing the relationship too far.

At one cookout, late in August of 2001, Art, Mara, and Lindstrom were sitting around after finishing grilled bratwurst and discussing current events.

"Can you believe Patterson is actually pushing through that constitutional amendment banning abortion?" Art was ranting. "I'm afraid he actually has the clout to pull it off."

"I'm afraid you're right, me boy," the old man answered, sipping his lemonade. "Although I don't necessarily disagree with him on that issue, it is just another example of how he is going about abrogating our freedoms, one by one. This just makes Avalon all the more important." He looked at Art and Mara sitting close together in their lawn chairs. "Well, you two are getting along rather famously," he said with a smirk. Art and Mara looked at each other with embarrassed little smiles. Lindstrom continued, "I like you, Art. In a way, I almost think of you as my son. I can tell you two have affections for each other, even if you hide it from yourselves. I've got a little secret for you, me lad." He leaned in toward Art. Mara's eyes flashed wide, but she didn't have time to say anything before Lindstrom confided, "She's my daughter." He winked at Art.

"I know that, sir. She told me you adopted her."

Lindstrom feigned frustration with stupidity. "No, you dense dolt. She's my *real* daughter."

Art looked uncomprehendingly at Lindstrom, then at Mara, then back at Lindstrom. "You mean…?"

"Yes. It's true." The old man was gleeful.

Mara was blushing. "Oh, Da, you promised!"

"Well, he's one of us now. He should know."

Art was stupefied. "I… don't get it."

"I have an estate in Ireland, just outside a little town called Doolin, on the western coast. My wife and I used to summer there every year. One year I met this charming lass, Mara's dear mother, and we, um, developed a passion for each other. I was already married, so of course everything had to be carried on discreetly." Mara hid her face in one hand and sank lower and lower in her chair. Nevertheless a smile could be glimpsed through her fingers. "I had no idea our love produced a child. One summer I heard My Love had died, and I went to attend the funeral. It was there I discovered Mara, and brought her home to the states. We made up that story about her being an orphan to conceal the truth."

Art, realizing his jaw was hanging wide open, shut his mouth and swallowed. He looked at Mara, and she seemed to be a completely different person. "Wow," was all he managed to utter.

"Now, I told you all that, young man, because I can tell you two care for each other. I'm not going to live forever, you know. I want you two to look out for each other, and take care of each other when I'm gone."

"Oh, Da, you know I hate it when you talk that way."

"Hush, darling, you know it's true. Now, if love could grow between you two someday, that would be splendid. You two have my blessing."

Art and Mara looked at each other, and were at a loss for words.

Chapter 16

The next morning Art got a frantic call from Mara. "Oh, Art, something terrible has happened. Can you come to the estate right away?" She hung up before Art could ask any questions.

"Who was that, dear?" Gwen asked, rolling over in bed and looking at Art.

"That was Mara. Something's happened. I've got to go." Art jumped out of bed and started throwing on clothes.

"You're always running off with that tramp. Have you got something going on with her?"

Art whipped around. "Don't you dare call her a tramp! I've got to go. We'll talk later."

"No we won't. I'm going to my sister's today, and taking Gary with me."

"Fine. Whatever." Art raced out of the room and left the house at a run.

Art rushed up the front steps of Lindstrom's estate after a frantic drive over there. Servants pointed his way up the grand staircase to Lindstrom's bedroom. When he burst through the open door, he saw a white-jacketed emergency crew tending to Lindstrom on his bed. Mara was sobbing in a chair in the corner. She looked up, saw Art, jumped up, rushed over to him, and threw herself into his arms. "Oh, Art, he's dead!" Art, not knowing quite what to do or how to react, hesitantly put his arms around her. Then the full impact of what he had just heard hit him. He looked over at Lindstrom, between the paramedics, who were preparing to wheel his body away on a gurney, and realized he was lying completely still. No breath made his chest rise and fall. He hugged Mara tightly. "How…?" He whispered almost inaudibly.

"They don't know yet. They have to take him to the hospital for tests."

The full weight of the implications of Lindstrom's death sank onto Art with the inevitable intensity of a hydraulic press. "So… what does that mean for Avalon? And what does that mean for you? We'll have to hold an emergency meeting."

"Don't go yet. Hold me."

"Yes, of course. Let's get out of here."

Holding each other, they went downstairs and sat on a couch in the great receiving room. They held each other without talking, intermittently crying.

About half an hour later a servant came up to them. "Excuse me, I know this is a troubling time, but Mr. Dulak has called an emergency board meeting of the Lindstrom Foundation. It will start at Lindstrom Headquarters at noon."

"Come on, Mara we have to go. We have just enough time to get there. Are you up to this?"

Mara sat up straight, wiped her eyes, blew her nose, and tried to tousle her hair back into shape. "I suppose so. I must look frightful. Give me a few minutes to freshen up."

"Certainly."

She got up and left the room, and Art was left alone with his thoughts. For the most part, he was numb, and could not think a coherent thought.

An hour later, Art and Mara arrived at Lindstrom Headquarters. The main administration building was abuzz with activity, which was odd for a Sunday.

"There you are," Dulak shouted to them as they entered the boardroom. "Come on, we're ready to start."

About half of the boardmembers were there, nervously talking in hushed tones. Art and Mara took their customary seats, side by side, trying to remain as calm and composed as possible. General Devere entered the room then, and came over to Mara. "My deepest sympathies, Miss Gann," he said, resting his hand lightly on her shoulder. Mara patted his hand and replied, fighting back tears, "Thank you."

The General took his usual seat as Dulak walked over and occupied the large chair customarily reserved for Lindstrom. "Well, not everybody is here yet, and some are out of town, but we have to get started. When the others show up, we'll bring them up to speed as quickly as we can. As I'm sure you have all learned by now, Mr. Lindstrom passed away in his sleep last night. I know it saddens all of us. I personally feel awful. Nonetheless, and this is the way he would have wanted it, we have to look after business. As Executive Director of the Lindstrom Foundation, and we all know that means Project Avalon, I am now head of the Project. I hereby appoint Morris Dredson as my Vice-Chair. We need to bring that to a vote. Do we have a second?"

The attorney Hector Maris seconded the motion, rather hastily, Art reflected.

"OK, we have a second. All in favor?"

All hands went up, except for Art, Mara, and General Devere. Devere turned to Art with a look that seemed to say "Chin up. Be strong."

"All opposed." Devere raised his hand. Art, seeing that, gained bravery and raised his hand. Mara raised hers.

"The motion carries. Dredson is also our Chief of Operations. We have been planning changes for some time, and now seems like the opportune time to instigate them. Morris?"

Dulak sat down and Morris rose to his feet. "Yes, well, the Project is carrying through rather well, but there are several areas which could be made more efficient. We need to crunch our timetable and get hardware in flight and on the lunar surface. As you know, the function of an organization stems from its leadership. Therefore, to streamline the Project, we must start by streamlining the board. I hereby move that we pare down the board by two seats." Dredson started straight at Art, and his eyes bored into him like daggers. "I move that Art LaFey and Henry Sagramor be removed from the board. Second?"

Again, Hector Maris seconded.

"All in favor?"

A majority of hands rose. Art could not believe what he was seeing. He was shocked into immobility.

"Opposed?"

"I oppose vehemently, you little shit!" Devere bellowed. "This is an outrage, and I won't stand for it!" He stood up quickly, knocking over his chair.

Dredson pasted an obsequious smile on his face. "Sir, the board has voted. It is completed. There is nothing you can do."

"We'll see about that!" He turned and stormed out of the room.

Dredson turned back to Art. He could not conceal the glee on his face. "Mr. LaFey, you are no longer a member of this board. Would you please leave the room?"

Art could not move. He was frozen in disbelief.

Dredson raised his voice. In very loud, precise syllables, he repeated, "Mis-ter LaFey, would you please leave the room?"

Mara stood up and touched Art's shoulder. "Come on, Art. There is nothing more for us here."

Dredson looked at Mara with a worried expression. "You are still a member of the board, Ms. Gann. You don't have to leave."

She cast a cold glance at Dredson. "I wouldn't stay after this mockery," she replied, the anger unconcealed in her voice.

Art turned and looked at Mara. How can she be so strong through this? he thought. He stood up very awkwardly, his legs wobbling. He almost tripped over the chair twice in the attempt to extract himself from his seat at the table. Mara held his arm as they walked through the wall opening to Lindstrom's office. As the wall-door shut behind them, they heard Dredson say "Mr. Sagramor, you are now no longer a member of this board…."

Art barely realized that Mara was leading him to the parking lot. His mind was racing, trying to comprehend recent events. Once they were back in Art's car, he finally said, "Where are we going?"

"I don't quite know. I don't want to go back to the estate. That would be too painful. I just want to go away."

"Let's go to my apartment. We can figure out what to do next there, in peace."

"Won't Gwen be there?"

"No, she said she was taking off to her sister's on Bainbridge Island, with Gary."

"OK, I'd like that. I need space to think."

"So do I."

Mara reached over and put her hand on Art's thigh. Art put his hand on top of hers and squeezed. They didn't let go for a long time.

They arrived at Art's apartment. "Can I get you something to drink?" Art asked.

"Sure. Ice water would be fine."

He went into the kitchen to get drinks. As he opened the freezer, he saw the flashing light on the answering machine which rested on the counter next to the refrigerator, indicating that there was a message waiting. He grabbed the ice tray, shut the door, and reached over to hit the playback button. He listened to the message as he twisted the plastic tray to loosen the ice cubes.

"Art, this is Sarah. Something's happened. Everyone is OK, but I think you'd better come out to Bainbridge. I can't tell you more right now." A click indicated that Sarah had hung up.

Art raced over to the phone, grabbed the cordless receiver, and pounded out Sarah's number. It took him three tries to get it right. Mara, hearing Art's frantic movements, came into the kitchen. "What is it, Art?" Art held up a finger as he listened at the receiver. He got Sarah's message machine. "Hi, this is the Winslow home. If you'd like to leave a message…" Art smacked the hang-up button and slammed the phone down on its stand.

"Something's come up. I've got to go to Bainbridge Island."

"I'll come with you."

"No, this is a personal matter. I don't want you to get mixed up in my troubles."

Mara spread her legs in a wide stance and put her hands on her hips.

"Arthur Roy LaFey, if you think I'm going to let you out of my sight, especially in the state you're in, after all that has happened, you are crazy. You need me right now. Besides," She paused, softening. She crossed her arms and looked out the window, trying to hide a forming tear. "I… I need you, too."

Art's heart melted. He walked over to Mara, slipped his arms around her, and held her tight. She melted into him. They stood there for a few minutes, silently weeping.

It was a beautiful day to be on the water. Art always enjoyed riding the Washington State ferries. He wished he could enjoy it more today, but he was preoccupied. He stood on the upper deck with Mara, looking out across the Sound to Bainbridge Island ahead of them. The wind blew their hair back, and seagulls chattered around them as they flapped their wings energetically to keep up with the ferry.

The ferry docked at Bainbridge Island, and Art drove straight to Sarah's home. As they pulled up the long gravel driveway, they saw several children running and playing around the house. Gary was amongst them. Art got out of the car. Gary saw him and came running. "Daddy!" he yelled, and leapt into Art's open arms. Art picked him up and swung him around. "How are you, Gary? Are you OK?"

"Sure. Do something funny to me!"

"OK," Art replied. He held onto Gary's wrists and spun him around in a circle, so his legs stuck straight out by centrifugal force. Art stopped spinning and set Gary on his feet. Gary tried to walk away, but he kept falling over to the left, giggling the whole time.

Art turned to Mara. "There. I got him toddler drunk." Mara laughed.

The other children ran up to Art. "Do that to me! Do that to me!" But Art had espied Sarah in the doorway of the house. "Maybe a little later. I've got to go see your Mama right now."

He and Mara walked up to the house, being pawed at by children the whole way. "Kids, go play nicely," Sarah called when they reached the steps. The children ran off, distracted by another child who had picked up a plastic bat and was swinging at a ball that lay on the ground.

"My, what a handful, Sarah," Art said walking up the steps. "Are those others the neighbor kids?"

"Yeah, this is the local Kool-Aid house. They all love to come here and play. Come in Art, and…."

"Oh, excuse me. This is Mara Gann. She is working with me on my Lindstrom Foundation project."

"I… see," Sarah responded, obviously seeing through the thin cover. She led them into the kitchen. "Sit down, won't you? Can I get you something to drink?"

"I'm fine for now, Sarah. I really want to know what has happened."

Sarah stared at Art for a moment, concern etched on her face. She then turned to a table in the corner and picked up an envelope. "You'd better read this," she said softly, handing the envelope to Art.

Art took it. The envelope was blank. "What is this?"

"Just read it," Sarah answered abruptly and left the kitchen.

Art shot a nervous glance at Mara as he pulled the letter out of the envelope. Mara reached over and put her hand on his forearm.

Art read the letter. It was in Gwen's handwriting.

> Dear Art,
>
> I could go into a long-winded explanation, but I'd rather get right to the point. Besides, I don't think I care enough to explain myself to you. I am leaving with Larry Dulak. Don't try to find us. Larry is loaded and well-connected. We will be far gone by the time you read this. I have already filed for divorce. You should get the papers in a week or so. I am giving you full physical custody of Gary. I've cared for him for six years while you traipsed around with your schemes of trying to get rich, none of which worked. He goes to school now anyway, and doesn't need me as much anymore. It's your turn to raise him. Good bye.
>
> Gwen.

Art dropped the letter and put his face in his hands. Mara put her arms around his shoulders. "What is it?"

Art absentmindedly waved a hand. "Read it. I don't care."

Mara picked up the letter and read it, one arm still around Art. When she had finished, she dropped the letter, put her hand over her mouth, and stared out the window. Art's body shook every now and then, and a tear occasionally dripped through his fingers.

Eventually Sarah peeked around the corner. Art was wiping his eyes with a napkin, and saw her. "Did you know about this?"

"Not until this morning. She wrote it right here, at this table, and made me read it. She's been coming out here a lot lately, but then she would leave

Gary here and go off somewhere. She never told me where, but she swore me to secrecy. She's my sister, Art. I had to keep it a secret. If I knew it was something like this, I… I don't know what I would have done."

Art looked at her for a moment, then said, "You're a good sister, Sarah. You did what you had to do. It's not your fault." Sobs overtook him suddenly, and he put his face back in his hands. Mara hugged him tighter.

"I'll go gather up Gary's things," Sarah said, and quickly left the room again.

After about five minutes, Art finally gained control over himself. "Well, I guess we'd better get out of here. Where's Sarah? Where's Gary?"

Sarah brought Gary's things, and Art, Mara, and Gary all piled into Art's car. Art drove back down to the ferry landing, and got in line to board the ferry. The next one did not leave for forty-five minutes. The three of them got out and walked on the beach next to the ferry dock. Mara slipped her arm under Art's and Art held Gary's hand with his other hand. The full weight of the day's events began to press on them both. They stared down at their feet as they slowly walked.

Art threw his head back and moaned. "What am I going to do? What are we going to do? It's all over. There's nothing left." He looked down and started crying again.

Mara wiped a tear from her eye. "It's not all over. We've been dealt some blows, but we must bear up and be strong. We can come through this."

Art stopped and looked at Mara. He let go of Gary's hand, who then ran down to the water's edge and tried to skip rocks on the gently rolling waves, oblivious to the adult's weighty concerns. "It *is* all over, Mara! Don't you see? The Old Man is dead, we got kicked off the board of Avalon, and now my wife has left me, all in one day. What else is there? It's hopeless!"

Mara slapped Art across the face. Art's eyes widened in surprise. "Maybe my father made the wrong choice! If he knew you were going to wilt at the first sign of adversity like a spineless jellyfish, he never would have brought you in. I'm hurting too, you know. My father is dead. It's painful, and I just want to curl up and disappear, but we can't do that. We're still alive, and have things to do." She grabbed him by the shoulders and wheeled him around. Art's eyes landed on Gary, unselfconsciously throwing rocks into the Sound. "Look. That's your son. You have to be strong for him. You're all he's got right now. If you give up, what happens to him?" She turned him back around. "We've got each other. We can make it." She hugged him tightly.

After a few moments, Art, still holding Mara, asked, "But… what are we going to do?"

"We'll go off to Ireland and rest a while. We'll heal ourselves."

"Ireland? What? How? Where will we stay? I don't have any money."

Mara pulled back enough from Art to be able to look at his face. There was a glint in her eye. "You forget who you're holding right now." She smiled wryly.

A wave of realization washed over Art. "You're Lindstrom's daughter! You probably inherit the estate in Ireland!"

"You see? It's not so hopeless after all. You just have to look past the present, past your own small concerns."

"Are you sure you want me and the little goofball tagging along with you? You're going to need your own time and space to work things out."

Mara squeezed him tightly for a second. "I wouldn't have it any other way. Don't you leave me now, mister!"

Art pulled her more tightly to him. "Thank you," he said in a whisper. And he kept repeating silently, thank you, thank you, thank you, thank you….

Chapter 17

The three of them rode the ferry back to Seattle and stayed at Lindstrom's estate that night. There were plenty of bedrooms at the estate, but Art and Gary decided to sleep in the same enormous bed. Neither wanted to be alone.

In the morning, Art took Gary back to their apartment to pack their things for an indefinite stay in Ireland. Art happened to have a passport, because two years earlier he had been scheduled to go on a trip to Japan to cover the exploding cyber-culture burgeoning there. He had gotten passports for Gwen and Gary at the same time, thinking he might be able to take them on the trip. Then the trip was called off, due to lack of funds at the Arts Review. Art was disappointed, but glad he had gotten the passports anyway, just in case. Now he was very grateful he had done so. When he opened the drawer in which he kept them, he noticed Gwen's was missing. He had to sit down, once again stunned by the events of the previous day. A thought occurred to him. He rushed to the closet in the bedroom. All of Gwen's favorite clothes were gone. He sat down on the bed and began to weep.

Gary came into the room. "What's wrong, Daddy? Where's Mama?"

Art grabbed Gary and held him tight. "Mama's gone away for a while. We're going away too. Have you ever heard of Ireland?"

"Yeah! There's leperkans there. Will we see a leperkan?"

"Sure we will. Pooky, it's 'leprechauns.' Can you say that? Maybe later." He swatted Gary lightly on the fanny. "Go gather up the things you want to take."

Gary ran out of the room, yelling "Yaaay!"

"Not too many toys," Art shouted after him.

Mara had told him that she would help him out for a while (after all, he was still officially on the payroll of the Lindstrom Foundation; Dredson had said nothing about that), so there was no need to hold onto his apartment. Art called his landlord and got his answering machine. "Bob, this is Art LaFey. I'm going out of the country for a while, so I don't need this place anymore. Gwen is gone, too." He had to stop and swallow a moment. "Keep my last month's rent and my deposit, and go ahead and rent it out as quickly as you want to. Anything I leave here, you can keep or sell. Heck, you could even rent it as a furnished apartment now. Sorry for the short notice. Bye."

He called Perry next. He got an answering machine there, too. "Perry, a lot has happened. I can't leave this stuff on an answering machine, but I'm going away for a while. I'll get in touch with you. I know, I'll send you email and explain it all to you. One thing: keep this a secret. I don't want anybody to know what has happened. If anybody asks, tell them I got my old job back at the paper and I'm gone on assignment. I'll explain it all later, I promise. I need a friend like you right now. Bye."

He called all the utilities and canceled services, then he and Gary finished packing. A couple of hours later, suitcases in his hands, he stood in the open front door and looked around at his apartment, his old life, one last time. A tear rolled down his cheek. "Come on, Daddy!" Gary called from the car. He shut the door, which he had already locked, got in the car, and drove away without looking back.

On the way to Lindstrom's estate, Art stopped by the post office to fill out a change of address card with the address in Ireland that Mara had given to him. When Gary and Art showed up at the mansion in the late afternoon, Mara was still efficiently taking care of her affairs. She was all administration and business, and there was no hint of the scared, vulnerable woman Art had seen the day before. "I've arranged a late night flight to Dublin, so you'd better get what rest you can now." Art and Gary went upstairs and took naps in Art's bed. At nine o'clock a servant woke them. "It's time to depart, sir." One of Lindstrom's limousines gave Mara, Art, and Gary a ride to Sea-Tac airport.

They sat in first class on their flight. Gary was excited. He had flown only a couple of times before, and never in first class. Art was just as excited, also never having flown first class. They played with everything within reach, and enjoyed the takeoff. After the novelty wore off, Gary settled down to watch a movie on the small, private video screen attached to his seat. Art turned to Mara, and saw she was weeping. "What's wrong, Mara?" She fell into his arms and sobbed uncontrollably. He patted her and tried to comfort her. "You go ahead and cry. It's all right. You've been a trooper through all this. You're amazing. I've been such a blithering idiot, you've had to take care of me as well as yourself. But now everything's in order. You've been so strong, but now it's alright to break down a little. I'll hold you." Mara, still shaking with sobs, kept her head buried in Art's shoulder, but her hand reached up and stroked his cheek.

The flight was uneventful. Mara recovered after a while, and she and Art talked about mostly inconsequential things. Gary caught up on a year's worth of cartoons. They all slept intermittently. When they landed in Dublin, Mara hired a van, which drove them across Ireland to the west coast. Art and Gary were fascinated by the countryside. They were enthralled by the stone walls which separated the fields. Those fields became smaller and smaller the farther west they traveled. They passed through little towns, each one more enchanting and picturesque than the last. Mara had bought bread, cheese, and wine (apple juice for Gary) back in Dublin, and they ate that as they rode and watched the scenery flow by. "Someday we'll tour around the countryside, but today I want to get home." Art was mildly surprised to hear her refer to the estate in Doolin as home. He looked at Mara, realizing there was a lot to her, and he had barely scratched the surface. He felt as if he was in the presence of a deep, rich soul, into which he could fall back and float, protected from the vagaries of common reality.

They eventually drove up a long, winding road to the top of a hill. At the top stood an impressive edifice that resembled a medieval castle. The van stopped, and the passengers piled out. Mara took a deep breath, and stood up tall. "Welcome to Castle Lindstrom, my true home." Art was too busy letting his jaw hang down to be able to respond. Gary took off instantly, running through the heather and chasing butterflies. Servants came out of the manor and began unloading the bags from the van. Mara turned and looked at Art, then beyond him. She breathed deeply through her nose. "Can you smell it?"

"What?" he asked, and sniffed a little.

"The sea. Look." She pointed over his shoulder. He turned around and dropped his jaw again. A breathtaking vista of rolling cliffs with a turbulent sea beyond them presented itself to his vision. Dramatic clouds were sweeping across the sky. It was one of the most beautiful sights he had ever laid eyes on. He turned back to *the* most beautiful sight and said, "It's magnificent!"

"This is my home, this is where I grew up, this is where I belong." She reached out and took his hand. "I'm so glad you are here to share it with me."

Art looked at Mara without saying a word. He was wondering how he could be so fortunate to find such a wonderful, beautiful, caring person. His heart swelled in his chest.

"Come on. Let me show you around."

Mara gave Art and Gary the grand tour, first of the castle, then of the grounds and surrounding countryside. After a long walk, they approached the cliff overlooking the sea.

"That is a strong wind," Art remarked. "Does it always blow like that?"

"Almost always," Mara answered. "Some say it's the blessed breath of the fairy folk, blowing out of their secret homeland in the West to bless Ireland. Look down there." She pointed off to the right. Along the coast, the cliff gently dropped down and curled away from the sea, to finally reveal a little town nestled in a valley. "That's Doolin, down there."

"What a wonderful little town. It looks very inviting."

"Yes, it is. The people are wonderful. We'll go there when we're settled in and feeling social."

The three of them stood there, gazing around them as the wind blew in strong gusts from the sea.

After a while, Mara said, "Well, there are some things I should take care of, and I should see to it that supper gets prepared. Do you two want to wander around for a little while longer while I go back?"

"Sure. Sounds good."

Mara reached around Art's waist and gave him a gentle hug, then walked off in the direction of the castle. She stopped suddenly, looked down, and called back. "Gary! Come take a look! I've found a fairy ring!"

Gary ran off after Mara. Art, watching Gary run off, was seized by a sudden melancholy. He turned and gazed back out to sea. The full weight of the last two days' events crashed in on him with an unexpected force. He realized with a grim finality that he had lost everything he had held of value back in Seattle, and he had no idea what the future would bring. He felt like a rudderless ship adrift at sea.

The wind coming in from the sea was very strong, and carried the sharp smell of sea salt. Art leaned at a steep angle against the wind, which yanked at his clothes. He leaned dangerously far out over the cliff, and stared straight down at the boulders below. What if I just let myself fall, right here, right now? Who would miss me? I'm not doing anybody any good. I couldn't save Lindstrom. I couldn't stop Gwen from leaving. I couldn't fight for my seat on the Avalon board, and now that bastard Dredson has control. What am I good for? It would be so easy.... He leaned farther over the cliff, into the onrushing wind.

"Daddy? We found a fairy ring! What are you doing? Are you trying to fly away? Take me with you." The sound of Gary's voice brought him back to his senses. He tried to pull back, but he had leaned over too far. He felt himself slipping with the inevitability of an imminent fall. He waved his arms, tried to lean back, but he was still falling forward. As a last ditch effort to save himself, he spun around, dropped straight down and dug desperately into the ground with his hands and feet. The edge of the cliff began crumbling beneath him, so he frantically scrambled as quickly as he could back away from the cliff. "Gary!" he called, "where's Mara?"

"She went back already, Daddy."

He was going to tell Gary to run for help, but his full attention was brought back to his predicament when part of the cliff broke away, and he found his feet dangling over nothing. He dug deep into the grass and dirt with his fingers, but he knew he could not hold on for long. The panic of certain doom gripped his mind like the claws of a hawk. Suddenly, a strong gust of wind came out of nowhere, up the face of the cliff, and Art felt himself lifted a little. He seized the unexpected opportunity, using the support of the wind to clamber back onto the cliff. As soon as he was able, he rolled several times away from the cliff, and stopped on his back, panting from fright. Gary ran over and jumped on his stomach. "That was funny, Daddy. Do it again."

"I don't think so, pooky," he responded, and gave Gary a tight hug. Thank you, thank you, thank you, he found himself once again silently praying. He felt as if he had just been given a miraculous second chance. He quietly resolved to try to overcome his sorrow, and that he would not burden Mara with the tale of his near-accident.

That night, they enjoyed a hearty supper of mutton soup, then Art put Gary to bed in what was to become his room.

"When will we see leperkans, Daddy?"

"We'll find some soon. I bet Mara knows where some are. Goodnight, pooky"

He joined Mara in the enormous, richly decorated sitting room, and they sat on a huge, comfortable couch in front of the most immense fireplace Art had ever seen. It was large enough for him to walk into without stooping. The fire roared and crackled, and periodically Art or Mara jumped up to throw another lump of peat on it.

Art reached out and took Mara's hand. "I can't tell you how grateful I am that you have opened your home and your heart to Gary and me. I don't know what I would have done otherwise."

"Nonsense," she replied. "What was I supposed to do? You heard my father, the day before... you know. He told us to take care of each other. I always respect my father's wishes. He saw something in you, Art. I see it, too."

They sat and looked into each others' eyes. Then, without warning, that same magnet that had attracted them on the cliff at Lindstrom's Seattle estate exerted its power again, and they found themselves in a deep embrace, kissing passionately. After what seemed an eternity, Art felt Mara's hands gently pushing against his shoulders. Although she was still kissing him, she obviously wanted to pull apart for a moment. He pulled back, and she looked down at her lap. Art sat up straighter, held her hand, and stroked her arm with his other hand, waiting for her to say what was apparently on her mind.

Finally she spoke. "I... I have a hard time trusting men. Even after my father came and adopted me, it took me a long time to forgive him for abandoning, as it seemed to me, my mother and me. You see, he loved my mother, but he could not have her in his life. He hired her as a servant at this castle, and I came to live here, too. My mother was deathly afraid he would find out about me, and therefore no longer be attracted to her, or think it was her fault. So every summer when the Lindstroms came to stay, I was sent to my aunt's in Belfast. All the servants here helped her keep the secret, and the Lindstroms never found out. I hated him for that, and it wasn't until I was almost a grown woman that I could forgive him. For by then I was in love and I understood.

"My mother loved my father deeply, and couldn't stand it when he went away at the end of every summer. She would become very melancholy, and drink to excess every night. One night, when I was eight, just after the Lindstroms had returned to America and I was still in Northern Ireland, she got very drunk, and was wandering around on the heath. She stumbled too close to the cliff, and fell off. She died instantly; for that I'm grateful, but to this day I am angry I didn't get to say a proper goodbye. I wanted to kill Lindstrom for what he had done to my mother, but when the servants finally broke their silence and told him the whole story, he made a special trip for the memorial service, and to meet me. His heart opened up so warmly and generously that I couldn't help loving him, just as my mother must have done. Still, it took many years for that wound to heal.

"As I said, it wasn't until I had fallen in love that I understood. I've only loved one man, a pigheaded brash youth from Belfast. He was my aunt's best friend's son, Brian, and I would play with him every summer when my mother sent me up there. After my mother's death, Lindstrom adopted me legally and took me to the States to live, but we still came back here every summer. He had revealed everything to his wife. They had a marriage of convenience by then anyway, and she didn't care about what had happened between him and my mother, so long as she could play the socialite and throw parties and travel.

"Brian came to stay with us every summer. Oh, those were glorious days. Our friendship turned into love, and we shared our first kiss the summer we were both fifteen. We were engaged by our eighteenth summer, and we were to be wed on our twenty-first. But the stubborn fool got entangled in the IRA in Belfast, and was killed in a gun battle with the English troops. I haven't been able to care for a man ever since. I am afraid he'll do something foolish or pigheaded, and I'll lose him again." She stopped and looked deeply into Art's eyes. "That is, until you. I care for you deeply. Art. Do you know we have the same color eyes?"

Art looked closely at her eyes. "Yes, you're right. Kind of hazel."

"I love you, Art."

When Art heard this, he knew the growing feelings that had been welling inside him were the same. "I love you, too." They hugged closely, then resumed kissing.

Mara pulled her head back. "I want you to stay with me tonight," she whispered, "but I'm frightened. I've been with one man, Brian, and I can't help feeling he abandoned me for some silly cause. I'm frightened you'll do the same. You men can be so maddeningly stubborn."

Art remembered his adventure on the cliff earlier that day, and thanked God for the opportunity to be here now. "I'll stay with you. I promise."

Mara squeezed him tightly. They lay down on the couch and intertwined arms and legs and lips. After a while, Mara whispered, "Make love to me." Art felt a powerful tingling in the pit of his stomach, as if a thousand butterflies had taken wing there. He could not believe his good fortune, and was overjoyed that Mara shared his feelings. He reached forward and stroked her hair. His hand slid caressingly down her neck, across her shoulder, then down to her breast. While softly kissing the base of her neck, he slowly unbuttoned her blouse, his lips following not far behind his hands. She arched her back and sighed softly with pleasure as the last button came undone and Art kissed her navel.

They tenderly undressed each other, pausing often to caress and kiss each other. When the last sock fell to the floor, Mara reached around Art's waist, then leaned back into the couch and drew him to her, her legs wrapping around his waist. Their kisses became very passionate, and their bodies responded to each other with increasing tempo as they explored each other with lips, hands, and the rest of their bodies. Mara reached down and guided Art into her. She let out a sharp gasp of pleasure as he entered. Slowly, lovingly, they developed a rhythm of interaction, with Mara drawing Art in deeper with each stroke. They pulled each other as close as they could, enjoying the blending of their bodies.

After several minutes of bliss, which seemed to go on forever, Art's quickening of tempo warned of his impending release. Suddenly he slowed down, and looked questioningly into Mara's eyes. She read his concern, and whispered, "It's OK. I anticipated this. We're protected." Art smiled warmly at her and kissed her passionately, once again amazed at her foresight and control. Their rhythm slowly increased again, until, after a few more wonderful minutes, amid moans of pleasure, they both released almost simultaneously.

They made love several more times that night. It was magical for them both.

Chapter 18

A couple of days passed uneventfully. Art, Mara, and Gary took long walks around the countryside, not talking much (except when Gary found something neat he just *had* to share with the others), trying to heal a bit. On one of the walks, Art asked Mara, "Don't you feel a little bit guilty, just leaving Seattle like that, and not staying around for your father's memorial service?"

"Not at all, because it hasn't happened yet. It will soon, though." She heard a noise and looked up. "Very soon."

A helicopter appeared from the east and landed near the castle. Servants rushed out to attend to it.

"Come, Art. It is time to put my father to rest properly."

Art saw one of the occupants of the helicopter descend, reach back into the compartment, and remove a small cubical black box. Art suddenly realized what was going on. "You're burying him here?"

"It was his fervent wish that he rest forever in the place he loved best. Let's get ready. The service is in two hours."

Two hours later, a small gathering, mostly servants, congregated around the gravesite where Lindstrom's ashes were to be buried, next to where his wife already lay. The parish priest of Doolin had come out with a small retinue to perform the services. Mara held Art's hand and stared out to sea throughout the service, the wind blowing back her hair that escaped from the black scarf she wore on her head. Art held Gary's hand on the other side. Gary, although bored, perceived that something important was happening, and dared not cause a fuss.

The priest concluded his eulogy, and silence fell on the small gathering. After a time, a soft cry came out of Mara's throat. It crescendoed into a high, wailing sound that did not remain on one note for very long. She dropped to her knees and reached into the cremation urn. She clutched handsful of her father's remains, and let them slip through her fingers as she continued her lament. The strong wind scattered the ashes over the surrounding heath. Art had never heard anything like it. It was strange, eerie, yet beautiful at the same time. Mara's pain and sorrow were evident throughout the song, but something ancient, timeless, and strangely comforting seeped through the indefinable melody she was singing. He felt as if that moment were the only one that had ever existed and would ever exist. Tears began to stream down his face as Mara's song filled his ears and the wind beat upon his face. He buried his face in one hand and hugged Gary close with the other.

After what seemed an eternity, Mara's song wound down. She bowed her head and remained kneeling in silence. Eventually a servant approached, took hold of her shoulders, and helped her up. They turned and walked slowly toward the castle, and the small party fell in step behind them. Art came back to himself and joined the procession. He happened to be walking next to Flanagan, the gardener. "Pardon me," he asked, "but what was that Mara was doing?"

"Aye, that was the ancient art o' keening, sir. She was wailin' for her lost Da, she was."

Art nodded appreciatively, and walked on in silence.

Early that evening, after the reception had concluded and the parson had departed, Mara suddenly said to Art, "Let's go into town tonight. I need diversion."

"Sure. Sounds fine. I'll put Gary down around eight, then we can go. Mary can watch after him, right?"

"Certainly. She really has taken to him. All the servants have. He's a wonderful boy."

Later, they walked down the long gravel road toward town as the sun set behind intermittent dramatic clouds. The last rays of the day shot through every now and then, illuminating the countryside in a deep red glow. They rounded a little hill and walked into the town of Doolin, which consisted of perhaps ten buildings, some of them with thatched roofs. Mara led Art to the door of one building at the other end of the small village. "Welcome to the O'Donnell's." She opened the door, and smoke assaulted them instantly.

Once Art's eyes cleared, he looked around. The room was cozy, with dark wood paneling, tables, and bar. There was no organization to the pub. Comfortable leather and wooden chairs were haphazardly arranged around tables, and inviting sofas lined the walls. A fire crackled at one end of the cheery room, and a small band of musicians were playing traditional Irish folk tunes in the corner next to it.

"Mara, me lass! So good to see ye." A big, grizzled old man sitting at the bar held up an arm and waved his hand loosely, signaling for them to come over. "I haird you ware in toown, an' I was lookin' forwaird to th' chance t' lay eyes on ye again."

"Paddy, you old dog! How are you?" She gave the man a big hug.

"An' who might this fine young lad with ye be?"

"This is Art. He is a friend of mine from America. He'll be staying with me a while."

"Oh, will he now?" Paddy replied with a wink and a wry smile. Suddenly his countenance changed. It seemed as if his whole face fell. "I haird about yer father. 'Tis a shame, it is. We'll miss the old poop. Give us a hug."

"Thank you." Mara hugged him again, tighter and longer. She finally pulled away and yelled at the bartender. "Nathan! Two pints, if you please."

"Aye, ma'am."

"Ah, Guinness fer strenth," Paddy remarked. "Ha' ye ever had the Mother's Milk, Art?"

"I can't say as I have."

"Ah, bless me soul. The poor lad hasn't been baptized yet." The pints arrived, and Mara handed one to Art. Paddy stuck his fingers in his own pint, and flicked the foam over Art's head. "You'll now be able to say you've truly lived."

They all clinked glasses and took long drafts from their pints.

"So how d' ye find the Blessed Isle, lad?"

"Well, I haven't been here long, and we're here under less than ideal circumstances, so I can't really say yet."

"Ah, ye've had some trouble, have ye?" Paddy slapped the top of the stool next to him. "You just sit right doown hare an' tell me all about it."

"Mara!" Someone called from across the room. Mara waved. "That's Thomas Flanery. I've got to go say hi." She put her hand on Art's shoulder. "You two stay here and get acquainted." She was off before Art had time to react.

"Sit, lad. Ye've got a tale to tell."

Art sat and took a long drink from his pint. Well, why not, he thought. Mara seems to trust him, and it might do me some good to unload it all onto a stranger. He launched into the events of his recent past, beginning with the Seattle Environmental Council and the red paint incident, and bringing it up to the present. He left nothing out, including the plans for Avalon. A couple of pints later, he felt warm, rosy, and relieved to have finally gotten it all off his chest. Paddy listened intently, his wise old eyes locking on Art's as he leaned over his pint, his head nodding in emphatic agreement from time to time.

Art finished his story and took another long drink. He was feeling rather lightheaded.

"Tis' the Good People what saved ye."

"How's that?"

"That time ye had on th' cliff, when ye almos' fell. That gust o' wind, 'twas the Good People. You have spirit in ye, lad, an' they don't care to see that go to waste."

"The Good…who?"

"The Good People. You know, the fairy folk. The *Shee-day*." Paddy almost whispered the last word.

"You think?" Art looked sideways at Paddy as he took another drink.

"Sure. They're overrunnin' the isle, an' they know who's worth savin' an' who's worth lettin' go. They've been doin' it fer centuries. Here, you think you've got it bad. Let me tell you the story o' Teigue. Nathan! Two more here, if ye please. Many years ago, when the Tuatha were still freely roamin' the daylight world…."

"The who?"

"The Tuatha. The children o' Dana. Ah, bless me soul, ye really don't know, do ye? The Tuatha De Danaan were the early rulers of Ireland. Tall, strong, magical people they were, proud an' noble an' beautiful. Alas, when men came with their petty ways, their betrayals an' disloyalties, the Tuatha grew sad an' retreated under the hills, where they live an' love an' laugh an' play to this very day. In Teigue's time, the Tuatha still regularly came out o' their exile to bless those who deserved it an' punish those who had earned it. Teigue was one o' merit. He was at home in his province o' Munster when a rogue named Cathmann invaded his land, laid waste the fields, burned the villages to the ground, an' made off with tremendous booty an' several hostages, among them Teigue's bride Liban an' two of his brothers.

"Teigue set off after Cathmann, who had retreated to his fortress on an island off o' Spain, with forty of his most loyal followers, an' a captive from Cathmann's party to lead the way. In their mighty, tall-masted ship they made their way through the choppy seas an' drivin' wind. They sailed fer months on end, stoppin' on strange isles to rest an' reprovision. Cathmann's man was obviously misleadin' 'em.

"Eventually they sailed into an engulfin' mist, which deadened all sound an' disoriented the crew an' the captive guide. A storm arose out o' nowhere an' assaulted the mighty ship. Teigue an' his loyal men fought the gale all that night an' into the next mornin', barely keepin' control o' their craft. Late in the mornin' the wind finally blew the mist away, an' the sun dried the deck an' their backs.

"After a spell they spied a shore off in the distance. They made fer it an' sailed up a little firth, with water so blue an' clear they could see schools o' fish playin' under the waves. Each bank was lined with tall, mighty oaks an' other trees. They anchored their craft an' climbed ashore. They walked through the thick woods until they came out the other side, an' were bewondered at the marvelous sight they beheld.

"On a wide grassy plain before them stood three hills, an' on each o' the hills stood a magnificent palace, colorful banners flyin' off the ramparts. The men approached the nearest palace. As they neared, a beautiful young maiden approached them from out the gates, an' greeted Teigue by name with a bright smile playin' across her face. She told them they would find what they sought at the next palace. The very same occurrence did befall them at the next palace, an' a blithe young slip of a lass directed them to the third palace.

"At that final palace, the gates were thrown wide. Teigue's company passed through the portico an' found themselves in the courtyard, where a magnificent apple tree spread its branches wide in the center o' the yard. Now ye know that apples are th' magic fruit o' the Good People, an' apple trees are sacred to them. No? Well ye know it now. From among the white blossoms drifted a woman like a flower, her hair resemblin' silvered petals. She regarded the mortals with a calm gaze an' greeted Teigue by name. An enchantment fell over him then an' there, an' all care fell from him like leaves from the trees in autumn. A wondrous calm took root in him, an' he listened peacefully as she told him these prophesies:

"She revealed she was a daughter o' the Tuatha De Danaan, an' her name was Cliodna Fair Hair. She told the company that they were privileged to be entertained on her isle. She said that the fruit of her apple tree was of such power that mortals who ate it would never hunger an' would always be drawn to her lands. An' she warned them that when a day passed in her realm, though it seemed but a day, a year passed in the mortal world.

"She then offered Teigue three enchanted gifts to aid him on his quest. First, she bestowed upon him a team o' three magical birds which would guide him to his place o' battle with Cathmann. Next, she gave him an emerald chalice, which would guard his life as long as he kept it by him. Last, she told Teigue the manner of his final passin', so that he would be heartened in his battle with Cathmann, knowin' the time had not yet come. He would pass his last day on the banks o' the Boyne, back in Eire, an' that she would be with him on that day.

"Strengthened an' emboldened with fairy magic, Teigue an' his company departed to finish their quest. They regained their ship an' set back out to sea, the magical birds now guidin' them. After a spell o' sailin', Teigue turned to gaze once again on the source o' his boon, but the mists had already come together, an' he couldna make where the blessed isle lay. A strange spell came over the men, an' they to a man fell into an enchanted sleep. The ship sailed on of its own accord, guided by the birds, which sang a fairy tune o' sleep.

"The birds finally stopped singin', an' the men awoke from their daze. Almost instantly, the ship grounded on the shore of a bleak, rocky isle, with stunted pines growin' sparsely about the shore. Not far from them they spied th' wooden ramparts of a crude fort, with a dirty pirate banner bein' whipped by th' stingin' wind on the uppermost spike. It was Cathmann at last!

"Teigue bade his men, who were itchin' fer a fight, to lay low while he scouted the scene. He arrived at the shore o' the dingy river that separated him from the fort, an' encountered a ferryman there. It was his brother, Eoghan! He had been forced into servitude by the bloody pirate. They hugged an' laughed. Eoghan's news was good: Teigue's bride was safe but a prisoner, an' Cathmann meant soon to take her fer his own, havin' been delayed only by her pleadin'. Teigue had arrived in a time o' conspiracy, for two o' Cathmann's kinsmen had armed themselves, an' Eoghan an' Teigue's other brother Airnelach had secretly joined them. Eoghan described Cathmann's defenses to Teigue in great detail, to better prepare him fer the onslaught. Teigue then went an' got his men, an' Eoghan ferried them silently across the river to the other shore. There Teigue allied his party with his brothers' band.

"Thus it was that seven hundred very angry Irishmen stormed the fort o' that blackguard Cathmann that very night, killin' all the inhabitants an' finally torchin' the stronghold. Cathmann, however, escaped, an' Teigue caught up with him on the banks o' the dingy river. There they fought like savage beasts fer hours on end by the angry red glow o' the burnin' fortress. Teigue took many a blow that would have killed a lesser man, but he had the emerald chalice o' the fairy lady by his side, an' he did not die that night. At last it seemed as if Teigue was beaten. He lay bleedin' on the ground, Cathmann towerin' over him. Cathmann, fiend that he was, paused to gloat over his fallen opponent.

"It was in this moment that Teigue used his last ounce o' strength to swing his sword one last time. It was a lucky stroke, perhaps guided by his fairy mistress. Cathmann's head fell from his shoulders, an' the tyrant was vanquished. Although Teigue was sorely wounded with thirty swordstrokes, he did not pass on that night. His crew took him back to the ship, an' in the mornin' he had miraculously recovered enough so that the whole troop of Irishmen could set sail for home. It is true that Teigue died many years later, on the banks o' the Boyne, an' his fairy mistress was there, but that is not o' this tale." Paddy, who had been leaning forward on his elbows and staring intensely at Art, relaxed, leaned back and put away almost a whole pint of Guinness at one swallow.

Art felt as if he were coming out of a trance. "That is a wonderful story," he said appreciatively as he sipped at his own Guinness.

Suddenly Paddy reached out with both hands, laid them on either side of Art's neck, and shook him vigorously. "Don't ye hear what I'm tryin' to say to ye, lad? I'm tellin' ye, even though it seems bleak now, don't give up! Never give up! That scoundrel Dredson you told me about, he's your Cathmann. Now, you can lie down an' die, like most other spineless whelps would do, or you can stand up an' fight back!"

Art was shocked. "But…how?"

"You'll find a way. An' the fairy folk'll take care o' ye. Look over there." Paddy turned Art's head with one hand as he pointed to Mara across the room with the other. She was talking and laughing with a group of friends at a table at the other end of the pub. "She's your fairy maiden, an' she cares fer ye. We here in Doolin, we've always known there was somethin' magical about her." He leaned close and whispered in Art's ear. "We believe she's one o' the Good People, come back to bless us all." He leaned back and looked into Art's face. "An' she's chosen to help you and love you. Don't ever betray that. Return that love, an' you'll both find a way out o' yer troubles." He slapped Art's cheek softly a couple of times, although it still stung a bit, while he drank again from his fresh pint that had miraculously appeared. Art now felt a need to take a deeper drink as he absorbed what the old codger had told him.

Mara walked up then. "Well, I see that you two have hit it off. That makes me happy. Paddy here was like a father to me when I was a wee lass." Art noticed that Mara's accent had thickened considerably since they had entered the pub. She gave Paddy a big hug. "I love you, Da." Paddy returned the hug and winked at Art over Mara's shoulder. "Well, are ye ready t' go, Art? I'm feeling a might tired."

"Yeah, sure. This has been a lot of fun, but I'm starting to really feel these Guinnesses." He stood up, slightly unsteadily, and extended his hand to shake Paddy's. "I really enjoyed meeting you, Paddy. Thanks for listening, and for that wonderful story. I hope we can talk some more."

Paddy stood up, pushed past Art's arm, and gave him a massive hug. "You just come right down here whenever you've a mind to, lad. You'll find me sittin' right here."

"Ain't that the truth!" Mara giggled.

Art and Mara walked back up to the hill, hand in hand. Mara sang a soft tune, which had the effect of reminding Art of Paddy's tale. For the first time in several days, he felt as if he were in the right place, and events were unfolding as they should.

Chapter 19

The next morning he wasn't so sure. He was moving very slowly, and the slightest noise sent an avalanche of pain careening through his skull. After a shower, several cups of coffee, an egg breakfast, and some unidentified pills from one of the servants, Art was feeling passable.

That day unfolded like several after that. Art, Mara, and Gary spent many hours walking the countryside around Doolin, sometimes talking, sometimes silent. They tried to get in touch with how they felt about everything that had transpired. Although Mara had lost her father, Art seemed more torn up over the whole matter. Occasionally he would suddenly yell "God damn it!" or some other epithet, then bounce around nervously, as if he were trying to break out of his body. He was very upset that Dredson had so completely caught him unawares and betrayed him. He wished he would not have let Lindstrom talk him into staying on the board. He wished he could wind back the hands of time and change several events, the outcome of which hindsight had given him a perfect understanding. Yet at the same time he was grateful to Mara, and was becoming increasingly attached to her every day. He could not imagine what he would have done had she not been there the day of what he had come to privately call the 'triple whammy.' He slowly began to believe Paddy that somehow he had been fortunate enough to have come into the graces of some magical fairy.

Mara amazed him. She seemed relatively at peace. There were occasions when she would begin quietly weeping, and Art would go over to her and hold her at those times. But for the most part she was steadfast and strong. There was an air of great sorrow about her that never disappeared, but it was a timeless grief, as if she was lamenting the fate of the world, not her own personal tragedy. Art gained strength from her strength.

In the first week, Art's mail began to arrive at Castle Lindstrom. The divorce papers Gwen had promised came through a week later. She asked for nothing except that Art retain physical custody of Gary. She did not even ask for visitation rights. Art signed them and returned them to her lawyer after only a cursory examination. He felt numb the rest of that day.

Gary sensed that something was wrong, and was more subdued that usual, but he viewed the stay in Ireland as somewhat of a vacation. Mara arranged it so that Gary could spend his days attending the local parish school. Gary loved it, and instantly made some wonderful new friends, with whom he often asked to run off and play. Every now and then they would invite Paddy up to dinner, and he would amaze Gary with wonderful stories of the Little People. Gary asked Paddy if he could show him a 'leperkan.' Paddy replied, "Ah, now, they're very shy creatures, an' not used to mixin' with mortal folk. But sometimes, at dusk, if you turn an' look quickly, ye might catch one ducking behind a rock, or diving into a hole." Gary spent the next two weeks diligently searching for leprechauns every night at sunset. Occasionally he would excitedly report to Art that he had seen one.

One day, not long after they arrived, Art sat down with Gary and had a talk with him about Gwen and what the changes meant. Gary seemed to understand, but some nights he would wake up crying for his mother. Art tried his best to comfort him at those times, but it was difficult. Gary seemed to naturally warm up to Mara, and held her hand a lot when they took their walks. The three of them nonetheless felt a sense of something missing.

Art's thought kept returning to Project Avalon. Endless scenarios played themselves out in his head. Was Dredson driving Avalon into the ground? Was he bending it to his own selfish purposes? Was he selling the whole thing off, and keeping the technology for his company? What about General Devere? Was he complicitous, or had he resigned? And Perry? What did he think of all this? Art sat down and wrote a lengthy email message to Perry, describing everything that had happened, and pouring out his emotions about it. Art asked Perry to let him know anything he could find out about the status of Avalon, but warned him about Dredson and implored him to be discreet.

Two days later he got a message back, saying "My God, I thought you had dropped off the face of the Earth! No news yet on Avalon. I'll write again later when I can find out more." The message went on for a bit, mostly about Perry's opinions on the state of world politics. Art had been perusing the International Herald intermittently, but due to his state of mind, he had not paid close attention to recent world events. Perry's strong opinions prompted him to surf the internet for the latest news. He discovered that President Patterson and his administration had pushed through the constitutional amendment banning abortion, and were now working on strengthening the second amendment, the right to bear arms, while limiting the first, the right of free speech. Two recent resignations on the Supreme Court had allowed Patterson to begin orchestrating a takeover of the judicial branch as well. Ironically, recent polls had been demonstrating that the majority of Americans were actually in favor of such measures.

Meanwhile, Moustapha Ali had solidified his leadership of the Arab world, and had founded a movement called the Party of Allah. He was openly calling for an end to all negotiations and cooperation with Israel. Terrorist attacks were on the rise, and Israel was retaliating in the occupied territories and major cities, and along the borders. Arab governments were denouncing Israel's actions, and were warning of serious repercussions. Of course, Patterson pledged his full support of the Israeli government, and threatened to send in ground troops if necessary. All this news gave Art plenty more to worry about.

Art and Mara went down to the Doolin Pub about two or three nights a week. Art got to know Mara's other friends who always seemed to be there, but he had a special affinity for Paddy, and often ended up on the stool next to him where he had passed the first night. Paddy would tell Art all sorts of Irish legends and fables, and Art was always entranced. He heard of the ancient struggle between the Tuatha De Danaan and the Fir Bolg for control of Ireland, of the heroic exploits of Cu Chulain and Finn McCool, and of the great and tragic tale of the Cattle Raid of Cooley. Paddy patiently listened to Art's tirades about the need to develop space, but it was obvious that the information had little to no bearing on his life. He treated it as fantastically as Art regarded Paddy's stories. They nonetheless developed a deep friendship, and more than once, after an evening of tall tales and heavy drinking, Art helped Paddy to his home at the other end of the row of buildings that was Doolin. Mara, of course, then helped Art home to Castle Lindstrom.

Art grew increasingly despondent over their situation. He saw absolutely no way out of their predicament, and, although the prospect was not unpleasant, he resigned himself to living indefinitely with Mara in Ireland, with no hope of fulfilling any of his former dreams. "I don't want to be a burden," he said to her one day. "Maybe Gary and I should go back to the States. I can probably get my old job back at the Review."

"I'll hear nothing of the sort," she answered. "You are staying right here with me, where I need you." Art silently thanked her for her diplomatic phrasing.

Art and Mara grew closer to each other. After the first week, Art kept his things in his room, but no longer slept there, except for an occasional nap. One night, after an exceptionally wonderful session of lovemaking, Art and Mara lay together, holding hands and stroking each other. Mara, looking deep into Art's eyes, whispered, "I love you, Art."

He squeezed her hand. "I love you."

"I love everything about you, and I want to know that you'll be in my life forever."

Startled, Art gazed closely at Mara. "Are you saying what I think you're saying?"

"Yes, I am. I want you to marry me."

He hugged her close and squeezed his eyes against the tears of joy that refused to abate. "Are you sure you want to mess up your life with me? I mean, I couldn't get it right the first time. I'm so scared I'll drive you away, too."

"Hush. That was different. You two were young, and hadn't experienced much yet. But you and I have already been through more than most married couples, and I still love you. You are kind and gentle. I love to watch you play with Gary. I can tell you are a wonderful father, and I know you would be a caring husband. Don't answer me now. Let's just be together for now. We still both have a great deal of healing to do. Let the idea grow on you for a while, and we'll talk about it later, in a few months, when the time is right."

Art hugged Mara again. "I love you so much, and I don't want to lose you."

"Me too."

They fell asleep in each other's arms.

The next day, at breakfast, Art asked Mara, "What are we going to do?"

"What do you mean?"

"I mean, are we just going to stay here? We don't have any income. And who knows what is happening with Lindstrom Industries and Avalon."

She came over, straddled his knees, and sat on his lap, facing him. She put her arms around his neck. "We are going to stay right here until we feel like rejoining the world. I, for one, don't feel ready yet. As for income, my father has made sure that would not be a problem for me." Art opened his mouth to speak. Mara put a finger on his lips. "And you are not allowed to worry about money. It's my money and I'll spend it how I want. I *want* you here, with me. Don't worry. Someday we will feel better, and we will resume what most people would call a normal life." She gave him a quick hug. "You worry too much. Just relax. We'll know when the time is right."

Weeks went by and melted into months. Art became increasingly morose. He saw no purpose for his life. His love for Gary and for Mara were the only things that sustained him. He would go into day-long depressions, barely talking. He took walks alone that lasted longer and longer. Despite Mara's reassurances and Paddy's wonderful stories with scarcely concealed moral messages, he felt like a complete failure. He missed Old Man Lindstrom and Project Avalon. It seemed as if his dreams of achieving space, once tantalizingly within his grasp, were now snatched away forever. A creep like Dredson was going to get there first, and ruin it for everyone else by turning it into just one more profit center for big business. Gone were the long-term plans of building a spacefaring civilization. Gone was the hope for tomorrow.

Art returned to Castle Lindstrom one evening after an especially long, hopeless walk. He entered the kitchen and almost fell over from shock. Perry was sitting at the kitchen table animatedly talking to Mara.

"Where did you come from?" Art exclaimed, grabbing a counter for stability.

They both turned to look at him. "There you are," said Mara. "We were wondering where you had gotten off to."

Perry jumped up, rushed over, and gave Art a big hug. "Man, it's so good to see you again. Come here and sit down, man. I've got some heavy shit to lay on you."

Art walked slowly over to the table and sat down hesitantly, noticing the grave expression on Perry's face. "What… what is it?"

Mara brought Art a cup of coffee. "Perry wouldn't tell me until you got back."

"How did you get here? How long have you been here?"

"I just got here, man, maybe ten minutes ago. Mara sent me an open plane ticket a couple of months back, and I'll tell you what, with this news I decided I'd better use it. I didn't want to send it by email, because if it got intercepted or anything, all hell would break loose."

Mara, who had sat down again, turned to Art. "I thought you could stand some cheering up, so I sent him a ticket a while back, and told him to come anytime he wanted." She turned expectantly back to Perry. "So what's the big news?"

"Woah, I'm shaking. This is intense, man. Are you sure you're ready?"

Art was getting impatient. "Just tell us, alright?"

"OK." Perry took a drink of coffee and swallowed hard. He spread his hands out wide on the table, as if he had to support himself against the weight of his own news. "Lindstrom was murdered."

"What?!" Art and Mara screamed in unison. Their hands groped for each other and clung fast once they contacted.

Perry was visibly shaking. His voice trembled. "No shit, man. I got this call, just out of the blue, just two days ago. It was that male nurse that you always saw with him, you know, the one who changed his oxygen bottles all the time."

"John. Right. Go on." Mara said with forced calm.

"Well, he called me, and said, 'Look, don't bother asking where I am. You'll never find me. But I can't take it anymore. I've got to tell someone. I killed Lindstrom. I injected some undetectable drug into his veins and gave him an embolism.' Well, actually he went into some technical detail about it, but I could barely follow it. I was in shock, man!" He nervously took a sip of coffee. "Anyway, he said, 'I'm just torn up about this. I mean, the old guy took care of me for years. But a guy named Morris Dredson got ahold of me and talked me into it.' The guy said that at first he would have nothing to do with it, and threatened to turn Dredson in, but Dredson threatened him back with killing him and his whole family. Then Dredson made the guy a sweet offer. He wouldn't tell me how much, but it was in the millions. He said he told Dredson he'd have to think about it. Dredson gave him twenty-four hours to decide.

"When Dredson called back, the guy said yes, but he recorded the conversation. Well, he did it, then left the country. He couldn't take it, he said. He tried to find you, Art, but you were gone, of course. He remembered me from that day when Lindstrom got all pissed off at me in his office, and he assumed I'd know where you were, and that you'd know where Mara was. Man, you should have heard him; he was on the edge. He was all whacked and stuff. He was barely coherent. He did manage to tell me, however, to go to one of those mail stores, you know, that have post office boxes. He told me to tell the guy there a password, and he'd give me a package. He hung up before I could ask any more questions. Here it is, man." Perry reached into his backpack and pulled out a padded envelope. He reached into it and pulled out a cassette tape and a piece of paper. "I listened to this tape. I hope you don't mind. It's the conversation between that guy John and Dredson. Dredson doesn't actually ask that guy to kill Lindstrom, but it's obvious what they're talking about. This is a copy. I have the original stashed away back in states, just to be safe. And this was in there, too." He handed over the piece of paper. "It's a copy of a deposit slip for three million dollars to a numbered bank account in the Cayman Islands."

Mara's eyes had grown increasingly wider as Perry went on. Now she dropped her head into her arms. Her body shook with sobs. Art rubbed her back, trying to comfort her. He stared out the window, not quite sure what to think. They sat there, silent, for a few moments.

"Man, you look terrible, Art," Perry finally said. "Are you sick? Is there anything I can do?"

Art was struck with a sudden inspiration. He sat up and looked at Perry with a gleam in his eye. "Yes, there is something you can do. You can help us regain control of Project Avalon!"

"Sure, man, but how?"

"We're going to use this information to drive Dredson out!" Mara had stopped crying and looked up at Art with red and puffy eyes. Art looked down at her. "But we'll wait a few days before we do anything."

Mara wiped away her tears with a napkin. "No, I'm ready now. I've been ready. I'm glad you're ready now, too."

"What are you talking about?" Art asked Mara, confusion on his face.

Mara sat up straight and regained composure. "Remember who I am?"

"Sure. You're Lindstrom's daughter. But I don't see...."

"Oh, come now, Art. Do you think I would let my father's most cherished dream die?"

"Well, I guess not, but what can you do about it?"

"Think for a moment. To whom do you think my father left his interest in Lindstrom Industries?"

Art lit up like a flare. "You're probably the majority stockholder now!"

Mara smiled, acknowledging Art's close guess. "Not the majority stockholder, but I have a significant interest."

"That means you can override anything Dredson tries to pull, at least on Lindstrom's end of Avalon."

"That's right."

"But why haven't you done anything up until now? Why have you let him get away with it all?"

"I haven't. I've been in regular contact with Scotty and the other managers at Lindstrom. They have basically concealed progress on Avalon from Dredson and his faction. From what I hear, Dredson is livid with frustration."

"You sneaky little weasel!" Art patted her shoulder. "But... why didn't you tell me any of this?"

"Art, you were hurt badly. You needed time to recover. You had to *want* to come back around on your own, not dragged back by me. Until you developed the desire to fight back, there was nothing I could do. Ever since we got here I've been waiting to hear the words you just said about fighting for Avalon. I've been waiting for you to come back to life."

Art leaned over and gave her a big hug. "I love you, Mara."

"And I love you."

After a few moments, Perry said, "And I love both of you. But how are we going to get Avalon back?"

Mara animated, like a field commander plotting strategy. "I've heard from good sources that General Devere is disgusted with Dredson's management. Dulak disappeared just after that board meeting that was held when my father died. Rumor has it that Dredson paid him off for control of the board. He retained Dulak's name as titular President, however, and has been voting his position by proxy. I guess Devere has been doing what Scotty has been doing, which is deliberately covering up progress on the Dark Stallion vehicle and the Oasis station. We've continued with research; we just haven't made it available to Dredson. I hear Devere has done the same. We can return to Seattle, get in touch with Devere, and join forces. Then we can take this evidence, confront Dredson, threaten him with prosecution, and drive him out. Once he's gone, we'll resume control, and finish the project." She sat back with an air of satisfaction.

Art got the distinct impression that he recognized the Old Man shining through in Mara's demeanor. A broad smile spread across his face. "People, this is going to be fun!"

They sat at the table and plotted strategy for another hour. Then they moved to the dining room and kept talking while the servants prepared and brought dinner. Gary, who had been playing outside, joined them for dinner, and was excited to see Perry again. Afterwards Art insisted on showing Perry the Doolin Pub, so he put Gary to bed, and they all walked down to town and drank several rounds of Guinness. Perry and Paddy hit it off instantly, and before long they were discussing the finer points of Irish mythology. Art and Mara just sat and listened, holding each others' hands and occasionally beaming at each other. At one point Mara leaned over and whispered, "I'm so glad you're ready to do this with me. Now my father's death will not have been in vain." They kissed.

After a glowing evening of storytelling and carousing, the three prepared to take their leave. Mara extended her arms to Paddy. "Well, Da, I guess this is it. We'll be leaving tomorrow. It was so good to see you again."

Paddy squeezed her tightly to him. "I'll miss you as always, me lass." He reached out for Art and pulled him into the hug. "You take good care of her, boy, or you'll have to answer to me!" He let go of them and slapped his hands down on Perry's shoulders. "And you have to watch out for both of them. Now go on out of here!" He shooed them, laughing, out the door.

Chapter 20

When they arrived back in Seattle, they contacted General Devere immediately. He came out to Lindstrom's estate for a strategy conference. Sukati attended as well. Devere was very agreeable to their plan, and informed them he had been waiting for just such an opportunity to wrest control from Dredson. Devere revealed that he had been attempting to form a secret coalition on the board to vote out Dredson, but it appeared that Dredson had a very loyal following of his own, so it would be best if they could convince him to resign voluntarily. They agreed to make Devere Chairman of the Board once the reverse coup had been accomplished. Sukati gave them details about how she and her crew had been sabotaging, but not damaging, progress on Avalon. She had a mischievous gleam in her eye as she described how she had foiled Dredson at every turn. Art clapped his hands. "Good going, Scotty!"

Scotty smiled at Art in appreciation. "I have some other news which will aid in our reverse coup. Although we have been dragging our feet on the primary Avalon development, we have been secretly forging ahead on some of the most crucial elements, especially energy production." She sat up straight and put her hands on the table. "My friends, we have achieved a net gain in energy from helium three-based fusion!" Everyone but Perry cheered and congratulated Scotty.

"I don't get it," Perry said with confusion on his face.

Art turned to Perry, almost too excited to contain himself. "Fusion is a way to gain energy from atoms by putting them together, rather than tearing them apart. It produces much more energy per reaction than fission, the other method, and is much less radioactive. And helium three is abundant on the Moon. The problem is, up till now, it's always taken more energy to start the process than the energy that resulted from it."

"You've been doing your homework, Art," Scotty said gleefully.

"Right," Devere chimed in, "and now that we can generate energy from the process, we will no longer be dependent on EnerCo for providing fission reactors. They have already delivered the first one, which we can outright buy, then we can slice them right out of the equation!"

"Now General, don't get too excited," Scotty cautioned. "We've only obtained our results under carefully controlled laboratory conditions. Our findings are indisputable, but it will still be a long time before we can count on it to produce energy."

"Of course, of course, but the major hurdle has been jumped." Devere uncharacteristically beamed a smile. "My friends, we are on our way to the Moon! Now," he whispered, leaning closer in across the table, gathering everyone into a conspiratorial circle, "the crucial element is to get Dredson to relinquish control without a fight. We have circumstantial evidence against him, this tape recording and this deposit slip, but it's not really strong enough to hold up in a court of law. Dredson and EnerCo really want to see Avalon built, so they can exploit it for their own purposes. We have to represent to Dredson that if he does not relinquish control, we will go public with this knowledge, and also reveal Avalon, thereby destroying anybody's chances to build it."

Mara gasped, and Art's eyes widened. Devere put up his hands reassuringly. "I know, it's a pretty dangerous bluff, but I've spent my life reading and commanding men. Dredson will growl and carry on like a cornered tiger, but in the end, if we hold firm, he will back down and slink away. Not only are the fortunes of his company staked on this, but also his personal rise to power. He won't want Avalon scrapped. But mark my words: He will slink off, and forever after be plotting against us, scheming over how to take back control. The EnerCo boys will try court injunctions against Lindstrom Industries, Federal Trade Commission investigations, anything they can think of to weaken our position without actually revealing Avalon to the public. We will always have to be on guard against Dredson."

"I'll do it."

Everyone turned to look at Art. "I want to do it. I want to confront Dredson. I owe him one."

Mara put her hand on his arm. "Art, are you sure? He can be dangerous."

Art looked around the room. "Look, I've always felt like a fifth wheel in this Project, sort of a hanger-on. I want to earn my place at the table. Think about it: General Devere, you would be the Chairman. You have to remain above the fray if possible, to maintain the highest degree of authority and control. Mara, you are running Lindstrom now. You don't want to give Dredson any weapons to use against you. Scotty, you shouldn't have to be burdened with this at all. Your job is to build excellent systems, and our job is to provide you the environment in which to do it. Perry, you're not deep enough into this. It's not your fight. That day, that terrible day, Dredson looked straight at me as he announced his cuts on the board. There is a certain… animosity between us." He clenched his fist and spoke in a low, determined tone. "I *want* to do this!"

Everyone sat back, stunned. Devere finally said, "Yes, I think you would be the best choice. But realize: You will be the target of his scorn and hatred ever after."

Art nodded decisively.

"Good, now here is how I think we can best accomplish this. If there are other opinions, please express them, but remember, I have spent the majority of my life as a military strategist...."

*****

"Mr. Dredson, General Devere and some members of the Lindstrom Foundation board to see you."

Dredson pushed his intercom button. "Well, by all means, send them right in." He leaned back in his leather chair in his richly appointed office at the corporate headquarters of EnerCo, on the east shore of Lake Washington in the suburb of Bellevue, across from Seattle. He put on his best public relations smile, and waited. The door opened. Devere walked in. Dredson jumped up, his arm extended for a handshake. "General Devere, how nice to see you...." He stopped, his arm dropped, and his smile faded as first Scotty, then Mara, then Art followed him into the room. Dredson's face writhed into a snarl as he growled, "What are *they* doing here?"

Devere, Scotty, and Mara all silently sat themselves in chairs around the room. Art approached Dredson and stood directly in front of him, closer than polite social interaction would dictate. His face was beet red, but his manner was resolute.

"Dredson, you will voluntarily relinquish control of the board of Project Avalon, and turn it over to General Devere. This will be done at the meeting later today." Dredson had moved the location of the Project Avalon board meetings to the EnerCo boardroom.

Dredson smirked and looked around the room at the others. "Is this some kind of joke? Oh, I get it, this is April fools or something. No, it's not April." Dredson turned cold, narrow eyes on Art. "Then it must be a sick, feeble attempt of humor on your part. Get out!"

After a moment's hesitation, Art reached into the manila envelope he was carrying, pulled out some papers, and threw them on Dredson's desk. "Before you make too hasty a decision, you may want to look over those papers." Art stared straight back into Dredson's eyes. He had never been so nervous in his life. He felt as if he were going to crumble into a million pieces at any moment, But he felt the strength of Devere, Scotty, and especially Mara behind him.

Confusion played across Dredson's face as he contemplated Art. He then slowly turned to look at the papers on the desk. He found there a copy of the bank deposit slip and a transcript of the taped conversation between himself and Lindstrom's nurse. He whipped around furiously. "Where did you get this?"

"Unimportant," Art responded with as much nonchalance as he could muster. "What is important is that we have it, and you will voluntarily resign Avalon."

"Devere, are you in on this?" The General sat as motionless as a stone.

Dredson turned back to Art. "This is ludicrous." He waved the papers. "You know this is circumstantial, and will never hold up in court. I have an army of lawyers. I'll beat you so badly you'll be the laughingstock of this town."

"That may be true, but in the process, all the details of Avalon will come out, and the project will die."

Horror flashed across Dredson's face. "You wouldn't do that! Not you. It's your dream. You can't kill your dream!"

Art silently, resolutely, returned Dredson's gaze.

"Devere, you wouldn't let that happen, would you?"

Again, Devere did not move.

Art spoke in a measured tone, betraying his seething anger. "Dredson, I would rather kill the Project than have a little dirtball like you run it into the ground for your own selfish profit. Turn the chairmanship over to Devere, and EnerCo will be cut in for thirty-three percent of all profits, as befits your contribution. But neither you nor anyone else at EnerCo will ever again have a controlling interest in the Project. That's your choice, Dredson: thirty-three percent, or nothing."

Rage welled up in Dredson. "You little shit!" He made a lunge at Art, but Devere was instantly there, with a restraining hand on Dredson's chest. "I'd advise you to seriously consider our offer, for, you see, we now have more evidence." He nodded in the direction of Scotty. Dredson looked over and saw a complicated electronic eyepiece in front of one of her eyes. She opened her jacket to reveal a microphone attached to her blouse. She had been recording and filming the whole interchange.

The tableau held for a moment as Dredson seethed and fumed, inches away from Art, but separated from him by Devere's arm. Art was terrified and exhilarated at the same time, but he held his stance and glowered back at

Dredson. Finally, fury still etched on his face, Dredson backed down. He straightened his suit, and stood up straight. "OK, I know when I've been beaten. Thirty-three percent it is."

Art smiled wryly. "You are a very agreeable and accommodating man, Mr. Dredson. In that stack of papers you will find a draft of your resignation letter. You will have it prepared and delivered to this afternoon's meeting of the Board. You personally will not attend."

Dredson exploded. "OK, you've won! Get out! All of you! Get out!"

They all calmly took their leave. Dredson shouted after them, "You haven't heard the last of this! I swear it!" Devere closed the door on his rantings.

Dredson fumed for a while after they had left, then calmed down, sat in his large leather chair, and stared out the window for a bit. He then wheeled around and banged his intercom. "Marcie, get me Jensen at the White House." The phone rang a few minutes later. "Hello, Bob? Yes, I'm fine, thanks, how are you? Say, I've got some very interesting information that I believe President Patterson would be most intrigued to hear. Can you arrange a meeting? Thank you. I'll make it worth your while. Goodbye."

Chapter 21

The meeting of the board of the Lindstrom Foundation at EnerCo went very smoothly that afternoon. As agreed upon, Dredson had his letter of resignation delivered, and General Devere read it to the board. A boardmember loyal to Devere's faction then nominated the General to be new chairman, and it was quickly seconded. Devere was expecting a fight from Dredson's camp, but he was pleasantly surprised at the overwhelming number of votes he received. He later found out that many of Dredson's followers felt coerced into supporting him, and were grateful for the chance to vote him out.

The General's first official act was to nominate Mara, then Art, for reinstatement onto the board. Both measures passed with a very comfortable margin, and they were brought in from a waiting room and warmly welcomed back in.

After many handshakes and pleasantries, Devere called the meeting to order again. He remained standing to speak. "Now, on to substantial business. I must inform you that the Pentagon has been put on active notice that there may be some military activity in the Middle East. Tensions are running high between the Israelis and Moustapha Ali's factions. It could turn into a hot war at any moment. If that were the case, a vast majority of the resources available to me will have to, of necessity, be turned to other ends. My first duty has been, is, and always will be to uphold the Constitution, defend the United States, and follow the orders of my Commander in Chief. It is irrelevant that I completely disagree with the policies of President Patterson. He is my superior, and I must obey him.

"Nonetheless, we have a window of opportunity right now, before things get dicey. I am not ashamed to admit to you, especially after seeing how the voting went today, that both Mara and I have been concealing the extent of our true capabilities from Dredson. Dark Stallion, although still experimental, is ready to begin performing significant operations, including transporting humans. Our space platform is operational. There are two crew members there even as we speak, preparing for refurbishing Dark Stallion units for the flight to the Moon. Mara informs me that the first habitat modules are ready to launch. We could conceivably have our first lunar colonists on the surface within six weeks.

"I am an officer of the United States Air Force. I love this country, and intend to defend it to my dying breath. But I tell you all here, privately, for we are all here for the same reason, that I don't like the turn the world is taking. Patterson and his gang are actively rewriting the Constitution, and they have enough control of the executive, legislative, and judicial branches to pull it off. Patterson is hot to take on Ali in the Middle East. He has even begun to inquire into the specifics of our tactical nuclear capabilities. Ali, on his part, wants nothing less than the total destruction of Israel and the continued expansion of fundamentalist Islam throughout the world. My intelligence sources inform me that he is considered to be the twelfth Imam, who has returned from centuries of hiding to complete the Islamic expansion across civilization. An inner circle even considers him to be the Madhi, the Muslim version of the Messiah, who has come to instigate the last days and prepare the way for Judgment Day.

"You are all no doubt aware of Patterson's thoughts on these matters. He has made no secret of them. He is very much a believer in the Christian version of Judgment Day, and his mouthpieces in their pulpits around the country endlessly point to the signs that it is approaching soon. My colleagues, I believe that both Patterson and Ali *want* Armageddon to happen during their tenure, so they can both claim righteous victory when *their* side, they each fervently believe, emerges as the winner, with Christ at their side. The Muslims believe too that Christ will return to rule, but only as an interim before the institution of the true Paradise.

"There is one problem with this scenario, at least tactically. Armageddon implies destruction of the world, and that implies destruction of the United States, and that runs completely contrary to my first duty. Therefore, I am left in a very precarious situation: do I obey my commander and destroy the world, thereby failing to preserve my country, or do I defend my country by deliberately disobeying my superior? My friends, I can assure you, a military man can face no more difficult a question.

"The resolution of this question is the primary reason I am involved in Avalon. I will follow my superior's orders, but I will also help create a 'nest egg,' if you will, of humanity and civilization, on the Moon, beyond the fray. Up until now, we have talked of economic expansion, return on investment, creating a spacefaring civilization, and other high concepts, but now let me openly add this to our list of reasons to build Avalon, way up toward the top. Many of you have expressed your private fears to me, so I know we are already thinking on a similar wavelength.

"Ladies and gentlemen, our true mission is nothing short of saving humanity. God willing, we will make the right decisions, and not cause Armageddon to occur, but if it does, we must have a way of carrying on beyond it. We must guarantee our survival. We must not let fanatical dreams of a returning messiah destroy billions of people and millennia of development. It is our highest duty to plant the seed of humanity on another world, to nurture it, to grow it as best we can with the absence of hatreds and malices and petty differences that guide so many of our actions here on Earth. There we will be beyond the reach of all terrestrial weapons, or we will see them coming three days out, and will be able to render them useless with our benign energy sources. That being our environment, we will be able to continue the noble experiment begun so long ago in ancient Greece, when the first democratic city-states emerged, and men were first awakened to their potential as human beings. We will have no less than an opportunity to perfect civilization."

Applause burst out around the room as everyone jumped to their feet for a standing ovation. After a minute, the General signaled everyone to quiet down and resume their seats. The next few hours were spent planning the strategy of most quickly landing the first colonists on the Moon. One of the motions made and passed was to return the location of the Lindstrom Foundation board meetings to the Lindstrom Industries boardroom. At the conclusion of the meeting, a few of Dredson's most loyal supporters quietly approached General Devere and resigned from the Project. Among them was Hector Maris, who had seconded the motion to remove Art from the board.

After that meeting, activity on Project Avalon reached the intensity of a tornado. Progress was pushed forward on all fronts, but special attention was given to the habitat modules, the Dark Stallion vehicle, and the fusion research. There was a general feeling that the clock was ticking, and no one knew how much time was left, before some event or another would prevent them from finishing the project and establishing a lunar base. Art was given a broader responsibility to oversee the development of the content of information and education systems at Avalon. In the event that everything operated nominally, his work would be the groundwork for tourist trips to Avalon, once the project was made public. Yet if the horrible possibility came to pass that the world was destroyed, his work would represent the repository of human knowledge. Art no longer felt that his contribution was irrelevant, for the tourism aspect of Avalon was expected to be one of the highest revenue producers. Perry was drawn into Project Avalon as Art's assistant, because Mara was swept up in her duties of managing Lindstrom Industries. She passed or delegated the major responsibilities such as CEO and President, but her position as a major stockholder gave her a powerful influence over the company, and she was elected Chair of the Board of

Directors of Lindstrom Industries.

Art delved deeply into his work during the day, while Gary was in school, but at 3:30 every day he picked up Gary from school and spent the rest of the evening with him. They would go to movies, play in the park, or play computer games. Art and Gary had moved into Lindstrom Estate with Mara, and Gary rode his bike around the neighborhood and made new friends. Through the hedges to the south of Lindstrom Estate was a house with a pool and a bunch of kids always playing and swimming, and Gary made friends with them and often ran off to play with them. The servants at the estate looked after Gary on the infrequent occurrences that neither Art nor Mara were available to do so.

Art and Mara became closer. They talked more of plans for marriage. An idea struck Art one day. "Hey," he said, rolling over in bed, "Avalon will be ready to accommodate people within six months. How would you like to be the first couple to get married on the Moon?"

Mara threw her arms around Art. "That would be wonderful! Let's do it!"

One day, a couple of months later, Perry was reading a paper in the office at Lindstrom Industries out of which he and Art worked. "Hey, check this out!" He leaned forward and showed what he was reading to Art. Art turned away from his computer to look at the article. "Hey, that's our old buddy Doug."

"Yeah, he's with Greenpeace now. He just got back from trying to ram a Japanese tuna fishing boat that's been careless about catching dolphins as well. It says here he's stationed in Seattle. They took this picture of him next to his boat when he got back."

"Let's go look him up!"

"OK!"

After calling the local Greenpeace office and reassuring the person on the other end, Mike, that they weren't with the FBI, Mike wouldn't give them Doug's number, but promised to pass him theirs. Ten minutes later the phone rang. It was Doug. "Yeah, sure I'll get together with you guys. How about down at the College Inn, for old time's sake?"

That evening Art, Perry and Doug were clinking pints of Red Hook together. Mara had graciously offered to watch Gary for the evening. "You boys go play," she had said as she playfully slapped Art's butt out of her office.

"Man, it's been a while." Perry said, wiping beer foam from his mouth.

"Yeah, it sure has," Doug answered. "Well, you saw me in the paper;

you know what I've been doing. What have you guys been up to?"

Art and Perry looked at each other, searching for confirmation of whether they should reveal their true activities. Art turned back to Doug. "Doug, something's been going on, something big. I want to tell you about it, but this has to be in the strictest confidence. The reason I want to tell you is that I think you can help. If this gets out...." The seriousness etched on Art's face caused Doug to silently, gravely nod.

Art took a long drink from his beer, then continued. "Remember way back when, when we were doing our Seattle Environmental Council thing, that I made a strong pitch for the development of space as a possible solution to environmental problems?"

"How could I forget? You wouldn't shut up about it. Are you still on that kick?"

"It's more than a kick. It's actually happening."

"What is?"

"I'm involved with a group that's building a lunar colony."

Doug chuckled derisively. "What, you work for NASA? I never thought of you as one of those techno-geeks. Besides, isn't Patterson trying to pull the plug on NASA?"

"It's not NASA. It's a private group."

"No way. What are you talking about? No private group has the money to build anything in space."

"That's not true," Perry chimed in. "I've seen it."

"What, you too? You're both crazy."

Art responded, "You mean, crazy like ramming a Japanese tuna boat?"

"You got a point, but hey, what am I supposed to do? The Earth is going to Hell in a handbasket. We've got to fight back somehow."

"You're right, we do. But how effective are your activities?"

Doug became defensive. "Hey, this is important work! We turned them back."

"Yes, but they'll be back, and they'll keep coming. Not just the illegal fishers, but the all the other polluters and spoilers. Have you ever considered why they do what they do?"

"Sure. To turn a quick buck, at the expense of everyone else."

"No argument there. But why do you feel they do those things, instead of investing in new technologies and systems that could be much more sustainable and profitable in the long run?"

"Hey, it's easier to grab the quick bucks and run, rather than care for the Earth."

"Precisely." Art stabbed the air with his finger for emphasis. "But what if someone could demonstrate that it is possible to construct new, benign, renewable systems that are magnitudes more profitable that current practices?"

"Well, they would probably go chasing after that stuff. But that isn't going to happen anytime soon. The multinationals have a lock on the economic conditions of the planet, and they aren't going to give up their superior positions for anyone. It's a zero-sum game, my friend."

"You are exactly right, if we stay on the planet. But if we can hop off the Earth, we gain access to an ever-expanding resource base. If we develop the infrastructure to move outward, it will be perceived to be much more profitable to go mine an asteroid than tear into the Earth, especially since the asteroids are untapped, and the Earth has been mined and depleted for millennia."

Doug scoffed. "You mean you advocate humans taking their dirty, polluting, warlike ways out to the other planets? You're worse than I thought."

Art shook his head. "No, you don't get it. As we move out, we develop benign systems like solar power satellites and fusion, and we mine asteroids which are lifeless anyway, and we let the Earth regreen."

"Yeah! Like that's going to happen."

Art was getting excited. He leaned forward, bouncing in his seat. "Yeah it is! Not right away, of course, but over time. You have to work at it, build the systems, demonstrate that economic development doesn't have to be a zero-sum game. Perry and I are involved with a group of people that are trying to do precisely that."

"So who are these guys?"

"I'd really rather not say right now, but I wanted to let you know about this stuff so you could see there was an alternative, and things aren't hopeless. This group is actually weeks away from establishing a lunar base and developing the technologies that, once perfected, can be exported to Earth to help the environmental crisis."

A wave of realization passed over Doug's face. "Say, you kind of faded out of the Seattle Environmental Council after that run-in with Lindstrom. You're hooked up with that swine, aren't you? He's building that base for his own profit, isn't he?" Art felt rage well up within him as Doug's expression changed to disgust. "I never thought you'd turn so completely that you'd get in bed with that rapist."

Furious, Art stood up abruptly. Perry put a restraining hand on his forearm. "Art, man, he doesn't know what you've been through." With clenched fists, Art glowered at Doug, then at Perry. He suddenly grabbed his pint and chugged the remaining beer in it. "I've got to go to the bathroom. You tell him, Perry." He wheeled around and stormed off.

Doug slapped his forehead. "Wow, what was that all about?"

"You're right, Art did link up with Lindstrom, because Lindstrom convinced him of all the things he just told you. Art developed a deep respect for him. But he's dead now. Art's engaged to his daughter, who is now the head of Lindstrom Industries."

Doug slumped back in his chair. "Wow, I guess I really put my foot in my mouth, didn't I?"

"It's OK, you didn't know. But Art really believes all that stuff he said, and you know, I'm starting to buy it all, too. I've met the people and seen them in action. They really do want to save the world."

"Well, I don't doubt their sincerity, but pardon me if I think they're going about it all wrong."

"Well, we'll just have to see about that. Only time will tell."

They sat and reflectively drank from their pints for a few moments until Art returned. As Art sat down, Doug said, "Look, I'm sorry, I didn't know the situation."

"That's all right. I've been through a lot lately. I shouldn't take it so personally. Once upon a time I totally agreed with you. Hell, I still agree with you about the problem. I just have a different take on the solution now. That's why I brought all this up. I think with your emphasis on environmental matters, you would be an excellent addition to this team. The lunar base is going to be ready for habitation in about a month or two. Join us. You could do so much good."

Doug put his hands up. "Now wait a second. I'm not ready to sell out."

Art became agitated again. "It's not selling out! It's the only viable alternative. Can't you see the way things are going? Wars, pollution, terrorism. We may well wipe ourselves out, or permanently damage our ability to survive here."

"I'm sorry, Art. I happen to agree with you, but I believe the solution is to stay here and fight. Despite all the problems, I just could not leave Earth."

"But Earth is going to leave you."

"Nevertheless, this planet is my home, my mother, and I prefer to die in her bosom than to live on that lifeless rock."

"But you could do so much to bring her back, once the storm has passed."

Doug picked up his pint. "I can't help feeling that that is a false hope. I wish you luck, but I just can't join you. I'm afraid we're just going to have to agree to disagree about that. Hey, the pool table just opened up. You want to play a game of cutthroat?"

They spent the next hour playing pool. Art periodically tried to bring up the topic of space development again, but Perry kept deftly changing the subject. Doug was grateful.

Chapter 22

Three days later, the next quarterly Project Avalon board meeting was held, following the one in which General Devere, Mara, and Art had engineered their reverse coup. The General announced to rousing applause that the first elements of Avalon were ready to be launched to the Moon aboard a Titan IV. After the meeting, he approached Art and Mara. "How would you two like to fly down to Baker Island with me tomorrow to watch the launch?"

Mara's eyes widened and Art dropped his jaw. "That would be fantastic!" He answered. "Can I bring Gary?"

"Sure. It would be good for him to witness this historic event. Scotty and a few of her team are going to fly down with us as well, to do some last-minute technical checkouts. We'll be leaving from McChord Air Base, south of Tacoma, at ten hundred hours. That's ten a.m. for you civilians." He winked. "Mara, I believe, between the excellent people in your company and my space command, that we're actually going to pull this off."

"I sure hope so," she smiled back. "My father would be so proud."

The flight to Baker Island was uneventful. They stopped for refueling at Hawaii, then headed south. Art and Gary were amazed as they came in for a landing. The whole island was one big launch complex. They stared out the window and saw launch pads everywhere, with towering, complex gantries. Some had gigantic rockets on them, seemingly ready for take-off. Huge buildings and hangars were placed strategically amongst the pads, to support the launches. Trucks, jeeps, and giant rigs were driving all over the place. The island was abuzz with activity.

Gary's eyes were wide with astonishment. Art was quite impressed, too. "I've never seen anything like this," he commented to Mara.

The plane stopped near an administrative-looking building. A mobile stairway was brought and attached to the plane, and Devere and the others descended to the tarmac. A sharply dressed officer with two aides met them at the bottom of the stairs.

"My friends, this is Major Wheaton. He'll escort you to the officers' dining hall, where we have a dinner prepared for you. He'll then show you to your quarters. Tomorrow morning at eight hundred hours, he will escort you to the launch observation site. I will meet you there then. Unfortunately this evening, I cannot join you, for I have business to attend to."

Art, Mara, and Gary followed Major Wheaton. Sukati and her team were led off in a different direction by another aide. Devere disappeared.

After a pleasant dinner and a good night's sleep, Art, Mara, and Gary were escorted to the launch observation site. The General was waiting for them. "I trust you had a restful evening."

"Yes, thank you," Mara replied. "Everything is so clean and orderly here."

"It is, after all, a military base." The General winked. "Hey, Gary, look over there." He pointed to a tall rocket that was closest to them, although still a good half mile away. Something resembling steam was streaming out of various openings in the rocket. "In fifteen minutes, that rocket is going to blast straight off into space."

"So that has the initial inflatable structures of Avalon on board?" Art asked.

"Yes, and various pieces of equipment. Let's see, the nuclear reactor from EnerCo is on there. We bought that outright from them, so they don't have any vested interest in the Project. There's drilling and mining equipment, and the material necessary for extracting oxygen from the lunar soil, and to begin producing glass and other building materials. Most of it will operate robotically. That's why we needed Scotty and her crew down here, to make sure everything was configured correctly for proper automatic deployment on the Moon."

"But how is it going to land on the Moon? Is it just going to crash land?"

"No. Attached to the final stage is a one-time use landing gear. We are going to set it all down gently as a feather."

Art whistled. "You guys are amazing. You've thought of everything."

"You can thank Scotty and her team for most of the innovations. We're just the trucking company, in a manner of speaking."

The clock on the wall counted down the remaining fourteen minutes. At about seven minutes, Art saw an interesting, stubby-looking aircraft land on a runway off to the left. "What's that, General?"

"That is Dark Stallion. That is how we've gotten our people to Oasis, and how we're going to get people to the Moon. That one is returning from delivering supplies and a new crewmember to Oasis, and returning one crewmember back to Earth."

Art's jaw dropped. "You mean, that thing just flew in from space?"

"Precisely."

"You told us about that in board meetings, but I didn't imagine it that small. Does it take off like a plane?"

"Yes, and it is refueled by another aircraft at sixty thousand feet, then continues on into orbit."

"Just like that?" Devere nodded. "How come we haven't done it like that all along?"

"Well, we had an army of public servants to keep employed on the space shuttle, didn't we? This is different. This is known as a 'black' program. The emphasis is on the result, not on the process. We can run that craft with no more staff than a conventional jetliner. In emergencies, less."

Art shook his head. "Maybe we are going to the Moon after all."

"Yes, we most certainly are." The General replied. Louder sounds emanated from the direction of the rocket. "Here we go. Final two minutes."

They all stood in rapt attention as the countdown proceeded to zero. Then, with a mighty roar, huge flames shot out of the bottom of the enormous rocket. Agonizingly slowly at first, but then with increasing speed, the rocket lifted off the pad and pushed its way skyward. In a minute it was almost out of sight.

"My friends," Devere announced, "it's for real now. Project Avalon is officially launched."

Art, Gary, and Mara gazed skyward, and watched the rocket dwindle to a speck, then disappear into the heavens. Art couldn't help feeling that the crew that had died in the shuttle accident a couple years back were properly honored by this launch. Now there was no way Patterson could halt space development, and cause their deaths to have been in vain.

Devere broke into Art's reverie. "Come on, let me give you a closer look at Dark Stallion."

They got in a Hum-Vee and drove to where the craft had just landed from space. It looked like a miniature version of the space shuttle, with short triangular wings that turned up just at the ends. The fairing was raised, revealing a two-seat cockpit.

"This is the two-seater, best used for transporting material. See that cargo bay there?" He pointed behind the cockpit to a sealed hatch. "We can transport two thousand kilograms of material to space in there. We have four of these that are operational. One is at Oasis now, being converted into a lunar transport. It will never enter the Earth's atmosphere again, except in an emergency. To get personnel to Avalon, we replace the cargo bay with a pressurized cabin that holds four passengers."

Art looked confused. "But how will they land on the Moon? There are no runways there."

"A team of engineers at Lindstrom has come up with a modification of the landing gear I told you was attached to the upper stage of that rocket that just lifted off. At Oasis, the landing gear will be mated to the back of the Dark Stallion, and it will be able to land vertically. This craft just came back from delivering, among other things, a set of landing gear to Oasis."

"You never cease to amaze me, General."

Just then Major Wheaton approached. "Begging the General's pardon, but Washington is on the line."

Devere glanced around at the small group, eventually landing on Mara. "I have a feeling I know what this call is about. I think it might be time to consider implementing Plan B."

"Right," Mara responded.

"Plan B?" Art queried.

"You'll get a full briefing on the flight back to Seattle, which will leave in two hours. I am afraid I cannot join you. I have a feeling I'm going to be summoned to Washington. I will meet you back in Seattle in five days, and we will finalize our course of action."

One of Major Wheaton's aides, Lieutenant Roon, accompanied Art, Mara, Gary, Scotty, and her crew on the flight back to Seattle. He debriefed them on Plan B, in which it was assumed that the Patterson Administration would discover General Devere's covert activity and would try to put a stop to it, most likely by removing the General as head of Space Command. In that case, all equipment and material that was ready to go would be launched on the remaining Titan IV and two Atlas IIAS launchers at Baker Island, all of which would be ready to launch within one week of the order. Devere had given that order before he left for Washington. The operations of the Dark Stallion vehicles would be transferred to the airstrip at Lindstrom Industries. Evacuation of key personnel to Avalon would commence at the earliest possible moment, after the launch of the last Atlas, which would contain all the freeze-dried food, seeds, and greenhouse material to begin lunar agriculture and keep a permanent settlement of thirty-six alive indefinitely. Scotty chimed in and reported that the life support team she oversaw was experiencing excellent progress in their hydroponic agriculture and closed-loop life support system experiments.

When the briefing was done, Art turned to Mara. "Are they saying we could be on the Moon in a couple of weeks?"

"Exactly."

"And you knew about this?"

"Devere had to consult with me as head of Lindstrom Industries, to make sure the plan would be enacted smoothly if it was ever needed."

"Wow," Art pondered, staring out the window and trying to imagine life on the Moon, while Mara placed several calls to Seattle from the phone in the seatback in front of her.

The plane landed directly at Lindstrom field, and a flurry of activity erupted once the plane touched the ground. Scotty and her crew ran off to make preparations. Lindstrom executives surrounded Mara and began asking innumerable questions. Mara stole a second to whisper into Art's ear. "You'd better go prepare your files for uploading to the Avalon computer. It will be online in four days and ready to receive information. Find Perry too and let him know what's going on. I'll arrange to have Gary driven back home, and he can go play next door for now."

"Right." Art was off.

When Art entered his office, he saw a sealed envelope lying across his keyboard. It was addressed to him at Lindstrom Industries, but had no return address. The postmark was from Nassau. Suspecting the contents, he tore it open. It was a card from Gwen. She very briefly wrote that she missed Gary terribly, and would like to see him again. She would be in the penthouse at the downtown Sheraton for three weeks, as of the day before Art received the card, and would Art please get in touch with her. He grabbed for the phone and dialed the number.

"Hello, this is Gwen."

Art, not knowing what to say, was silent.

"Art?" Her voice was trembling.

"Yes."

"Oh, thank God you called. I thought you might not call at all."

Art was silent again. His mind was in a turmoil.

"Can I see Gary?"

"I suppose. How about tomorrow, around noon. I'll meet you there, and we'll have lunch together."

"That would be fine, if you're OK with that."

"Yeah, that'll work. See you then."

"OK. Bye."

Art hung up and stared out the window for several minutes, lost in thought. He then snapped out of his reverie and threw himself into his work of preparing his and Perry's catalog of knowledge for uploading to Avalon.

The next day Art and Gary drove downtown to see Gwen. Art talked to Gary as he drove. "Hey, pal, how would you like to take a trip to the Moon with me?"

Gary's face lit up. "Yeah!"

"You wouldn't be scared?"

"No. It would be fun."

"Well, we might just do that."

They rode on in silence for a bit, then Art asked, "Are you exited about seeing your Mama?"

"I think so. I don't know."

During the rest of the drive Art pondered the pending Moon trip, and whether it was the best decision to take Gary along. Perhaps it would be better to leave Gary with Gwen. Living on the Moon could be dangerous, and was not necessarily the best place for a young boy. Nonetheless, the world was becoming more unstable and frightening all the time. Patterson was restricting as many freedoms as possible, and Ali was ranting madly in the Middle East. Environmental disasters seemed to occur almost daily. Perhaps it is best to take Gary to the Moon, Art concluded. This might be our last, best chance. This might be our only chance.

As they entered the hotel from the parking garage, Gary was uncharacteristically quiet, and appeared rather sheepish and shy. He held Art's hand tightly as they rode up the elevator and approached the door of the penthouse. Art knocked. A few moments later, the door opened, and Gwen stood there. She looked down, saw Gary, and burst into tears. She knelt down and reached out for a hug. Gary was hesitant at first, but then slowly walked forward and returned the hug. Gwen picked him up and held him close, and Gary hugged back tightly with arms and legs.

"I've missed you, Gary. You're so big now."

Gary just rested his head on her shoulder. Gwen looked at Art. "You're looking good. Come on in. I've ordered lunch to be served up here, on the terrace."

Still holding Gary, she turned and walked back into the penthouse. Art followed her out to the terrace. She set Gary in a chair and sat down next to him. Art remained standing and leaned against the railing. It was a pleasant sunny summer afternoon. The soft breeze blew Art's hair back as he gazed out past the buildings of downtown Seattle to Elliott Bay. "Pretty nice view you got here. Is Larry renting this for you?"

"As a matter of fact, yes. He had to come back to town to do some business with EnerCo, and he brought me along. I'm going to go see my sister a lot."

"He doesn't have time for you anymore?"

"Oh, of course he does. About half the time he's a perfect gentleman, always courteous and romantic. But half the time he becomes a businessman, and he's on the phone for hours on end. It sometimes gets a little boring."

"You're bored living on a boat in the Bahamas?"

"Well, the same thing all the time does get old after a while. There's a hole in my life, Art. I want Gary back."

Art whipped back around and looked out across the city. He was silent for a long time, then said, "You made your choice almost a year ago."

"I know that, Art. I was swept off my feet. Larry was such a dapper gentleman. I... I couldn't help myself."

"But now you're having second thoughts."

"No, I still want to be with him. He promised me he'd marry me and we'd have our own child, but that hasn't happened yet."

"So now you want to come take Gary back, just like that."

"I *am* his mother."

Art turned and glared at her. "And *I'm* his father. You gave me legal custody. I'm keeping him."

"Oh, Art, that's so unfair. You have your work on that Lindstrom Foundation, and I've heard through Larry's contacts that you and Lindstrom's daughter are together. I have nothing." She started weeping.

"You have Larry and a boat in the Caribbean. That's what you said you wanted. Be happy with it."

Gwen sunk her head into her arms and cried. There was a knock on the door. Art went to answer it. It was lunch. "Just put it on that table, there," he said, indicating the table just off the kitchenette. The porter put down a platter of ham and cheese sandwiches and salads. Art tipped the porter and showed him out. Gary came in from the porch. "Daddy, I'm hungry."

"Go grab a sandwich, pooky." He walked back out to the terrace.

Gwen was drying her eyes. "So that's it, then. Well, can I come visit him?"

"As often as you'd like." Art kept to himself that she might have to fly to the Moon to do it.

"Well, I'll be coming to see my sister every few months or so. Can I have him for, say, a week at a time?"

"Sure."

"How about now? I'm going out to Bainbridge Island this afternoon."

"Now is not exactly a good time."

"Why not?"

"Gary and I might be going on a little trip in the next few days. Maybe next week."

"I see. Well, I guess I'd better be content with that. Let's have lunch."

"I'm not so hungry anymore. It looks like Gary has finished his sandwich. We should be going."

Gwen became agitated. "Please, just stay a little longer." She ran in and gave Gary another hug. Gary wrapped his arm around hers to get the last bite of sandwich in his mouth.

"I'm going to the bathroom. You two have some time together."

Five minutes later he came out. "Time to go, Gary. Say goodbye to your mother."

Gwen, who was holding Gary on her lap on the couch, did not want to let go. She squeezed him tight. "I love you, Gary."

"I love you, Mama."

Tears of joy streamed down her face when she heard those words. Art let them hug a little longer, then went over and took Gary's hand. "Come on, pooky." They walked toward the door.

"Next week, then?" Gwen called after them.

"Maybe. We'll see."

He shut the door behind him and fought back tears as they waited for the elevator.

Chapter 23

Three days later Mara called Art into her office. General Devere was there, as well as a few members of the board.

"Hello, General," Art said, taking a seat. "How was Washington?"

"It's worse than I thought. Patterson called me in and personally asked me to resign my post as head of Space Command. I said I'd need a month to effect a transition. He told me I have one week, and if I didn't voluntarily turn over command to General Hawthorne, who, by the way, is much more sympathetic to Patterson's agenda, they would institute marshal law and arrest me for treason. He then went on a tirade, telling me he knew all about Project Avalon, and how dare I carry on a secret mission like that without his knowledge, and that it was tantamount to treason. I asked how he had acquired his information. He pressed a button on his desk, and a panel to my left opened up, and there stood Morris Dredson. I knew he would cause us trouble. I should have had him expedited."

Art, grasping the General's meaning, swallowed hard.

"So what do we do?" Mara asked.

"Proceed with Plan B. It was fortunate I ordered the go-ahead before I left Baker. I knew we couldn't keep Avalon secret forever, but I had no idea they were ready to pounce so soon. The Titan IV with the hydrogen supply lifted off two days ago, and the Atlases are scheduled to launch today and three days from now. Once those are aloft, we will no longer need Baker. We can conduct personnel operations from here. In addition, two crew members from Space Command are due to land on the Moon any time now, on a converted Dark Stallion, to begin preparations to receive personnel."

Art almost choked. "You mean, for the first time in over thirty years, two people are going to land on the Moon, with no fanfare or ceremony? They are just going to *be* there?"

"This isn't Apollo, Art. This is the last hope for Avalon. We have to be as expedient and covert as possible. Another crew of two will land three days from now. In two days, we will commence a general ferrying of Avalon personnel from here to the base aboard the six-passenger Dark Stallion vehicles. First Scotty and essential team members will go, then the Avalon board members who choose to go. In a little over a month, we should achieve our current maximum capacity of thirty-six personnel. We might be able to get a few more people up there, if we rearrange a few things. I'm having a rotation roster for transport to the Moon drawn up even as we speak. I believe we'll have enough time to get everyone up there, because I'll very graciously turn over operations of Baker to Hawthorne, and cooperate fully to buy time so that they won't necessarily figure out that we're continuing operations from here. Once they do figure it out, since Lindstrom is private enterprise and not a government facility, it will take them time to trump up justification to shut us down or confiscate our assets. That should give us the window of opportunity we need."

"Are you going, General?" Art asked.

Devere paused. The answer was obviously difficult for him. He finally answered, "Yes. I am. The alternative is to get arrested and get court-martialed for treason. I've uncovered other news that has helped me make my decision. It appears Patterson is seriously considering using tactical nuclear weapons against Ali and his troops, if fighting breaks out."

Everyone in the room gasped.

"It's getting bad, people," the General continued. "It gives me great pain to say it, but I no longer trust my government. Ali isn't making things easier, either. He has demanded publicly that Israel grant full citizenship and rights to Palestinians, and establish inalienable Palestinian states on the West Bank and the Gaza Strip, or face dire consequences."

"Like what?" another boardmember asked.

"We don't quite know, but we are putting nothing past him." Devere leaned back, stuck his arms straight out, palms forward, interlaced his fingers, and stretched. "This isn't a dress rehearsal, my friends. This is the real thing. We will have an emergency board meeting in a few days to inform the rest of our partners. Mara, can you see that everyone is notified?"

"Certainly." She picked up the phone and punched the line that connected her to her assistant.

Everyone in the room stood up to leave. Devere and Art found themselves in close proximity. "Are you ready for this, son?"

"I think so. I guess part of me never thought it would really happen, especially not this soon."

"Nor did I," the General replied, and sighed heavily.

Devere disappeared for a few days after that, and everyone at Lindstrom was in a mad rush to complete final preparations. When the General returned, a final meeting of the Lindstrom Foundation board was held. The board members were given the offer to emigrate to Lindstrom Base, and, if they had spouses and children, to bring them along. Devere warned all of them that going to Avalon could possibly be a permanent move, for if they remained on

Earth, they could be found guilty of treason. He made an offer to any board member to leave then, and he and his organization would do all they could to mask the connection between any given board member and Project Avalon.

"If you come with us, it will change your life forever," Devere warned. "It's not going to be a picnic. It will be rough at first, with very few comforts. You will no longer be an executive, an accountant, or a lawyer. You will be pioneers, and you might live the rest of your lives there. We will be a government in exile, and once Patterson figures out what we have done, he will try to come after us. You will be expatriates; you will be leaving the country without a passport. You will be exiled.

"On the other hand, you will be doing something no one else has attempted. You will be crucial in establishing a permanent settlement on another world. What we are doing is similar, yet greater in scope, to the Pilgrims coming to Massachusetts. We will be founding a new country, and changing the destiny of the world forever. Our next board meeting will be held on the Moon."

A little over half of the boardmembers took him up on his offer to sever ties to Project Avalon. Five board members actually decided to go, and two of them declared they would like to bring their wives. One of those people, John Brandiles, said he had two children as well, ages eight and ten, that he wanted to bring along. Art felt better about his decision to bring Gary when he heard that news.

Art, Mara, Gary, and Perry all ended up scheduled on the same flight, sixteen days from the last emergency board meeting. A week prior to their flight, they were all given physical examinations by Space Command medical personnel. None of them were found to have any problems which would prevent them from flying in space or living on the Moon. They discovered, however, that two of the board members that wanted to go were not so fortunate. Art was relieved to hear John Brandiles and his family were not among them, because he was glad for Gary's sake that there would be other children on the Moon.

Art and Perry furiously labored to get their information catalog in final shape. Since all the supply flights had been allocated to delivering essential supplies and materials for surviving on the Moon, they had to abandon their plans to export original books and works of art. Art was disappointed, but saw the logic of that decision. Avalon's computer on the Moon came on line a day after the payload from the last Atlas IIAS landed, and Art and Perry commenced the upload process through several relays across Space Command communications satellites. It took ten days of continuous transmission to upload all they had electronically amassed of the world's great art, literature, and technical knowledge.

The day finally arrived. Art had butterflies in his stomach, and did not sleep a wink the night before. Perry stayed at the Lindstrom Estate that evening, so they would all be together in the morning. They arrived at Lindstrom Airfield about nine a.m., and there on the tarmac sat a Dark Stallion awaiting them. The two Space Command personnel that were to fly the craft gave them a thirty-minute briefing on the procedures of the flight. As part of the briefing, they received a packet of pills to take. It was explained that, among the various vitamins and medicines in the packet, there was an agent that would have the effect of constipating them for the three days that the lunar voyage would take. Also, their diet en route would be low in fiber and other elements that would necessitate a bowel movement. For urinating, they were shown how to connect a hose apparatus to an outlet near the crotch of their spacesuits. The inner lining of the suits in the genital area was hyper-absorbent, and the hose produced a mild suction. During the flight, they could attach the hose and urinate where they sat. The lining would draw the urine away from their bodies, and the hose would suck it away for storage and later recycling on the Moon. Despite Art's admonishments, Gary giggled throughout the explanation, and Mara found the whole process rather crude. They all realized, however, that this was part of the requirements for getting to the Moon, and resolved to make the best of it.

The Space Command crew then helped them suit up in pressure suits with oxygen feeds, in case the passenger module decompressed, and helped them stow their allowed fifty pounds of luggage, held in specialized containers they had packed the night before, in the storage area behind the last row of seats. They were shown how to operate the compact radio control panels on their left forearms, so they could communicate with each other and the crew. The crew then strapped them into their seats and shut the hatch. Art noticed that there were two heavily-tinted windows mounted in either side of the compartment, and he became excited that he would be able to view Earth during the flight up to Oasis.

A few minutes later the craft started moving, and accelerated quickly, faster than any aircraft Art had ever been on. Gary was sitting next to him, and he held onto his hand as well as the bulky pressure suit glove allowed. They left the ground and climbed at a very steep angle. The swift acceleration pushed all of them deeply into their seats. The vehicle climbed swiftly for about half an hour, then leveled off. After a few minutes, they heard and felt a clunking on top of the craft. The pilot spoke to all of them over the radios in their suits. "Don't be alarmed. That is the support plane attaching the boom that will feed oxidizer into our tanks necessary for the flight to Oasis. We should be refueled in about fifteen minutes."

Fifteen minutes later there was more clunking. Then the pilot announced. "Prepare for orbital acceleration in one minute. Hang on for the ride of your lives, folks!"

Art waited that minute, which seemed like ten, with cautious anticipation. Suddenly, a loud roar filled his ears, and he felt as if a giant hand were pressing him down into his seat. He concluded the aft engines must have kicked in, as the pilot had explained to them on the ground. Gary turned to Art. Art couldn't hear anything, but he could plainly see that Gary was frightened and crying. He reached over and held him as best he could. He fumbled with switches on the unfamiliar comm panel on his forearm, trying to connect to Gary. "Gary, can you hear me?"

Perry answered. "You got me, buddy. Try again."

After several more attempts, he finally established the right connection. "Gary, can you hear me?"

"I'm scared, Daddy!"

"It's all right. That noise is the engines firing. We're going to the Moon."

"Make it stop, Daddy!"

"I can't do that, pooky. It will be over soon. Just hold onto me, you'll be all right. I'm right here."

Gary held onto his Dad as best he could. The pressure slowly eased up, and Gary calmed down a bit. The pressure kept easing until they all were rising a little out of their seats and pushing gently against the straps of the restraints.

"Hey, Daddy, this is fun!"

"Yes, you're right. We're weightless now. We're in space!" He glanced out the window beyond Gary and had to catch his breath. Through the low-positioned window he saw the rim of the Earth, brightly gleaming, spread out under him, the blackness of space stretching out beyond it. "Look, Gary. Isn't that pretty?"

"Yeah!"

None of them could take their eyes off of the dazzling sight below them. As the flight progressed, they witnessed night envelop the world as the terminator glided across the globe.

Their flight lasted another hour. They all giggled silently and played around with the phenomenon of weightlessness, letting their arms and legs float around as much as their straps would let them. Suddenly there was a bump, and they sensed they had reached their first destination.

The pilot's voice came over the radio. "We have reached Oasis. Please sit tight while we complete docking procedures. We will be docked three hours while we take on fuel for the flight to Lindstrom Base, attach the lunar landing gear, and take on supplies. In just a moment, we will open the hatch, and you can enter the waiting area. We will serve you some space rations and prepare the passenger module for our three-day flight to the Moon."

Two minutes later the hatch popped open. Directly above them was a narrow tunnel which had been extended from the station and had been sealed around the hatch. One by one they unbuckled their harnesses and pushed themselves up through the opening. Art pushed Gary along in front of him and helped guide him through the hole.

Once they were all on the other side, the hatch to the tunnel automatically shut, leaving them in a small passageway. A glowing green arrow on the far wall pointed in one direction; there was no longer any up or down, for they were weightless. They grabbed the handholds along the corridor and pulled themselves in the direction of the green arrows, which led them, after several turns, into a small cubicle with six 'seats' into which one could strap oneself. One wall of the cubicle was a large tinted window, and they all gasped as they saw the beautiful blue-green globe of Earth spinning majestically beneath them. The terminator was now retreating, leaving day in its wake. The hatch they had just come through sealed automatically, and they could feel a change in pressure as they heard a loud hiss. A couple of minutes later, a voice came over their radios. "It is now safe for you to remove your helmets. Place them in the receptacles above your seats and strap them in. The small compartments below the helmet receptacles contain space rations. Please strap yourselves into the seats and enjoy. We'll call for you when it is time to board again."

They spent the next three hours alternatively eating the bland but filling freeze-dried space rations in plastic packets, staring out the window at the Earth, or doing ad-hoc microgravity experiments with the empty food containers.

At one point Art turned to Mara and said, "Did you ever think we would really be here doing this?"

"Not really. It's all so unreal. But I love it!" She wadded up a food packet and threw it at Art. The motion knocked her farther back into her chair. Gary reached over and intercepted the packet before it hit Art, and sent it flying at Perry. He batted it with his hand, and it sailed off at an oblique angle. "This is great, man! I can't believe this is really happening. I mean, look out there. You always see pictures, but that is just amazing. No picture does that justice."

Just then North America was appearing under them. "Can you spot Seattle?" Art asked Perry.

"There it is, I think. At least that's Vancouver Island. It's pretty hard to tell with all those clouds in the way."

"Look, Gary." Art tried to point at Washington State. "We were down there only three hours ago." Gary just stared out the window, mesmerized.

The three-hour wait went by fairly quickly, then the announcement came to clean up the cabin as best they could by stuffing the empty packets back into the compartments out of which they had come, put their helmets back on, and proceed back up the passageway back to the Dark Stallion. Pretty soon they were strapped back in their seats and ready for their final journey. The hatch closed, there was bumping and grinding, and they could sense motion. "Prepare for escape acceleration in three minutes."

Here we go again, Art thought, and held Gary as best he could, but this time when the acceleration kicked in, Gary seemed genuinely excited. Well, what do you know, Art mused. My kid is taking naturally to space. Just then a wave of nausea overcame him, and he spent the next ten minutes fighting the mild urge to vomit. Fortunately, he was successful.

The next three days passed uneventfully, and became even somewhat tedious toward the end. There were video monitors in front of each seat, and Art was pleasantly surprised to recognize his catalog of information was available on the menu. Art had spent some time at Oasis mastering the comm panel on his forearm, so Art called up Perry and said, "Check out the screen in front of you. Our stuff is all in there!"

"Yeah, I've been looking at it. We did a good job, and Scotty's people have done excellent work making it accessible." Fortunately, Art and Perry had included plenty of movies in their catalog. They amused themselves by watching "2001: A Space Odyssey" and other science fiction classics, and comparing the spaceflight depicted in them to the real thing.

They were allowed to take off their helmets long enough to eat from the rations that were in a compartment immediately below the video screens. There was a ring on the front of the helmet, and they attached that to a breakaway Velcro strap beside them, in case they had to grab it quickly and put it on in an emergency. Art always ate when Gary did, so he could help him. By the third day, they were all getting tired of the mostly bland and liquid food, and the method of going to the bathroom was becoming rather burdensome. Unused to the lack of gravity, they all slept fitfully, in short naps, several times in a 'day.'

At last, just before severe boredom and cabin fever set in, the pilot announced, "Ten minutes to lunar touchdown." They had not noticed, but the craft had slowly turned around so the aft was facing the direction of their flight, and now the engines softly began firing. They felt a mild increase of pressure pushing them back into their seats. Eventually there was a mild bump, and all motion ceased. They all looked around at each other with open mouths. They strained to look out the windows, and saw the dazzling white reflection of a horizon that was perpendicular to the direction they expected it to be. They had landed with their backs toward the surface of the Moon. As their eyes became used to the glare, they began to make out rocks, ridges, mountains, and other features in the distance. The foreground, however, was shrouded in darkness. They sat in stunned silence, trying to comprehend what had come to pass.

Eventually the hatch opened with a strange silence, and they looked up to see the passenger compartment opening covered with an inflatable enclosure. As they unstrapped themselves, they noticed they were no longer weightless, but neither were they anywhere near as heavy as they were on Earth. They had to carefully navigate their way over the sideways seats and make their way down a ladder at the aft of the compartment. They climbed down to the ground and walked, or rather awkwardly bounced, down a round tunnel resembling a giant encased Slinky. At the end was a hatch, which, as they approached, separated into three triangular sections that retreated into the wall, leaving a circular opening. On the other side was General Devere and several others who had recently arrived at Avalon. They were all wearing pressure suits.

Devere flipped a switch on his forearm, connecting everyone in the vicinity in a radio link, and said, "Welcome to Avalon. As I recall, Art, you suggested the name."

"Actually, to be quite fair, it was Perry's idea."

"Well, congratulations, Perry. Welcome to Avalon!" He extended his arm, indicating that they should all walk forward. They looked up and around and found themselves in one of the inflated domed structures Art had only seen in the models on Earth. Equipment was everywhere. There seemed to be little organization. The dome was about five meters high and fifteen meters across. There were three other hatchways spaced evenly around the perimeter, all of them sealed.

The crowd drifted away back to their various duties, but the General stayed with them. "Come. I've got a few spare minutes, and I need a break from all this hectic set-up work. Let me show you around. Be careful and walk slowly; the difference in gravity takes some getting used to. It's been extremely hectic, but we've built the Base up to the Phase Three configuration, pretty much. There are four inner domes arranged in a square, then eight domes surrounding those, all connected by tubes. This is one of the outer domes, known as the equipment dome. Let me show you some of the equipment."

They approached one of the small wheeled vehicles scattered around the dome. It roughly resembled a riding mower with a cabin and interesting attachments. "This is one of our all-purpose excavators. We can use it to clear or move regolith, or employ it in the lunox or helium three manufacture process. It can be driven by a person, or guided robotically. When we are not accommodating the landing of a Dark Stallion, we use that hatchway you came through to get the vehicles out to the surface. We keep the other hatches sealed, to protect against oxygen leaks from the other compartments."

They moved toward one of the hatchways, which was closed. Gary, holding Art's hand for balance, bounced around as they walked, playing with the reduced gravity. Devere pressed a button on the wall, and Art was amazed at the speed and smoothness with which the three triangular sections of the door separated and retreated into the wall to reveal another Slinky-like tunnel. The General led them in, stopped just inside, pressed a button on the outside wall of the dome, and the three sections of the hatch door slid back in from the wall of the dome to create a perfect seal. Devere commented, "For safety reasons, we keep all the hatches closed. Normally you can operate these hatches like I am doing here, but in an emergency, we could remotely seal all the domes in the complex within six seconds. A hatch closes automatically after twenty seconds, if you neglect to do so. But don't worry; if you're in the path of a door, it will rebound, like an elevator door on Earth." They walked down the short tunnel to another hatchway. Devere pressed another button, and the hatch sections separated silently.

They stepped through the opening, into the new dome. There was more of the excavation equipment in this dome, and several of the vehicles, some driven by people, some not, were moving about on various duties. Some were moving up or down a ramp in the middle of the dome which descended into the ground. Devere explained what they were seeing. "These are the drills, hoes, and moon-movers that have begun digging out our permanent homes down below. Once we finish excavation and construction, we'll be able to pressurize and seal the area down there, and we'll be able to work and live in a shirt-sleeve environment. Until then, I am afraid we'll have to live in these pressure suits for a while. Some of the braver souls have moved down there, to test the quality of our construction, but most of us still sleep in our sleep dome, a couple of domes over. I'll show that to you in a bit, but now you have to see the brains of the operation."

They proceeded through a hatchway on their right, which led them to the inner square of domes. The dome they entered was packed with electronic equipment, barely allowing any room for people to move around. A couple of operators were busy manipulating various panels. The gloves of their suits had been modified to be very thin, allowing them the greatest dexterity possible. "This," Devere said with a flourish, "is the computer dome. Your project is stored in here, Art."

"I know. We viewed some of it on the way here. Pretty impressive."

"You liked that trick? Here's how it happened." He moved over to a bank of electronics at which one of the crew worked. "How's it going, Daniels?" Devere said after flipping a switch on his comm panel.

"Fine, sir," Daniels replied.

Devere turned back to his guests. "This is our communications center, and Daniels here is our Communications Operator, or CommOp for short. We've already set up an antenna on the rim of the crater we're located in. It barely peeks over the horizon back to Earth, so that it will remain relatively undetectable from down there. Here, let me show you." He reached over the operator's shoulder and tapped a button. One of the eight video displays on the console showed what was obviously the view from a camera positioned outside the structure. "Look out there," he said, pointing to the screen. Not too far off, on what appeared to be the top of a ridge, they saw a complex tower rising above the surface of the Moon with several instruments at the top, illuminated by floodlights. "That's the radio tower. That is our main communication link to Earth. Signals are sent to a satellite in our network orbiting Earth, which can then be transmitted to Earth, to Oasis, or to a Dark Stallion vehicle en route. The tower also acts as a local repeater. From time to time we may want to share information with the entire Avalon staff here on the Moon. Notice this light here on the panels on your forearm." He pointed to a specific light-emitting diode on his comm panel, and they all found the matching one on theirs. "That will flash in the case of an emergency or other need for mass communication."

"You'll be interested in this as well." He tapped another button on the console. The display showed a squat structure quite a distance from the camera, also lit by floodlights. "That's our radioisotope thermonuclear generator. That's how we're getting power until Scotty can set up her fusion reactor. That might take a while, but that's OK, because that generator will supply power at expected rates of consumption for ten years. And look over here." He flipped another switch. They saw several of the vehicles they had seen earlier moving around outside, digging at the ground. "Those are digging up regolith, for production of Lunox (that's lunar oxygen), helium three, and raw material for glass and bricks."

Art noticed that the areas Devere was showing them outside the base were for the most part blanketed in darkness, with only a few areas here and there illuminated by floodlights. He asked the General about that. "That's because we're in a crater, son, on the south pole of the Moon. Sunlight doesn't directly hit us here. We have erected floodlights around the perimeter of the crater we're in, so that we can direct light where we need it. Because there is no atmosphere, everything outside the beam of the lights is pitch dark. Although that can pose a problem at times, we derive three advantages from being located here that more than offset the inconvenience. First, we don't receive the direct radiation from the Sun either, especially during a solar flare. Second, we have begun erecting towers on the rim of the crater which will support solar collectors. Here, take a look." He flipped a switch on the console, and a monitor showed a squat, unfinished tower, lit by floodlight, on the rim of the crater. Two space-suited figures were working near the top of the scaffolding. "The solar arrays we'll install at the top of that tower when it's completed can be rotated to always face the sun, thereby constantly generating power. If we were on a limb of the Moon, under the sun, we would experience two weeks of down time each month when the sun swung behind the Moon from us.

"The last and perhaps most important advantage of building in this crater is that we may find water ice down here. Look how close we are to the edge of the crater." He flipped another switch, and Art almost jumped back in surprise. The wall of the crater was right in front of him, illuminated by the floodlights outside the structure. "We have just begun a serious search for water ice in the bottom of this crater, because the sun has never shined here, and if comets impacted here, they may have left their debris, which we know from studying other comets could very easily be ice. If we find some, half our supply problems will be instantly solved. We'll have an abundant supply of hydrogen and oxygen, which we can breathe and make water and rocket fuel from. We can manufacture oxygen from the regolith, but it is a long, slow, painstaking process, and all the hydrogen we have was sent up from Earth by rocket. There is no natural source of hydrogen on the Moon. It is too light, and the Moon's gravity can't hold it. It just floats off into space. We're pretty confident we'll find cometary ice, however."

"Why, General," Mara chimed in, "you seem positively giddy."

"Why, I am, my dear. This whole project is the fulfillment of a lifelong dream. Come, let me take you down below and show you where we're building the greenhouse. I understand you three chose to work on that project, once you arrived? Gary, too, as much as he can?" They all nodded.

They walked back through tunnels and hatchways to the dome that contained the ramp into the Moon, and Devere led them down the ramp. Gary held Art's hand and stared around in awe. They were soon out of the glare of the main structure's lights, and were seeing by benefit of a row of small unobtrusive lights strung along the rocky corridor. Devere's voice came over the radio as they walked. "We're hoping to be able to pressurize portions of these tunnels within about a week. Once we do that, we'll be able to work in a shirt-sleeve environment." They turned a corner and stepped through an open hatchway. Several technicians were working in the rather large cave they had entered, arranging complex rows of benches and digging with odd tools overhead.

One suited figure noticed them entering and came over to greet them. It was Scotty. She flipped a switch on her forearm and said, "Welcome. I've been waiting for you guys. This is the beginnings of the greenhouse. We ought to be ready to plant in about a week and a half. These guys here, up toward the roof, are digging tunnels up to the surface so we can pipe down sunlight. We'll direct it down here by way of mirrors and concentrators arranged along the crater rim. Those are a lower priority than all the other things we have going on around here, and will take some time to construct. We want to try to build them out of lunar material. In the meantime, these artificial lights powered by the nuclear generator will work just fine. I'm doing too much here already, but this is my special interest. It will be fun working on this with you guys."

Art turned to Devere. "You've got a lot accomplished in a short time, General."

"We didn't have much choice. It was do or die. From all the initial results we've gotten, I think we'll do just fine."

Scotty said, "We'll have a chance to catch up later, but now I've got to finish a couple of things here, then run off and work on the fusion reactor. See you." They all waved as Scotty went back to her work.

Devere led them back out of the hydroponics cave. "Let me show you your sleeping area. You might want to think of taking a nap. You've never had jet lag until you've flown to the Moon!" He led them back out the tunnels, up the ramp, and through several domes and hatchways until Art was quite confused. They finally entered a dome compartmentalized into several sections, each big enough to hold two people apiece. Devere pointed toward two of them. "Those are your temporary bedrooms. Sorry the accommodations are so spartan. We ought to have all the permanent sleeping and bathing quarters finished down in the tunnels within two weeks. For now, there are the washing facilities." He pointed to a larger partition a few meters away. "It is pretty self-explanatory, but you may want to read all the directions on the inside of the door, because we want to conserve as much water as possible. Also, this dome is pressurized, and each sleep tent has its own oxygen feed, but it would still be a good idea to stay in your suits for now, just to guard against emergencies. I've got to go attend to some other business now." He smiled broadly and put his gloved hand on Mara's shoulder. "I'm so glad that you all made it here safely. This is the beginning of a new chapter in humanity, and you helped it to come about." He patted her shoulder, then waved. "See you around." He turned and walked off through a hatchway, which he closed behind him.

Art yawned. "Well, I am tired. Who gets to wash up first?"

Perry had walked over to the wash area. "No need to take turns. There's six separate washrooms here."

They each entered a separate washroom, Gary going with Art, and had an interesting time figuring out the novel arrangement of familiar but high-tech bathroom items. Along one wall were arranged dispensers for common items such as soap and toothpaste. The instructions asked that everyone use these supplies, because they had been specially engineered to break down and filter out easily in the water recycling process. Fresh new toothbrushes were supplied along a rack on one wall, which could be cleaned in a small ultrasonic cleaner embedded in one wall, and reused. Among other things, they were amazed when they spat into the sink after brushing their teeth, because their spit fell slower, due to the gravity of the Moon, which was one-sixth of Earth's.

The shower and the toilet were recognizable but complex contraptions. With a bit of a struggle Art removed his suit and Gary's as well and stowed them in the provided compartment. It felt wonderful to be out of the suits for the first time in three days. After many attempts and false starts, he finally figured out the operation of the shower and washed himself and Gary. While still in the watertight stall, he shut off the fine but pressurized stream of water and turned on the air vent that completely dried them in two minutes. They stepped out of the shower stall and noticed that next to the suit compartment was a dispenser of new liners for the insides of their suits. The instructions told them to place the old liners in a tube that sent them to the recycling plant. This is all going to take a lot of getting used to, Art concluded.

After about half an hour, they gathered one by one back at their compartments. They decided to let Perry have one to himself for now, and to fit Gary in with Art and Mara. Each compartment had two air mattresses on the ground, with pockets along the walls and small shelves held up by supporting polyurethane ropes, to hold personal items. Someone had brought their luggage containers and stowed them in the space designed for them along one end of each compartment. Small pillows were provided that could fit right inside the helmets, so a sleeper would be comfortable while still remaining fully encased in a suit. They settled down for naps, and although the novelty of the situation made it somewhat difficult to get comfortable, the one-sixth gravity helped them relax. Art left his radio turned on and tuned in to Gary's frequency, just to be able to check on him and make sure everything was all right. Soon they were dozing peacefully, remembering through dreams their flight through space and the weightlessness they had experienced.

Chapter 24

Art awoke with a start to the sound of loud crying in his ear. He recognized Gary's voice, and turned to look at him. His eyes were closed, and he still seemed to be sleeping, but he was thrashing around and wailing. Art reached over and hugged him. His movements awoke Mara, who flipped on her comm set and asked, "What's wrong?"

"I think he's having a nightmare. All this change has obviously upset him." Art flipped on his radio connection to Gary and gently shook him. "Come on, Gary, pooky, wake up. It's all right, I'm right here. Come on, you're OK."

Gary opened his eyes and looked with confusion at Art. Tears welled up in his eyes. "Daddy, I'm scared. I want Mama."

Art hugged him as well as he could, with both of them wearing suits. "Oh, pooky, it's OK, you're here with me. Remember, we're on the Moon. We're going to have fun here."

"I know, Daddy, but I want Mama here, too."

"Mama's back on Earth. Maybe you can talk to her on the radio. Would you like that?"

"Yes."

Art held Gary and looked at Mara over Gary's shoulder. He flipped the radio control so only Mara could hear him, and said, "I forgot to tell you, with everything going on, but Gwen came back to Seattle the other day. Gary and I went to see her." Mara's eyes widened. "I guess that reminded him how much he missed her. That must have been what the nightmare was about. I wish there was something I could do." Art got a distant look in his eyes, thinking about Gary's mother, so far away on Earth. Mara reached out and put her hand on Art's shoulder.

"Well," Art said, snapping out of his reverie and flipping a switch to get Gary back on the radio loop, "Let's go find something to eat, then look around some more." He held Gary by the shoulders. "Then we'll go to the comm center and see about making calls to Earth. What do you think about that?"

"OK, I guess," Gary sniffed.

"That's a good boy. Remember, I love you."

"I love you too, Daddy."

They emerged from their compartment and looked around. Perry's compartment door was open, and he was gone. They asked a passing technician where to get food, and she described an intricate route through domes and tunnels to the public dome. After several wrong turns and more questions of personnel, they discovered a hatchway labeled 'Public Dome.' They walked through the tunnel, opened the hatchway at the end, and found themselves in a makeshift mess hall. Several small plastic tables were arranged around the dome, and at one end were contraptions that resembled refrigerators and microwave ovens. A few people were sitting at tables, their helmets resting on the tables beside them, so they could eat. They recognized Perry at one of the tables, and went over to him.

He pointed to his head and made motions pretending to take off a helmet. Picking up his cue, they took off their helmets. "They pressurized this area separately so you could take off your helmets and eat. Go on over there, grab something out of the fridge, and nuke it. There's some pretty good stuff."

They set down their helmets on the table and went over and looked in a refrigerator. Neatly labeled packages read "Roast Turkey, 6 oz., gravy, 2 oz., broccoli, 4 oz., scalloped potatoes, 4 oz." or some other food combination. They chose three dinners and put them in the microwave ovens. While the waited, they noticed a tray of plastic utensils next to the ovens. Next to the tray was an interesting device labeled "Ultrasonic cleaner. Please place utensils and food trays in cleaning tray, put in loader, and press start." Next to that device, at the end of the table, was a trashcan-like receptacle. A sign over it read "After ultrasonic cleaning, please place food trays in here, so they may be returned to Earth, refilled, and brought back."

When their food had been heated, they grabbed their trays and took them over to the table where Perry was. They sat and began eating.

"Isn't this wild?" Perry said excitedly. "Everything here is so different. You can't take anything for granted. It's going to take a long time to get used to all this. That constipation pill wore off while I was sleeping, and I spent a good half hour in the bathroom, shall we say, 'cleaning the pipes.' That water-and-air suction method of cleaning up your behind when you're through is a trip."

"I wonder if we'll ever really adjust." Mara pondered. "I'll bet you a lot of people will get homesick, and will want to return to Earth."

"Yeah, they'll get 'Earthsick,' " Perry joked.

They all chuckled. They talked some more about their novel experiences as they ate. In general, the lighter gravity seemed to be the phenomenon to which they had the most difficulty adjusting.

All of a sudden Art noticed several other people were rushing into the dome from the airlock. "I wonder what's going on?" he said, pointing out the activity to the others.

"Look," Perry said, glancing at his comm panel. "That emergency broadcast light is flashing." They all simultaneously put on their helmets and flipped the switch that brought in the broadcast channel.

"...continual updates. Please proceed in a calm and orderly fashion to the Public Dome for the latest information. If you are unable to do so, you can hear the audio portion of the updates on channel Z-4. Repeat: A significant event has happened on Earth. We are receiving reports from several sources, and we are receiving continual updates. Please proceed in a calm and orderly fashion to the Public Dome...."

Art, Perry, and Mara all looked at each other with worried expressions. "What does it mean, Daddy?" Gary asked Art with a quizzical expression.

"I don't know, but all these monitors around the walls have come on, and there's Devere saying something. Look, there's 'Z-4' being flashed at the bottom. That must be the channel we need to tune into to hear the update."

They frantically fumbled at their comm panels until they tuned into channel Z-4, and General Devere's voice began accompanying his image on the monitors. He was standing at the communications console, periodically checking with Daniels the CommOp and glancing at the monitor panels on the console. Devere's voice boomed in their ears.

"...begin again and repeat everything we know up to this point. If you have heard it before, please be patient. If you have questions after I complete the entire briefing, please signal the CommOp on channel Z-3, and I will acknowledge you.

"Here is the crux of the matter: Several independent reports have confirmed that at 5:17 p.m. local time, which translates to 9:17 a.m. Eastern time in the U.S., a thermonuclear device was detonated in the heart of the coastal town of Haifa, in Israel. It has not been determined precisely how the device was delivered, but it is assumed to have been launched from a ground launcher of some type located in southern Lebanon. Haifa and its surrounding suburbs have been mostly leveled. Casualty counts are extremely high. Wait..."

Devere switched to a private channel and conversed with the CommOp for a few moments. He tapped back into the broadcast channel. "Moustapha Ali has just made an announcement from an undisclosed location. He says he warned the Israelis that if his demands weren't met, there would be dire consequences. Now the western infidels, as he put it, have felt the wrath of Allah. He further said that this was just the beginning of the plagues he intends to send upon Israel and the rest of the world, if the heads of state of Israel and the G7 countries do not agree to meet with him within twenty-four hours. He said there will soon be another warning delivered that will demonstrate that he means business. Hold on…"

He switched to the private channel again. His conversation with Daniels seemed to get a bit excited. Then Devere suddenly became calm, and turned back to the crowd. His face was drawn and severe. He took a few moments before he switched the broadcast channel back on. "We have new reports." He spoke very slowly and deliberately. "It appears that a high-explosive device has been detonated outside the U.S. Capitol Building. Half the Capitol has been demolished. Congress was in session. There is as of yet no confirmation of casualties, but it is feared to be very high."

The crowd became very subdued and hushed as Devere turned back to the CommOp for more details. After a couple of minutes, the monitors around the public dome came alive with an image of President Patterson, looking grave and tired, and a new channel identification was flashed across the bottom of the screen. Everyone scrambled to tune into that channel.

"…with great regret and sorrow that I announce to you that the United States has become the unfortunate victim of a heinous terrorist attack. At 10:42 a.m. Eastern time, the Capitol of the United States of America, while Congress was in full session, was struck by an enormous blast, destroying half of the structure and trapping many people inside. Rescue efforts are already underway, and we have pulled out several people, but we fear the number of casualties may be very high.

"We know who is responsible for this cowardly and reprehensible assault. Moustapha Ali, I know you are listening. Wherever you are hiding, you will never escape us. We will find you, and we will punish you for your inexcusable acts on this terrible day. You have twenty-four hours to surrender, or we will take our own measures to ensure that you are no longer capable of waging terror on the innocent citizens of the world.

"Citizens of the United States, be brave and courageous. We have been under attack before, and we have always triumphed over adversity. This situation is no different. Rest assured that your government is taking all necessary steps to safeguard the lives of Americans. I hereby declare that, for the duration of this emergency situation, martial law has been enacted within the boundaries of the United States. Please do not take any unnecessary trips out of your houses. Your local authorities will inform you of the appropriate course of action. We will survive, and we will prevail. Good day, and God bless us all." The screen went black.

Devere reappeared on the monitors, and the original broadcast frequency was displayed in the lower left corner. Everyone tuned into it, and heard Devere say, "My friends, I know precisely what Patterson meant by 'our own measures.' I was in on the joint chiefs of staff meeting where it was decided. Patterson intends to target with tactical nuclear weapons all the known and suspected hiding sites of Ali. Against my objections, the plan was approved. Also, martial law means that Patterson can commandeer any resources which he deems necessary for the defense of the country. I am afraid Plan B was not good enough, because I believe Patterson will try to commandeer, among other things, the assets of Lindstrom Industries. We don't necessarily need it as a base of operations anymore. The Dark Stallion vehicle with the last round of passengers left Lindstrom field yesterday.

"We must now go to Plan C. I must devote my attention to implementing that plan. Benhurst." He motioned to someone to his left. A young communications technician walked into view. "Benhurst here will communicate with the CommOp and continue to inform you of developments. Please extend him the courtesy you showed me, and please do not bother the CommOp directly. Thank you." Devere walked off to the right and out of view.

Mara tapped Art's shoulder, and he tuned into her frequency. "The General has summoned me for a meeting. I have to go."

"Let me come with you."

"I'm sorry, Art, the General didn't call for you."

Art's gaze bored into Mara's eyes as he squeezed her shoulders. Mara hesitated, then made a snap decision. "OK, come on."

Art quickly switched over to Perry's frequency. "Can you watch Gary for a few minutes? Mara and I have to speak with the General."

"Sure. I want to stay here and pick up all the news anyway. Man, this is heavy. What are we going to do?"

"I don't know, but I think the General has an idea."

They joined Devere in his sleep compartment, which was a bit larger than the others and had a makeshift office area set up in one corner. Four small foldable chairs were set up around a small table, on which rested a computer terminal which had a connection with the main computer of Avalon. Art and Mara packed into the General's compartment with about four other individuals, two of whom were officers of Space Command, the two others being Scotty and one of her lead engineers. Art and Mara were the last to enter. The General said something that only one of his Space Command aides could hear. That fellow went over to the tent entrance and made sure that it was correctly sealed. Devere then motioned with his hands, indicating that everyone should take off his or her helmet. When everyone had done so, he commenced speaking. "We ought to be just fine in here for a few minutes without our helmets. In fact, we should be just fine indefinitely, but it is a violation of safety protocol. The reason I wanted to do this is so that our conversation could not be overheard or accidentally tapped into by the others. Now Mara, I noticed you brought Art. He is not necessarily part of the Plan C loop, but you obviously have your reasons."

"Yes, sir, I want him here as part of this. We'll need a balancing, disinterested opinion."

"Fine. That's your call. Ladies and gentleman, it is time to seriously consider Plan C. As you all heard just a while ago, Patterson has declared martial law in the United States. That means he can take extraordinary measures in the name of defending the country. Now we all know that he is fully aware of Project Avalon, and we know that Dredson is his source of information. Therefore, we can assume he is aware of Lindstrom Industries' involvement in the whole Project. Under normal circumstances, Patterson has no recourse to commandeer or mandate the operations of private industry, but having declared martial law, he can stipulate it is in the 'national interest' that the government take over temporary operations of crucial industries, such as defense. And Lindstrom Industries is clearly a defense contractor. Therefore, I don't doubt that it won't be very long before Patterson tries to slap a government injunction on Lindstrom and shut Avalon down, or at least try to take us over. We have one slight advantage, however: we're up here, and they're down there. The last Dark Stallion is on its way here, so there is no vehicle currently on the surface of the Earth that can deliver personnel to the Moon.

"That is, nonetheless, not the end of our problem. We have been operating on the theory that we could run Avalon from Lindstrom for at least six months to a year. I am even shocked at how quickly events have progressed. We have brought everything necessary up here to function indefinitely on a nominal basis, although things will be tight, and we'll have to make sacrifices. There are other supplies we could use from Earth, but we have everything we essentially need, and we can accelerate our schedule to begin manufacturing local lunar material. Nonetheless, if we leave our infrastructure in place down there, they could quickly build a new Dark Stallion-type vehicle, and try to come get us. All the schematics, plans, and molds are down there, ready to start production. I have it from good sources that General Hawthorne, who took over Space Command from me, has already begun dismantling my team, and reassigning my key personnel all over the Air Force, and even forcing some into early retirement.

"It is time to seriously consider Plan C, which is this: Before we left Earth, we positioned high explosive devices all around the main Lindstrom facilities, against just such an emergency. They can be detonated remotely through our satellite link. It is time we consider detonating those charges, before Patterson and Hawthorne gain control of the assets and use them to come after us. Our opportunity is now, or never. The benefit is that the information and technology of Avalon will not fall into Patterson's hands. The drawback is that we will be completely, irrevocably, on our own, with no more supplies coming from Earth. Please take a moment to think about the gravity of that situation, then I would be happy to entertain questions."

After about a minute of silence, Scotty spoke up. "About how long do you think until we're ready to begin Plan C?"

Devere answered, "The remote command can be given any time. I have a code and Mara has a code. When those two are given together, the detonations can be triggered."

Mara spoke up. "I know you've explained this to me before, but I just want to get it clear: if we destroy Lindstrom, will we ever be able to return to Earth?"

"Certainly. Dark Stallion can land on any conventional runway. Whether political and social conditions permit return, however, is another question entirely. As part of Plan C we will bring up our personnel from Oasis, then destroy it as well. Once the crew leaves Oasis, we'll no longer have the infrastructure in place to continue operations from Earth. We would have to build the Earthside systems from scratch."

Art spoke up. "So, we are certain we have all the material we need to survive here, on the Moon, indefinitely?"

"Yes, according to our baseline models. It will be tight, but as soon as we get our food production and manufacturing processes online, we will be in fine shape." Devere noticed the growing concern on the faces around him. "Look, people, I know this is a serious and intense decision. I do not undertake it lightly. Yes, it's true we will be completely on our own after this. But you are all aware that the models we ran support the possibility of our doing this. You all participated in those model constructs. Yes, this is the real thing, and it is a bit frightening. But I know Patterson. I have talked to him, I have heard his scheming, and I know the megalomaniacal nature of his desire to control the world, or see Armageddon come to pass. He knows we are beyond his reach, and that infuriates him. He will come after us any way he can. If we do not protect ourselves with extreme measures like this, we are vulnerable to him, and he will not hesitate to utterly destroy us. This is our last chance." Devere looked around the room at each face in turn. He ended on Mara. "Mara, it is ultimately your call. You are Lindstrom Industries. If we do this, it will destroy everything your father, and his father, and his father created. There will be no turning back."

Mara looked around the compartment slowly. Art reached out and put his gloved hand on her arm. She finally turned to Devere, swallowed slowly, and said "We won't be destroying *everything* my father created. We're here, aren't we? Let's do it."

Devere looked around the compartment at everyone present. Each in turn nodded in silent approval. Art felt a lump in his throat as he indicated his assent. "That's it, then. We have buyoff from the technical team. We will have to call an emergency meeting of the present members of the board to get their approval, but we have pretty close to a quorum present in this tent already. We should be able to commence the operation once we get that approval. Thank you for your attention and diligence in this matter."

With grim determination, everyone put on their helmets and exited Devere's compartment.

Chapter 25

Several hours later, the same group of people were gathered around the comm console in the communications dome. The emergency board meeting had approved Plan C. Once Mara had demonstrated her assent to the plan, there was not much objection from the others. Mara was visibly under great stress, but she remained resolute. Now Art stood with her at the comm console, holding her shoulders. Devere was giving commands to Daniels and consulting with Scotty and his Space Command personnel. Devere had requested that the rest of the Avalon personnel return to their normal duties, and had informed them that Benhurst would continue to report general updates every half an hour. The General wanted to keep the specifics of Plan C confidential, so as to not cause confusion or panic to those who were not fully briefed on the situation. He also desired that people concentrate on their work and not on their predicament, and in light of their pending independence from Earth, he wanted all systems brought up to speed as soon as possible.

"The call is coming in now, sir," the CommOp told Devere.

Immediately after the board meeting, Mara had put a call through to Terry Slattery, General Manager at Lindstrom. He was aware of Project Avalon, but not directly involved. He had been informed, before Mara left Earth, that there may at some time in the future be a need to quickly clear the Lindstrom premises. On the earlier call, Mara told him to do so, and to cancel the second shift in the plants that night. The call coming through was from Terry. Daniels switched the channel over to Mara.

"Hi Mara."

"Hi Terry."

"Second shift has been canceled tonight. We made up a story about a toxic leak in Plant Four. Everybody is gone, except for a few admin people here with me. We'll be gone in fifteen minutes or less."

"Thank you, Terry. I really appreciate this. You'll all be compensated well. I arranged a 'severance package' against just such an emergency, and I made a call earlier to enact it. When you go to the bank tomorrow, I believe you'll be pleasantly surprised."

"Thanks, Mara. It's been great working with you. How is it up there anyway?"

"It's all so new, and so much is happening, I haven't had time to figure out how I feel. How is it down there?"

"Everybody's in a blind panic. Military people are driving around everywhere in jeeps, patrolling the streets. No one is allowed out of their homes, except to go to work, or to a grocery store and back home. People are being stopped for random searches. Patterson has really put a tight lid on everything."

"Well, good luck. Maybe I'll see you again someday."

"Yeah, maybe. Bye."

Devere, who had been listening, said, "OK, we wait twenty minutes, then detonate. Let's do a survey of the grounds to make sure everyone is gone."

Before Scotty and her team left Earth, they had rigged the security cameras on the grounds of Lindstrom to feed through the satellite uplink to Avalon. The CommOp now tapped into that link, and four of the video monitors on the console showed images of Lindstrom Industries. Each scene changed about once a minute on rotation, so that one scene changed every fifteen seconds. Some of the cameras were stationary, some swiveled slowly. After ten minutes, they had cycled through every camera on the premises, and began cycling through a second time. They did not see anyone on the grounds, except for Terry and his small staff, who, when the camera showed a portion of the administration building, were exhibiting obvious signs of preparing to hurry out of the building.

After the first cycle was complete, Devere sighed and said, "Good. It looks pretty empty down there. Let's just wait through one more cycle to be certain."

They continued to watch the cycle again. Everything looked quiet. About three minutes into the cycle, when the image shifted to the administration building where Terry and his team had been, it was empty. An image a minute later showed cars driving out of the parking garage. After the last car left, a steel grate descended over the entrance to the garage, preventing any other cars from entering.

"That's it. They're gone." Mara said with grim finality.

"Let's finish the cycle, just in case," Devere responded.

Everything seemed still for the rest of the cycle. As they looked at the last images of the cycle, Devere said, "OK, when this is done, we will proceed. Wait for my command."

"Hey, what's that?" Daniels queried, pointing to a screen. One of the final images showed a gated entrance to the premises. There was motion outside the gate. Several military jeeps and armored vehicles pulled up.

"Hold that screen!" Devere barked.

The CommOp hit a button, and the image did not change at the end of the minute. They watched as a soldier got out and tested the lock on the gate. He turned and shook his head, signaling to one of the jeeps that he could not open it, then ran back to the vehicle he had come from. The armored vehicle closest to the gate backed up, then raced forward quickly toward the gate. It hit the gate and smashed through in a shower of sparks. The other vehicles followed.

"They've done it, damn it!" Devere cursed. "They've appropriated Lindstrom under the martial law code. We're too late. Give me the four cameras nearest to that gate. I want to see their progress."

They watched as the military personnel spread out all over the complex. One jeep headed straight for the administration building.

"Follow that jeep there," Devere pointed. "I have a sneaking suspicion about who we'll find in that one."

The CommOp switched the cameras to follow the jeep's progress. It stopped outside a back entrance to the admin building. Two soldiers climbed out and approached the door. One of them shot through the lock with his rifle. Two other occupants of the jeep got out and followed the soldiers through the door. Daniels switched the camera, and they saw the intruders heading through the hallway to the main offices. They were all wearing caps, and their faces were obscured.

"They know precisely where they want to go," Mara remarked.

The CommOp switched the camera again, and Lindstrom's office, which had become Mara's, was now showing. Nothing happened for half a minute, then the door burst open in a shower of bullets. The four intruders entered the office. One went behind the large mahogany desk and turned on the personal computer sitting there. As it warmed up, he took off his cap. Everyone gasped except Devere, who said, "I suspected as much."

It was Morris Dredson.

One of Devere's aides asked, "Sir, what about Plan C?"

"We can't kill U.S. military personnel needlessly!" Devere snapped.

Art spoke up. "Sir, they're into Lindstrom's computer system. They have access to all the records and systems. They'll come get us!" He felt an overwhelming hatred for Dredson welling up inside him. The thought of him being blown up gave Art a certain pleasure.

Mara added, "He's right, you know. We are finished if we let this information fall into their hands."

"I can't kill my own soldiers," Devere agonized.

"Then you doom us all, sir," Scotty threw in.

Devere became agitated. "Let's warn them, give them a chance to get out. Open the channel to Mara's office."

The CommOp flipped a few switches. They could see a red light begin to flash on the phone next to Dredson, who was typing at the computer. A surprised look passed across his face as he glanced at the phone. He stared at it for a few seconds, then slowly picked up the receiver and punched the button next to the red light. "Yes?"

"Dredson, this is General Devere. You are in great danger. You and all the other personnel have ten minutes to leave Lindstrom property, or you will no longer be able to after that."

A malicious smile spread across Dredson's face. In mock sincerity, he replied, "Why General Devere, how nice to hear from you again. Where are you calling from, as if I didn't know?"

"You know full well where I am, and I will not allow you the means to come here or stop our plans. Leave Lindstrom now, or face the consequences." Due to the distance between the Moon and the Earth, there was about a five second delay before the response came back.

"How melodramatic of you, sir. Whatever can you do to me from up there?"

"Plenty." He signaled Daniels to cut the communication. "Switch to the Plant Four camera. That's the main Avalon plant, right?" Scotty and Mara both nodded. "Show me if the soldiers have reached it yet."

Two of the cameras switched views, showing an exterior and an interior shot of Plant Four. There was no activity inside. Outside, two jeeps and an armored vehicle were approaching. They were still at least five hundred meters away.

Devere turned to Mara, "Mara, the code, quickly."

"407QYEW318." The CommOp punched in the code.

Devere urgently delivered his code. "934BODF654." That was hastily punched in as well.

"System armed," Daniels reported.

"Detonate Plant Four, now!"

The CommOp punched several buttons. Nothing happened. The military vehicles were approaching the plant, about one hundred meters away. Suddenly, a blinding flash filled the exterior camera. The interior camera went dead at the same instant. When the overexposed image on the exterior camera came back into focus, Plant Four was gone, replaced by flames and twisted metal. Chunks of burning material were flying through the air. The jeeps and the armored vehicle has been blown over on their sides. The soldiers were scrambling out of the vehicles and running away from the carnage. One soldier had the arm of another over his shoulder, and was dragging him away. The other soldier had an obvious wound in his left leg. On the screen showing Dredson in Mara's office, Dredson apparently had heard something. He rushed to the window and was frantically looking about. He locked his gaze in one direction, and stood up slowly straighter. He could obviously see the burning remains of Plant Four.

"Damn!" Devere cursed. "I don't want this! Get me Dredson again."

The red light flashed on Mara's phone again. Dredson turned, saw the light, rushed over, and grabbed the phone.

"This is your last warning, Dredson. Get out, or we do the same to the whole facility."

"Your little firecracker doesn't scare me, Devere. We've already begun the uploading process from the computers here. We already have most of the information we need." He slammed down the receiver.

Devere turned to Mara. Mara turned to Scotty. She said, "He's bluffing. There's barely been time for the link to the mainframe to be established, much less to crack the necessary codes, then to establish a link to wherever they wanted to upload."

Devere's lips were drawn taut. "Get me Dredson again."

The light blinked on the phone. Dredson ignored it and kept working at the computer.

"Damn him! Can you tap into the PA system?"

"Yes, I think so. Scotty, can you help?" Daniels and Scotty conferred for a few seconds, punching buttons. A few moments later, she turned with the thumbs up sign. "OK, sir, you're live."

"Dredson, you have five minutes, not one second longer. You have been warned." He signaled to cut.

They saw Dredson look around, as if he were looking for the source of the sound. He turned toward the camera that he obviously had spotted and clearly mouthed the words, "You won't do it." He then turned back to the computer and rapidly began typing again.

"Sir, look at this." The CommOp indicated a different monitor. Soldiers were transporting boxes out of a building and onto a jeep.

"They're stealing dies!" Scotty exclaimed. "We can't let them leave with those, sir. They'll build a new Dark Stallion and be after us in no time!"

Devere turned away from the small gathering and flipped a switch on his comm panel, cutting off contact with the others. They all knew he was making the hardest decision of his life, and they respectfully waited in silence.

"Uh, sir," the CommOp interjected, patching into Devere on an emergency channel. Devere abruptly held up his hand for silence. "Sir, I really think you ought to know something." Devere whipped around and glowered at Daniels, who continued with a shaky voice. "Sir, you ordered me to inform you of any communications anomalies whenever they arose. Well, in all the recent excitement, I didn't notice something until just now. Oasis has not submitted its regular orbital report. The call is about fifteen minutes late."

"What?" Devere shouted, switching back to the channel they could all converse on. "They're never late. Give me visual from the station."

The CommOp punched some buttons. "Nothing, sir."

"Show me telemetry."

After some frantic control manipulation, Daniels reported, "nothing there either, sir. It is as if they're not there."

"Those bastards!" Devere cursed. "They blew up our space station! We still had two men aboard her! That's it! They're done! Detonate all Lindstrom charges. You already have the codes."

The CommOp started deliberately manipulating buttons. Mara softly said to him, "Give us cameras 33 and 12 on two of the monitors." Two images appeared, one showing the Lindstrom Industries grounds from the front gate, another showing a view from the opposite direction. It appeared as if the camera was up above the grounds, a little distance away. Mara pointed to the faraway shot and explained to everyone that it was a view from a hill behind the compound that was still part of Lindstrom property. The other two images showed Dredson, still feverishly working away at the computer at Mara's desk, and military personnel loading a jeep with material from a warehouse. For what seemed agonizingly long moments, nothing happened.

Suddenly, an intense brightness filled all the images. The two located on the Lindstrom property instantly went black. The two other cameras showed immense fireballs reaching into the air. With no sound, the scene seemed eerie to Art, almost dreamlike. It was horrible yet thrilling at the same time. From the two different vantage points, they could see the entire Lindstrom compound become engulfed in a raging tempest of fire. Periodically, new explosions threw material high into the air. After a while, the inferno died down, leaving fires scattered around the property. There was no sign of movement, neither of people nor of vehicles.

Everyone at the comm station breathed a collective sigh, and their shoulders seemed to sink half a foot. Devere finally, quietly, said, "We've done it." Then, after a brief pause, "What have we done?"

Mara replied, "We've severed our ties to Earth. We're on our own now.

We've given birth to a new life, and we just watched the birth pangs."

They were all silent for a few minutes, staring at the images of the smoldering flames where the Lindstrom facilities once stood.

Chapter 26

"Sir, I hate to do this again, but my monitor panel is going nuts."

"What is it, son?"

"Well, it seems reports are coming in from all the news wires and info services. It seems as if some sort of epidemic has broken out in Israel. People are dying by the hundreds."

"Monitor all the news channels on a rotating basis and report the significant findings." There was a sense of urgency in Devere's voice.

The CommOp frantically manipulated controls and periodically told everyone his discoveries. A major epidemic of unknown origin had overrun Israel. Anyone contracting the disease died within six hours, and the disease was spreading so rapidly there was no way of quarantining or containing it. Oddly enough, it seemed as if no Arabs or Palestinians were contracting it.

"Sir, CNN has reported that they've been contacted by Ali's people to tap into a transponder on Arabsat One. Ali is uploading a statement there within five minutes."

"Can you tap the transponder directly?"

"No, I have to go through the CNN link."

"OK, do it. And patch it through to the public dome monitors."

One of the blank monitors began showing CNN coverage. They saw several reports about the conditions in Israel. Apparently Israeli, American, and NATO officials were not allowing anyone to leave or enter Israel. CNN had one correspondent still inside Israel, there to report on the tensions between that country and Ali. That reporter was frantically submitting a report from a rooftop in Jerusalem. Behind and below him could be seen and heard frantic activity in the city. The reporter was coughing raucously, and was appearing to weaken in front of the camera. "I will hold on and continue reporting as long as I am able, but I fear that this will be my last report. I have been told that there is no hope of me being allowed to leave the country, and I am afraid I have contracted the mysterious virus. I (he paused and turned to cough) I don't mean to be grim, but I want to say goodbye to my loving wife Rachel, and my children. I love all of you." He began weeping, and his hand holding the microphone fell as he covered his face with the other hand.

Instantly a splash screen reading "CNN Special Report" flashed across the screen, and the announcer said, "We now bring you a live teleconference with Moustapha Ali, head of the Arab coalition, from an undisclosed location. We are receiving the report from an unknown location via satellite."

The scene changed to an image of Ali behind a podium, surrounded by two well-armed militia types. Ali began speaking almost instantly in animated tones, his arms waving and slamming the podium for emphasis. He was speaking in Arabic, but a voiceover with a thick Arabian accent gave an English translation.

The voiceover translated, "We have, for many years, offered to work with the Jewish people. They have repeatedly rejected our overtures. They have continually denied the rights of the Palestinian people, and rebuffed the Arab world in general. Therefore, we have visited the righteous destruction of Allah upon the godless infidels known as Israelis. They will be exterminated, to the last individual. Maybe then the rest of the world will realize that we are serious in our claims to our ancestral lands. All Israelis will be dead within twenty-four hours, and we will move in to claim our rightful heritage. The rest of the world should take note: we are prepared to take the same measures against any aggressor to secure and defend our rightful position." The transmission abruptly ended.

The CNN picture switched to an anchor desk in Atlanta. The newscaster spoke. "That was Moustapha Ali speaking from an undisclosed location somewhere in the Middle East. We have just gotten an update from our correspondent at the Pentagon. Apparently intelligence sources have discovered that a biological agent has been released in Israel which leads to severe illness and death within twelve hours, sometimes much less. Very few Palestinians or Arabs are contracting the disease, leading defense analysts to suspect that Ali's forces have distributed an antidote to the Palestinians in Israel and the neighboring Arab people. NATO forces have set up a tight blockade around Israel, allowing no entrance or exit from Israel by any means. The Pentagon fears that if individuals leave, they will carry the disease to the rest of the world. We will bring you updates as the situation develops." The anchor looked down at a panel. "It seems we have a live report from the White House. President Patterson is preparing an emergency address. We will now switch to the White House briefing room."

The scene abruptly changed to the familiar blue backdrop, with the Presidential podium and seal in front. Patterson walked in from the left, grim-faced, and took his place at the podium.

"My fellow Americans and citizens of the world, a very serious situation has arisen. Moustapha Ali has maliciously and willfully taken steps to destroy Israel. According to the latest reports, about a quarter of the citizens of Israel are dead, and most of the rest are dying. There is, unfortunately, nothing we can do. We have appealed to Ali's people to release the antidote. We have promised all sorts of things, from direct negotiations to instant and de facto Palestinian homelands. The response has always been the same: 'The time for talk is over. Now is the time for action.' I say to you, then, people of the world, the same thing: The time for talk is over. Now is the time for action. We cannot allow this to proceed. We have done everything we can for the Israeli people, but the situation is beyond our control. What we can do is contain the epidemic so it doesn't affect the rest of the world, and at the same time punish the heathens who have committed such an atrocious and despicable act. Even now the first wave of our wrath should be falling upon the heads of Ali and his evil minions. They will not profit from their activities today. Thank you."

Amid reporters clamoring for recognition, Patterson walked back off to the left and disappeared. The scene switched back to the Atlanta anchor.

"We are now receiving reports from the Middle East of widespread destruction." He looked down at a monitor, and said very slowly, "Oh...my...God." He snapped out of his trance. "Uh, excuse me. It appears as if nuclear devices have been released over several Arab localities. Sites in Lebanon, Syria, Jordan, Egypt, and Iraq have all been targeted. More detonations are going off even now. It appears as if the whole Arab community surrounding Israel has been targeted."

Devere, who had been leaning over the comm panel, slowly stood up straight. His face through the helmet glassplate was taut and grim. His gloved hands were clenched tightly. The others were exhibiting various states of horror and shock. "Give us Earth visual," Devere said calmly to the CommOp. There was no trace of emotion in his voice. One monitor began showing a distant view of Earth. Daniels increased the magnification so it filled the screen. Clouds obscured the surface, but a glowing layover of computer-generated orange lines showed the contours of the countries below. The Middle East was just rotating into view from the left side of the globe, where night still shrouded the surface. As soon as the image was displayed, they all could see intermittent flashes in the Middle East region. They were bright and intense, but brief and small. They watched in silence for several minutes.

"It looks like lightning," Art finally said with a cracked voice.

"It would be beautiful, if it weren't so horrible," Mara added.

"Sir," Daniels called to Devere. "We have anomalous telemetry coming from Earth. It appears as if there are several objects headed to the Moon from

Earth."

Devere whipped around and stared at the comm panel. "That's impossible."

"There they are, sir." The CommOp indicated a screen which showed a computerized schematic of the Earth-Moon system. Three red lines were leaving Earth at a tangent, headed roughly for the Moon.

"Damn it! Get me Hawthorne at the Pentagon."

Three minutes later, the connection was established. "Hawthorne, this is Devere. What the hell are you doing?"

"General Devere, how nice to hear from you. Are you enjoying your exile on the Moon?"

"How dare you launch nuclear weapons in a first strike?"

"I was given orders by my Commander-in-Chief. We will not tolerate renegades and flagrant violators of international law. That includes yourself. Your heinous act of sabotage at Lindstrom Industries cannot go unpunished. Good men died in that criminal act. You ought to hang your head in shame. By now you no doubt have noticed a few… presents on the way."

"Yes, we've picked them up. What are you planning?"

"Those are nuclear charges we have reserved for you. If we cannot bring you to justice, we will simply destroy you. You are outside of the law, you are a rogue element, and your presence cannot be tolerated."

"Damn you to hell! Did you take out our space station?"

"Yes, that was our first little surprise for you. We're now working on destroying your satellite link."

Devere was livid with fury. He made a sharp chop with his hand, and the CommOp cut the link. The General started pacing like a caged animal. Art, Mara, and the others backed slowly away, giving him plenty of room. They were all confused and scared, and didn't know what to do or say.

Devere paced for about a minute, then wheeled quickly to Scotty. "Scotty, I think it's high time to unpack Excalibur. How long do you estimate it will take to get it operational?"

"It will take two days of around-the-clock work. But let me remind you, sir, it had never been used in operational conditions."

"Well, then, this will be the ultimate experiment, won't it? Get going. Requisition whatever materials, supplies, and personnel you need. We're all counting on you."

Scotty nodded, tapped her colleague on the shoulder, and they sped out of the communications dome.

Art turned to Devere. "Excalibur?"

Mara gently grabbed Art's shoulders. "Come on, Art, I'll explain it to you. The General has a lot to attend to. Let's go find Perry and Gary. I'll bet you they're in the public dome, with the Brandiles'."

As they slowly walked out of the dome and through the tunnel to the public dome, Mara explained. "Lindstrom Industries was developing a laser system that could be used as an anti-ballistic missile weapon. We decided, in keeping with the name of Avalon for the Base, that we'd call it 'Excalibur'. We had not gotten it perfected before we had to evacuate to Avalon, but we brought it along, in case just such a situation as we're in were to arise. It has been tested extensively, but never in field conditions. Frankly, we don't know if the thing will work."

Art stopped and looked at Mara through their glassplates. "There is so much about you I don't know. I feel very close to you, yet I had no idea you knew of anything like this, or a lot of the other stuff that goes on around here."

Mara grabbed Art's gloved hand. "There are things I had to keep secret from just about everyone, because of the nature of our project here. But I am not keeping my feelings for you secret. I love you very much, and I'm glad you are here with me. You and Gary."

They squeezed each others' hands. Hugging would have been awkward in their suits.

Mara continued. "We did the right thing to evacuate up here. Civilization on the Earth seems to be drawing to an end, and there's nothing we can do about it, except survive here, and one day return."

"It's so unbelievable. Everything was there just yesterday, and now it's all falling apart. It's almost too much to take."

"We have to take it, Art. We came up here because we knew this was a distinct possibility. Now it seems we have made the right choice."

They walked on in silence, through the domes and interconnecting tunnels to the public dome. There they found Perry, John Brandiles, and the other adults glued to the monitors, absorbing every scrap of news. Gary and the Brandiles children were entertaining themselves as best they could with computer games on the public user terminals. Art rounded up Gary and approached Perry, who looked away from the monitor with a concerned expression. Art and Mara tapped into his radio frequency. "I've been following the updates. Looks pretty hairy, huh?"

"That's an understatement," Art returned.

"Hey, why don't we all take a break, clear our heads," Mara suggested, including Gary in the radio link. "Let's see if we can get permission to take a walk on the surface."

"Yaaaay!" Gary clapped his hands, which eerily didn't make any sound.

Chapter 27

Because it was Mara making the request, they got permission from Space Command personnel to leave the base for forty-five minutes. They were issued hardsuits, which were fully pressurized and contained an adequate supply of oxygen for two hours on the surface. Even though they were protected by their position in a crater at the south pole of the Moon, they were shown the special warning light on the comm panels that signaled a solar flare, which meant they were required to get back to the dome as quickly as possible, or risk a severe overdose of radiation.

They were shown on a schematic map the best places to explore, and strictly warned from venturing beyond certain boundaries. A display on their comm panel would show their location on the schematic at all times. This was accomplished by setting a signal on their comm panels to beacon, so their location was always known to the central computer. Although floodlights were positioned around the perimeter of the crater to facilitate work, the entire crater was not illuminated. Beams from lamps on the foreheads of their helmets would light their way through the dark crater.

After other instructions, they were finally allowed to leave the main airlock in the equipment dome. They entered through one hatch and found themselves in a short tunnel. The hatch closed behind them, and they could feel air pressure tug at them as it was sucked back into the habitat. Then the outer hatch opened, and blackness confronted them. They stepped out onto the lunar surface, then stopped to look around, letting their eyes adjust to the lower level of light from their headbeams. They noticed that there was no gentle fading from light into shadow. The change was so abrupt that shadowed areas beyond the floodlights and their headbeams were as impenetrable as solid rock to their eyes.

They turned around to look at their home. They could only see the closest dome, the entrance to which was lit, for the benefit of entering and leaving vehicles. It was orange and squat, covered with intricate ribs, wires and pipes, and resembled the dome of an astronomical observatory, without the opening for the telescope. Behind and above it, a little distance off, they could make out the illuminated wall of the crater, with space-suited individuals scurrying over it.

As they turned and gazed around, they could see activity all over the crater floor, under the sporadic floodlight beams. A short distance off, to the left, they saw one of the small tractors digging away at the lunar surface under a floodlight. Not far off to their right was the landing pad, with three of the Dark Stallion vehicles resting vertically on the landing gears attached to their tails. Leading away from the airlock toward the other side of the crater ran a wide, flattened path which appeared, from the lit portions they could see, to be heading in the direction of the communications tower, which rose to a seemingly impossible height above the rim of the crater. Perry pointed toward the tower and said, on the channel they were all tuned in to, "Let's walk up this track to the crater rim. I'll bet we'll get a good view of Earth from there."

They began to hike, and they all laughed as they tried to become accustomed to the hardsuits and the difference in gravity. They felt much lighter than on Earth, but the weight of the suits held them down a bit. They eventually adopted a sort of hop-walk, which Gary found very amusing. He bounced slightly ahead and swayed as he walked, looking like a caricature of a chimpanzee. Art took pleasure in seeing Gary play, then suddenly became wistful. He switched to a private channel with Mara, told her as much, and said, "He doesn't know what's happened yet. How can I tell him?"

"It will be hard, but you have to find a way. You can't hide anything from him. I'll be here to help."

After about ten minutes of hop-walking, which became increasingly difficult as the slope increased, they reached the rim of the crater. As they came over the last rise, the Earth was there, hanging low in the sky like a large blue jewel. They all stopped and gasped at its beauty. It was about three-quarters lit by the Sun, and was much larger in the sky than the Moon was from Earth. East Asia and the Pacific could be made out under the clouds.

"Look, Daddy, there's Australia."

"You're right, Gary. How did you know that?"

"Don't know. Just do. Why is it upside down?"

Art chuckled softly. "It's not upside down, pooky. There really is no such thing as right side up and upside down, when you're talking about countries on the Earth. We're just used to seeing North at the top of our maps. But we're at the South pole of the Moon, which points in the same direction as the South Pole of the Earth, so everything back on Earth looks 'upside down' to us.

"It looks really funny. Are we going back soon, Daddy? I miss Mama. We never got to call her."

Art looked at Mara, who returned the glance, but they couldn't see each others' faces through the tinted glass. Mara reached out and brushed her glove in Art's. The lack of feeling was disappointing.

"Gary, I've got to tell you something," Art started in. "I think it will be a long time before we go back to Earth."

"How come, Daddy?"

"Because something has happened there, something... not so nice. You see, there's been a war. People got mad at each other and started fighting. They sent some big bombs at each other and really hurt each other. Right now it's safer if we stay up here."

A hint of fear crept into Gary's voice as he asked, "Will Mama be OK?"

"I don't know, pooky."

Gary started crying and clung as close to Art as best he could in the bulky suit. Art did what he could to hug back. "I want to go home," Gary sobbed.

"We can't, Gary. This is home now."

"Art, Mara, this is Perry on a private channel. I didn't know if you wanted Gary to hear this. It's getting worse down there. I've been monitoring the news briefs ever since we left. Apparently some Israelis made it out of Israel before the NATO blockade was established. Several boats made it to Cyprus, and one private plane has landed in Italy. The people in Italy have been quarantined, but the people who landed at Cyprus just got off the boat and headed for the nearest doctor. Now people in Cyprus have contracted the virus, and no one knows how many have left the island, carrying the virus. NATO has expanded the blockade to Cyprus and Turkey, but the Turkish government is not cooperating, especially after the nuclear attacks on other Arab countries. NATO is threatening extreme actions if the Turks don't cooperate soon."

Art looked at the Earth, tears welling in his eyes. "How can we be so foolish, to do such things? All supposedly in the name of God. How can God let this happen?"

"God gave us free will, to succeed or fail by our own devices," Perry replied. "We were given our chance. God gave us everything we needed to make it work. If we blow it, God will try again in a few million years with another species."

"We're not done yet," Mara added. "God also gave us the ability to jump off the planet, to give birth to a new order of people, and it looks as if we did it just in time."

"Yes," Art continued. "If they can't contain that virus, then we will be the last hope of the human race." Art switched back to the channel that included Gary.

"Gary, it is very important that you understand something. We could quite possibly become the last people alive, up here, on the Moon. It is very important that we stick together and help each other. We need to survive, and to grow strong, so that one day we can return to Earth and make it a safe and happy place to live again. It's going to take a lot of hard work, but I know you can do it. I know it seems hard and scary now, but I'm here, and Mara, and Perry, and everyone else. We can make it together. Can you do it?"

"I... I think so, Daddy. Is everyone on Earth dead?"

"No, pooky, but I'm not going to hide anything from you. A lot of people are dead, and a lot more are going to die. What we have to do up here is remember that, and remember the bad mistakes that we made that caused all this to happen, and try to be our best so that it doesn't happen again."

"I'll... I'll try," Gary replied, still sniffling.

"Good boy. You know we can make it together."

They all silently gazed on Earth for a few more minutes, then turned and made their way back to the dome. As they returned, they were treated to the spectacular sight of the landing of the last Dark Stallion vehicle. Its engines blazed brilliantly against the backdrop of the shadowed wall of the crater as the craft gently settled down next to its companions, a short distance away from the equipment dome. Instantly a crew pulled the extension of the pressurized tube to surround the passenger compartment. Art, amazed at the efficiency of the Avalon crew, gained a bit of hope in the success of their venture.

Chapter 28

Over the next two days, to take their minds off the impending crisis of the approaching nuclear warheads, Art, Mara, Perry, and Gary threw themselves into their assigned task of helping with the construction and operation of the hydroponics cave. Now that all contact and resupply from Earth had been abruptly and irrevocably cut off, it was imperative that they bring the hydroponics system into operation as soon as possible. Most other operations of Avalon carried on as usual, although at a more hectic pace, because everyone was nervous about the three angels of destruction soaring their way. Scotty and her team were working frantically on Excalibur. They were erecting it on the rim of the crater, to give it the clearest possible shot at the incoming missiles. She kept reporting to Devere, "It's going to be close, but I think we can make it."

More emphasis was given to digging out the living and working quarters below the inflatable domes, because The General wanted to make sure there was room to shelter everyone underground when the hour of judgment arrived. Certain areas of the tunnels were ready to be pressurized, but Devere decided not to do so yet, because he didn't want to create a false sense of security, then risk drastic decompression if a warhead exploded too close. Space Command personnel conducted hour-long drills on emergency procedures with the entire crew of Avalon, in teams of four on a rotating schedule. Everyone received three hours of this training, and most felt prepared to withstand Armageddon if necessary.

Some good news from closer to home made the situation seem slightly more bearable. A search team comprised of Space Command personnel and some of Scotty's techs had found ice deep in the crevices of the crater, behind the domes. It was a minute amount and very dirty, having been mixed in with the regolith when the comet that had brought it had impacted, and required a good deal of processing before it could be useful. It was nonetheless there, and the team now had a better idea of where to search for more. When the news was reported to the base, widespread cheering, backslapping, and high-fiving broke out.

Under the feeling of impending crisis, and knowing full well that they may be spending their last days together, Art and Mara made the decision to exchange marriage vows. A small group gathered in the public dome the day before the missiles were to arrive. General Devere, as commanding officer, sanctioned the marriage, but asked Perry to conduct the ceremony, such as it was. Scotty attended as well, along with the Brandiles family and a couple of others with whom Art and Mara had made friends over the course of the Project. Scotty had arranged the lighting and decor to be as intimate and festive as possible, under the circumstances. Due to the pending emergency and the frantic pace of activity at the Base, Devere insisted they all remain suited, but allowed everyone to remove their helmets. Art and Mara stood in the center of the small group, holding hands as best they could and facing Perry. Gary stood by Art, smiling up at his Dad.

Perry cleared his throat. "This is a unique situation in all of humanity. At the moment of civilization's most severe challenge, two people have chosen to come together in the greatest possible act of hope in the future. May you enjoy happiness together as long as you yet live, and may your optimism in the future be rewarded." He stopped and smiled broadly. "I've always wanted to say this. You may now kiss the bride." As Art and Mara shared a passionate kiss as best they could in their bulky suits, Perry announced with a smile, "I now pronounce you husband and wife. You are now forever after Arthur Roy and Mara Gann LaFey." The small group of friends clapped and cheered. At the conclusion of the ceremony, by way of a honeymoon, Art and Mara retired to their sleep compartment, and were left undisturbed for several hours.

Reports of catastrophe and devastation kept pouring in from Earth. NATO forces were not able to contain the virus released by Ali, and it spread, first to Istanbul, then throughout Europe, then Africa and Asia. The United States and Canada enacted a severe restriction on anyone entering or leaving the country, but nonetheless the disease somehow crept up through South and Central America and penetrated the States. Within forty-eight hours, half of the world's population was dead or dying. They did not go peacefully, either. Violent civil unrest shook most countries, and intense but brief clashes occurred between neighboring states. Russia, severely angered with the United States for launching nuclear weapons against the Arabs, some very close to Russian borders, threatened retaliation against the States, but never launched. The leaders of Russia, witnessing the damage caused by the nuclear blasts and knowing that they would be retaliated against, and perceiving the futility of that act in the face of the spreading plague, decided not to play that card. India and Pakistan, however, were not so restrained. A full nuclear exchange was carried out between them a day after the NATO blockade of Israel failed. Many western observers remarked that the people who died instantly in the nuclear inferno might have been the lucky ones.

As time passed, fewer and fewer reports were transmitted from Earth. News organizations, with increasing numbers of their staff falling victim to the virus, were not able to maintain operations. Finally, only a few newsgroups in the United States were able to provide any significant information. Devere could not get access to any other information; General Hawthorne had ordered a general rescrambling of military frequencies, and Devere could no longer tap into them. Moreover, six hours after Hawthorne had revealed that nuclear warheads were on their way to Avalon, the satellite network that Space Command had assembled for Avalon went dead. Devere could only assume that Hawthorne had destroyed one or more of the birds. "We're as blind as bats up here," he muttered to no one in particular, anxiously pacing in the comm center as he waited for any scrap of information.

Scotty, however, still had a few tricks up her sleeve. She left the work on the laser in capable hands as she stole a couple of hours to work with the CommOp on restoring communications. There were some little known and, due to the plague on Earth, unused channels on satellites that Lindstrom Industries had built and operated. She reestablished basic communications, then instructed Daniels on how to improve the system before she went back to finsh work on the laser. "I knew there was a reason we called you Scotty," Devere remarked, congratulating the chief engineer.

Finally the decisive moment arrived. Devere had ordered that the comm center be moved to the assembly hall in the excavated area below the domes. Three hours before the arrival of the warheads, he ordered everyone to gather below in the hall in full pressure suits, to guard against sudden decompression. In the past two days, the construction crew had devoted the greatest amount of attention to the hall to reinforce its structural integrity. Metal salvaged from the Titan IV and Atlas II upper stages, which had originally delivered material to the Moon, was used to strengthen the walls and ceiling. If any place could survive a direct impact, it would be the hall.

"How's it going up there?" Devere called on the radio link. Above the comm center, which had been set up on a temporary platform at one end of the hall, everyone could watch Scotty and her crew on a large monitor. The image was being transmitted from a camera attached to the radio tower, usually used for visual sightings of incoming Dark Stallion craft. Scotty and her team were still outside the Base, putting final touches on the laser weapon and making sure the connection to the nuclear generator was operating optimally.

"It looks pretty good here. We'll be ready to come down in about fifteen or twenty minutes."

"Good. Don't take any longer than that."

"Remember, General, that this baby is going to need at least twenty minutes to recharge after each firing."

"Yes, I know. We've plotted the trajectory of the incoming missiles, and we're pretty sure we'll be able to get them all with a decent safety margin."

"I sure hope so, sir. I'll see you in a few minutes. Over and out."

Art, Mara, Perry, and Gary were huddled together against one wall, watching the monitor. Art tuned into Perry's frequency and said, "Twenty minutes between each laser blast? That sure sounds like they'll be cutting it close."

"Well, it's about all we've got to work with. I'm sure those Space Command boys and girls know what they're doing. I love the name they chose for that thing: 'Excalibur.' It's appropriate. Let us just hope that it is as effective for us as the original was for King Arthur. By the way, don't you find it ironic that we have to fight off an attack from people who are most likely already dead?"

"Yes, bitterly ironic," Art returned without laughing or smiling.

A suited figure approached them. The person inside conducted some kind of exchange with Perry, then got closer to him. He put his arm around the person and pulled the person close. Art and Mara both glanced over to see the face of a young female technician from the hydroponics crew. Art and Mara exchanged smiles, and Art tapped into Perry's frequency again. "Why, you sly dog."

"Art, you know Connie from the hydroponics crew, don't you? Well, it seems as if a certain... something has developed. After all, if we have to repopulate the world, we have to start somewhere, you know." He winked at Art. Art waved to Connie, and Mara reached out and squeezed her hand in support.

Just then Scotty and her team came through the hatchway to the assembly room. They shut and sealed the hatch behind them, and Scotty took a position at the comm console while her crew melted into the crowd. Devere opened a broadcast channel and told everyone, "Now comes the hard part. Now we wait."

Everyone tensely watched the exterior monitor for the next half hour, anxiously waiting for the first glimpse of a missile. Art was glued to the monitor like everyone else, but Gary had fallen asleep, his head slumping in Art's lap. Suddenly there was commotion in the hall. People were pointing to the monitor. Earlier, only a few motionless stars could be seen on the screen.

Now, it appeared as if one of them was slowly moving. A moment later, another mobile star appeared. A few seconds later, a last one came into view.

"Now, everyone, calm down," Devere admonished from the platform where the comm console was located. He stretched out his arms, palms down, and made downward motions, signaling everyone to remain calm and seated. "I will open the comm link so you can hear our activity, but it will not be two-way. We need to be able to concentrate. If you have something urgent to impart, you can contact Benhurst here, and he'll pass it along to me if it warrants my attention."

He turned to the CommOp and Scotty, who were both rapidly flipping switches and manipulating controls on the panel. The three moving stars on the monitor seemed to grow increasingly brighter as time passed.

"The first missile ought to be in range in five minutes, General," Scotty reported.

"Good. Track telemetry, calibrate range, and prepare to fire. Wait for my order to fire."

Daniel's and Scotty's hands were a flurry of activity in the console. The moving images on the screen actually began to take on dimension, and for the first time, it was noticeable that they weren't stars. Unaware of his actions, Art pulled Gary increasingly closer with one arm, and squeezed Mara's hand tighter with the other.

"First missile in range, sir." Art felt reassured by the steady calmness of Scotty's voice.

"Let's wait one minute, to account for margins of error."

That minute passed excruciatingly slowly. Finally, Devere said, "OK, on my mark... fire!"

A thin red beam shot out from the lower left of the monitor toward the approaching objects. Nothing seemed to happen.

"I'm sorry, sir, I missed. The calibration was off by a fraction of a degree. That gave me enough information, however, to recalibrate. I won't miss next time."

"That's very good, Scotty," Devere replied, visibly agitated, "except for the small problem that we now have to wait sixty minutes before we can fire at the last missile. They have been calculated to be arriving in forty-seven minutes. Accounting for the recharge time, we can only take out two of them now."

Even though the people in the room could not hear each other, their movements expressed a noticeable anxiety.

Scotty spoke up. "Sir, there is an alternative. We could launch one of the Dark Stallions on an intercept path. It would reduce our return to Earth capability, but it could very well save the Base. It would probably be best to launch a cargo version, so that we minimally reduce our ability to transport people."

The bodies in the room, which had been sinking lower in despair, suddenly started rising in hope again.

"Do it!" Devere barked. "And don't miss."

"No, sir. I want to remain alive as much as you do."

It seemed impossible to Art, but Scotty's fingers flew over the console faster than before. The missiles continued to grow on the screen until their shape could be discerned. At one point, Devere glanced up, saw how close the missiles looked, turned and told the crowd, "We have this monitor set to extreme magnification. They aren't really that close, yet." He turned to the CommOp. "Drop to five hundred percent zoom." Instantly the missiles shrank by half their size. The whole room seemed to breathe a sigh of relief.

Five minutes later, Scotty reported, "Ready to launch, sir."

"Please check your telemetry one more time, then have Daniels confirm it."

"Yes, sir."

Three minutes later, Scotty said, "Telemetry confirmed, sir."

"Switch monitor to launch pad." The screen shifted to show the four Dark Stallion vehicles sitting side by side on the lunar surface.

"Launch."

Nothing happened for a moment. Then the rockets beneath one of the center vehicles erupted furiously to life, and the craft lifted from the pad atop a blazing column of fire. It quickly rose out of view of the camera.

"Switch back to radio tower view," Devere ordered.

The darkness of space once more filled the screen, but the missiles appeared menacingly closer. Art almost jumped a little.

"Laser ready to fire again in two minutes, sir."

"Check and recheck calibration, and have Daniels confirm. Make that a standing order for each firing."

"Yes, sir."

After two minutes of frantic activity, Scotty said, "Calibration checked, sir."

"Decrease zoom to two hundred percent."

The missiles shrank appreciably.

"OK, on my mark… fire."

The thin red beam shot out again from the lower left. Again, nothing seemed to happen. Art realized he had been holding his breath too long, and forced himself to exhale. Gary was squirming under the tight grip Art had inadvertently applied to him.

Suddenly a blinding flash filled the monitor. Art had to shut his eyes against the intensity of the light. When he opened them and his eyes readjusted to the light levels around him, he could only see two objects approaching on the monitor.

"We got it, sir!" Scotty yelled exuberantly.

Almost everyone in the room jumped up in a spontaneous dance of joy. The eerie lack of sound and dreamlike slowness of the revelers' movements did not seem to dispel anyone's mirth. Art gave Gary, then Mara, then Perry, then Connie in turn, big hugs of celebration.

"Calm down, people. That's only one. We've got two more to go, and they'll be more dangerous, because they'll be closer."

Despite Devere's protestations, it took everyone a good five minutes to calm down. Then the realization that the remaining two missiles were still growing on the screen, and that the next laser blast was soon coming, finally brought everyone back into rapt attention to the image above the comm panel.

"Drop zoom to one hundred percent." The missiles shrank almost back to stars. "That is actual distance, people," Devere told the crowd.

For the next thirteen minutes, everyone watched the missiles slowly grow again into ominous shapes, knowing this time that that was their actual size and distance.

"Laser ready in two minutes, sir." Scotty's calm voice once again noted.

"Check calibration."

"Certainly, sir."

Two minutes later, Scotty said, "Laser ready."

Once again, Devere ordered, "On my mark... fire."

The bright red beam once again shot out toward the approaching missiles. This time Art squinted, and just in time, for another enormous blast filled the screen. There was celebration again, but not as exuberant as the time before.

"That's it for the laser, sir. The remaining missile is due to impact in seven minutes."

"How are you coming on guiding the Dark Stallion into position?"

Scotty checked her telemetry readout. "Seems to be on course, sir, but it's going to be touchy. That missile is moving at ten times the speed of the Dark Stallion. Interception estimated at four minutes."

"That gets that missile mighty close, Scotty."

"I know, sir, but it's the best we can do."

The next four minutes were the most tense of Art's life. All he could see on the screen was the growing missile, which now almost filled the monitor. He held Art and Mara as close as he could, and he saw to his left that Perry and Connie were clinging tightly to each other as well. Everyone in the room was very still, riveted to the monitor.

"Scotty," Devere said with a slight urgency in his voice, "it's been four minutes."

"I know, sir," she replied, frantically manipulating controls on her console. "I had to make a few last-minutes adjustments."

"Scotty, don't miss." Devere sounded very agitated.

Suddenly a streak zoomed in from the right of the monitor and collided with the oncoming missile. There was a flash brighter than any previous, then the monitor went black. At the same time, it seemed as if an earthquake, or more properly a moonquake, had erupted around the hall. The room shook violently, dust and chunks of rock fell from the ceiling, and the lights temporarily dimmed. They regained their normal brightness a few seconds later, and everyone could hear Scotty say to the General, "Don't worry, sir, I won't miss." She had turned to face the General, and Art was close enough to make out a broad, beaming smile through her faceplate. The room spontaneously burst into a raucous celebration dance, wilder than the first one. Devere ordered the CommOp to throw the broadcast wide open, so everyone could hear everyone else, and congratulate each other on surviving the impending crisis.

Devere let the celebration go on for about ten minutes, then broke in. "OK, people, we're not out of this yet. That last missile exploded pretty close. We have to make a thorough sweep of the compound and check for structural integrity. If we find that the tunnels are sound, we can begin pressurizing, and we can have a real party."

Cheering broke out again.

Epilogue

Three days later, a full structural inspection had revealed no significant damage. What little there was could be repaired on the spot by the crews that found the damage. Devere had approved the pressurization, and announced a no-suit party for later that evening (the base was run on nominal Greenwich Mean Time, for standardization of working and sleeping shifts). The Avalon inhabitants would still have to wear an emergency oxygen supply, with a mask ready to slip over one's head at a moment's notice, but everyone was looking forward to getting out of their suits, if only for a little while.

The news from Earth was not good. Reports had faded to a trickle, and then only from HAM operators or the few official stations that could maintain operations. It appeared as if about ninety percent of the population of the Earth had died from the virus released by the Arabs. The few people that were left were reduced to subsistence living. Neo-tribalism quickly took hold, and the Earth seemed to be headed into a new dark age. These reports significantly quelled everyone's spirits at Avalon.

The time for the party came. All the staff of Avalon gathered in the recently-pressurized assembly room and gratefully shed their suits. The mood was distinctly suppressed from the exuberance of the other day, when they had survived the missile attack. The radio tower, which had been severely damaged by the last missile's blast, had been repaired, and a new camera mounted on it. That camera was now projecting a view of Earth on the monitor over the comm console. The zoom had been increased so that the planet filled the screen. The sun was shining directly on it, showing it as a full, round globe.

General Devere called the gathering to order. "My friends and colleagues, we have cause to celebrate, and cause to lament. We have survived, but the people of the Earth have not. Look at it." He turned and gazed at the screen. "It is so beautiful, isn't it? It doesn't look like anything is wrong from this distance. Can you see any national boundaries? Can you see any religious differences? I can't." He turned back to the crowd, and a tear ran down his cheek. He covered his face, wiped the tear away, and quickly regained control. "I'm sorry. I've asked Perry Vale to say a few words."

Devere stepped down, and Perry stepped up on the platform in front of the comm console. "The General asked me to say a few words about what we have been through. I'm not all that technical, but as a student of comparative literature and mythology, I'm about the closest thing to a chaplain, or something like that, that we have up here. We have to realize what has happened, and what our responsibilities now are, what it all means to us. Essentially, we are now the stewards of humanity. All social order has broken down, down there." He pointed to the bright blue globe on the screen. "The male-dominated hierarchy has played its final card, and everyone lost the game. We now represent the highest form of human civilization. We are on the Moon, the very symbol of womanhood. We must try to develop a technically competent and capable society, letting our masculine desire to achieve and conquer carve out a life for us here in this hostile environment. But we have the opportunity now to listen deeply to our feminine sides as well, to develop the nurturing and caring attributes that we will need to heal the Earth. We must remain cohesive and united, and grow strong. Then one day, when we are ready, we can return to Earth and attempt to bring her back to life. In this respect, the name we gave to our new home, Avalon, is amazingly appropriate. Here, let me read you something. This refers to King Arthur and Britain, but it can easily be applied to our situation, in relation to the Earth." Perry pulled a piece of computer printout from a pocket of his jumpsuit and read:

"Arthur was wounded   wondrously sore....
And these words spoke he   with sorrowful heart....
'And I shall fare to Avalon   to the fairest of all maidens,
To Argante the queen,   a fay most fair,
And she will make sound   all my wounds,
And make me all whole   with healing potions;
And afterward I shall come   again to my kingdom,
And dwell with the Britons   in very great joy.'
The Britons believe yet   that he is alive,
And dwelleth in Avalon   with the fairest of fays;
And the Britons still look ever   for Arthur to come.
There was never man born,   of any maiden chosen,
Who knoweth the truth   more to say of Arthur.
But there was once a prophet   Merlin by name;
He foretold in words —   his sayings were true —
That an Arthur must still come   To help the Britons."

Perry folded the piece of paper, looked down and stood silently for a moment, then stepped down. Everyone in the room silently gazed at the image of the bright blue Earth, suspended majestically in the blackness of space. Occasionally soft sobs and weeps could be heard around the room.

Art held Mara close on one side and Gary closer on the other. He thought to himself, My God, what have we done? Patterson, Ali, Dredson, Paddy, Doug, Gwen, and everyone else, all gone, just like that. God forgive us all.

Gary, looking up at his father, then gazing on the beautiful image of Earth, floating tranquilly in a sea of stars, vowed in his heart that it would be his life's goal to bring the Earth back to peace and prosperity.

Ninety-Eight Years Later: Monday, January 3, 2101

Awestruck, Gary slipped his holohelmet off, and sat quietly. He was astounded by the intensity of the events that had brought about Avalon. He had not fully assimilated all he had just witnessed, yet he already had a growing respect for the Lunar settlement and its importance in the affairs of humanity. He was still unclear on one matter, however, and he pressed the signaler on his armrest.

"Yes, Gary?" The Programmer asked.

"I've heard of a conflict that arose between Gary and his father Art. Can you tell us about that?"

"That happened many years later, and is not part of this section of the datafeed. We will be streaming that at a later time, but we have plenty to discuss and comprehend here for now."

Although burning with curiosity, Gary resigned himself to waiting for the answer.

He was more sure, and prouder than ever, that he had made the right decision in choosing to join the astromining corps in the asteroid belt. This activity would take him to the current frontiers of the human endeavor, and allow him to contribute significantly to the development of the solar-system wide civilization. Like his forebearer, Gary vowed that he would work toward the peace and prosperity of human culture, as it yearningly reached toward the stars.